ChangelingPress.com

Shotgun/Fury Duet

Marteeka Karland

Shotgun/Fury Duet
A Bones MC Romance
Marteeka Karland

All rights reserved.
Copyright ©2022 Marteeka Karland

ISBN: 978-1-60521-841-0

Publisher:
Changeling Press LLC
315 N. Centre St.
Martinsburg, WV 25404
ChangelingPress.com

Printed in the U.S.A.

Editor: Katriena Knights
Cover Artist: Marteeka Karland

The individual stories in this anthology have been previously released in E-Book format.

No part of this publication may be reproduced or shared by any electronic or mechanical means, including but not limited to reprinting, photocopying, or digital reproduction, without prior written permission from Changeling Press LLC.

This book contains sexually explicit scenes and adult language which some may find offensive and which is not appropriate for a young audience. Changeling Press books are for sale to adults, only, as defined by the laws of the country in which you made your purchase.

Table of Contents

Shotgun (Black Reign MC 3)...4
   Chapter One..5
   Chapter Two 21
   Chapter Three...42
   Chapter Four...55
   Chapter Five 65
   Chapter Six..75
   Chapter Seven 93
   Chapter Eight..108
   Chapter Nine 122
   Chapter Ten 134
Fury (Black Reign MC 4) 149
   Chapter One..150
   Chapter Two 158
   Chapter Three...170
   Chapter Four...182
   Chapter Five 205
   Chapter Six..224
   Chapter Seven 235
   Chapter Eight..249
Marteeka Karland..261
Changeling Press E-Books 262

Shotgun (Black Reign MC 3)
Marteeka Karland

Esther: I was born and raised Southern Baptist -- a preacher's daughter at that. If Daddy had his way I'd be a preacher's wife, just like my momma. I want more. I want out. The only way I see to escape my father's rule leads me to University of Miami to study cyber security. That is until I walk into the wrong bar on the wrong night and... look up to see my knight on a shining Harley. Shotgun's about as far left of Daddy's expectations as a woman could get. And I may be damned for my sins, but I want him. He doesn't know it yet, but he's met his match.

Shotgun: My real name is Moses. Moses Blackstone... no relationship to the firm. For some gods forsaken reason El Diablo has decided I'm going to learn Cyber Security. I got no clue why he thinks I'd be any good at this. Give me some heads to bash and I'll be fine. But computers? I hate computers. But if I can't learn this shit I'll fail in front of my club, and in the eyes of El Diablo. When I wandered into that bar I was looking for a good fight. Or a good lay. Either would do. Instead I find a preacher's daughter. And maybe my own salvation...

Chapter One
Esther

"Let me get this straight, Esther." I could tell by the way my dad was pinching the bridge of his nose he was about to blow a gasket. "You're moving to *Miami*? Like, Miami, Ohio? Because I might be able to work with that. I have some friends through the church in Camden who can keep an eye on you."

"No, Dad. I've been accepted to the University of Miami in Florida." I tried to keep my voice even. Respectful. Even though I felt like he was disrespecting me by deliberately misunderstanding what I'd said. "And I've accepted a scholarship in the Computer Science program. I'll be majoring in Cyber Security. When I'm done, I'll have a double major in English from BBC as well as Computer Science from the University of Miami." BBC was Baptist Bible College in Springfield, Missouri, Dad's *alma mater*. It wasn't a bad school. It was just geared toward individuals going into the seminary and was a very male-oriented, Southern-Baptist-rooted school.

"You majored in English so you could teach at a good Christian school and help your husband. If you marry a church pastor, you'll need that English degree."

"Dad, I'm not getting married any time soon. You've never even let me date."

He crossed his arms over his chest, taking up a defensive posture. Was he preparing for battle? If so, he was in for a letdown. I didn't come here to fight. Only to inform him of my plans out of respect. "Which begs the question of how you plan to survive on your own in the world. You're not ready. Springfield might be a college town, but it's nothing like places like

Miami. Even Cincinnati would be pushing it for you." He sighed and stepped close to me to cup my face gently before brushing a curl back and tucking it behind my ear. "Baby, you're just not ready for places like that. The secular world."

I sighed. "You might be right." He grinned and opened his mouth to say something. Probably to tell me I'd made a wise decision. I continued before he could speak, though. "But I'm going to try. If I fail, I'll have no one but myself to blame."

He looked shocked. "What?"

"I'm going to Miami. Classes start in two weeks. I need to get a job and a place to live."

He chuckled, the sound more exasperated than humorous. "You mean you're headed to Miami and you don't even know where you're going to live? That's not very smart, Esther. Now. Get along upstairs. We'll talk about this tomorrow when you've had time to reflect on all the ways this could have gone wrong." My dad turned away as if the conversation was over. I suppose it was, but I had to make sure he knew why it was over.

"This isn't a spur-of-the-moment decision. And I would already have a job and an apartment lined up if you'd let me go two weeks ago when I had the trip planned."

"I needed you here at the church. You knew that."

"Then why did you wait until the day I was supposed to leave to tell me that? I was home the week before. I even asked if you'd need me that week. You said no." He'd lied to me, then, just to keep me here longer. He hadn't needed my help with anything. I'd had a hard time finding anything to do other than watch.

"I forgot," he said, waving a hand dismissively. Which just made me angry because I knew he was lying. Again, he wasn't showing me any respect, while he demanded I give him mine at all times. I'd been a good daughter all my life. Even in my childhood years, I'd never given him a moment's trouble. Not when Mom died, not during my teenage years, not when I agreed to go to the college of his choosing because he didn't want me corrupted by what he always called "the secular world." He saw it as a world without God, or Christ, or any of the other things that compelled young men and women to be good people. In his eyes, the college that was a rock of our community represented all that was good and holy in life. To me, it was just one more disappointment in a long line of them. Starting with my father.

"It doesn't matter. I stayed then. I'm not staying now."

"Esther Ruth Haney." He used his sternest voice, the voice that had always sent me scurrying off to follow his commands as a child. "As long as you live under my roof and rely on me for financial support, you will do what I say."

"I understand," I said. Then I picked up my purse and jacket.

"Where do you think you're going, young lady?"

"To Miami. Look," I said before he could start into the tirade I could see building. "I'm keeping the same phone number. Once I get settled, I'll let you know where I'm staying and where I'm working."

"Not with my money you're not."

"I have my own money, Daddy."

"You can't use the trust your mother gave you for something like this. She'd turn over in her grave!"

"I'm not. I worked while I was in college. I saved

and bought a car, a computer, and anything else I needed. I also saved money specifically for this, knowing I'd need a down payment and extra in case I needed to stay in a hotel for a while. Everything you and Mom bought me is upstairs in my room. The only thing I'm taking with me I didn't buy is the doll Mom made me. But if you want that back, I'll get it out of the car."

He looked hurt. "I'd never take that doll from you, and you know it. It hurts that you'd suggest I would."

"It hurts that you'd lie to keep me here," I said softly. "Christians aren't supposed to lie, Daddy. You taught me that."

He shook his head, but stopped. "You know, Samuel Sebastian has wanted to ask you out for a long time. I made him promise not to distract you at school, but he has plans to see you this weekend."

I couldn't help but smile and duck my head. "Daddy, trust me when I say Samuel is the last person who should be leading a congregation. No one at BBC is as pure and Godly as they pretend to be. Samuel is not a man I want as a prospective mate."

"You'd rather have some heathen?"

"Not saying that. I just want someone who's real. I'd rather have an honest heathen than a dishonest Christian. I don't tolerate being lied to, Daddy. Not by anyone. I know for a fact Samuel has done things at college he'd prefer not get out. I won't be a party to helping him cover up his behavior."

"Those are some pretty wild accusations."

I snorted. "Well, there were some pretty wild nights." I sighed, taking a step back. I wanted to hug my father, but if I did, there was a very real possibility he'd hold me there bodily. "I'll keep in touch."

"This life you're so eager to run into is leading to nothing but sin," he said. Dad looked like he was pleading, but his eyes said he was angrier than he was letting on. It was just one more way to control me. "Sin will lead to trouble. Possibly more trouble than you can run away from."

"You're just going to have to trust that I can recognize sin and trouble when I see it. You raised me to avoid sin. I'll follow the path you taught me."

"If you could recognize trouble, you wouldn't be so ready to disobey me now."

"I just knew you'd say that," I muttered under my breath. "Look, Daddy. I want more in my life than marrying someone I don't love to fulfill your dream for me. I'm intelligent. I can do some great work if given the chance. I want to do this. To go to University of Miami and see exactly what I'm capable of."

"Esther, if you defy me in this, if you run off to Miami, there's no coming back home. This is it."

OK, that hurt. I sucked in a breath. If I'd been less committed to this, to a future where I controlled my own destiny, I'd have caved. My father had been my whole world since my mother passed away when I was twelve. To have him say he'd basically disown me hurt. But what he was doing hurt more.

"You can't use my love for you to control me, Daddy. If this is the way you feel, then I'm sorry for you. I won't contact you. You can call me anytime you want. Goodbye."

As I left the house, I could hear him yelling at me. He meant business, and I was to get myself back in that house immediately. He'd change the locks on the doors. He'd make sure I wasn't welcomed in the church. All things I knew he wouldn't do, but it was still a pain to my heart. And the neighbors heard. Oh well. He could deal with his outburst on his own.

I got in my car, started it, and backed out of the driveway. I had a twenty-hour trip ahead of me and two weeks until classes started. I was starting a new life in a new city. Was life going to be perfect? Probably not. But it was *my* life. *My* choices. I could do this.

Two hours into the trip, I had the windows down and the radio on, singing at the top of my lungs while I learned a whole new genre of music -- eighties hair metal. How had I not listened to this before? Life might not be perfect when I got to Miami, but I was going to give it my all. I could do this.

I could do this.

* * *

Shotgun

"Software Hacking and How to Avoid it Happening to You" as taught by Giovanni Romano of the Shadow Demons wasn't exactly what I would call a bunny course. In fact, I called it fucking torture. The man was a fucking sadist of the worst sort.

"If I have to look at that man five more seconds, I'll put a fuckin' bullet in his goddamned brain. Then we'll see how smart he is."

"It's not that bad, Shotgun." Fury picked up a glass full of whisky and downed it in one gulp. "Besides, even if you shot him in the head he'd still be twice as smart as you." I threw Fury a look that he totally ignored as he got another drink.

The bar, though near the middle of Palm Beach, was a dive. The only people who frequented it were roughnecks and bikers. It was a hell of a good time most nights, but I just wasn't in the mood. At least, not for fun. I needed a good knock-down, drag-out brawl. Fury didn't seem to want to be here either, but then, he was rarely in a good mood unless he was in the presence of the little girls currently taking over the men of Black Reign. Little Bella was Rycks and Lyric's daughter while Holly was the daughter of Wrath's woman, Celeste. Fury was still gruff, but only if it made the girls giggle. If anyone called him out, he beat the fuck out of the bastard and everyone else shut the fuck up.

"This is a waste of time," I muttered. "I'll do whatever El Diablo needs, but I ain't gonna learn anything from that fucker Giovanni. He makes it purposefully difficult so no one can get what he's talking about, and he looks all superior and shit."

"Don't know about that," Fury said as he downed his second shot. "But I know you can get it if you want to bad enough. Ain't never seen anything you couldn't do once you set your mind to it."

I raised an eyebrow. "You sick or somethin'?"

Fury didn't even look at me. "No. So don't get used to it. I just happen to think that Giovanni character needs taken down a fuckin' peg or two."

"You're speakin' my language now."

Fury snorted. "'Course, I happen to think you're a dumb shit from time to time as well, so…"

"Fucker."

We sat in silence for a while, casing out the place. Seemed pretty tame tonight. Only three women and they all seemed to be claimed by one man or another so no fighting over women.

"I'm done," I said, slapping down a twenty and standing from my stool at the bar.

"You ain't goin' to the docks, Gun. El Diablo specifically said no fighting. He's tryin' to keep the club outta shit for a while."

I ground my teeth together. "Then let's go to

Beach Fit. I gotta work off some steam, and physical exercise after a day of staring at a fucking computer screen sounds perfect."

"I think I can allow that."

My gaze snapped to his. "*Allow*?"

"Yeah. I'm your keeper until this shit's done." When I just stared at him, Fury added, "You didn't think I was hangin' with you for your stellar personality, did you?"

"Motherfucker," I muttered, shooting the last of my whisky. "I'm gettin' the fuck outta here."

Just as I spoke, the entire bar went silent. I'd heard the door open and close, but hadn't registered much else until the only noise was the hard rock coming from a speaker in the corner. I let my gaze quarter the area.

"So, that's what all the commotion's about," I said softly.

"Fuck," Fury bit out, standing and dropping a twenty beside mine. "Get ready."

"No shit. Hope El Diablo don't get too angry, or our heads will roll."

"Just don't kill anyone."

As if not realizing the whole bar was watching, a curvy woman waltzed in like she owned the place. Her head was up and her nose in the air, like she was better than everyone in the place and knew we all knew it. She wore a sundress of the palest green, the hem hitting her just above the knees and swishing around her legs as she walked. Modestly heeled sandals adorned her feet, the thin straps wrapping around her slim ankles several times. The heels were just high enough to make her calf muscles flex ever so slightly. Smooth, creamy skin beckoned every fucking biker in that bar. No doubt they were all imagining tossing her on one of the now-abandoned pool tables, pulling her legs wide apart and fucking the sweet pussy beneath that skirt.

"What'll it be, sugar?" The bartender leaned against the bar as he polished a glass, biceps flexing as he did. Yeah, he was thinking the same thing we all were.

She cleared her throat delicately. "Um, a Coke, please." Her voice was high-pitched, like she was young. I knew that on first sight, but now I questioned whether or not she was even legal to be in here.

The bartender pointed to a little door off to the side next to the restrooms. "Coke's in there. Buck twenty per gram. You pay before you go in."

She nodded her head, then opened the tiny purse she carried around her neck and across her body. Girl actually pulled out a dollar and a quarter and handed it to the bartender. Now, he looked less than amused.

"One-twenty," he snapped. "Even for a pretty little thing like you."

The girl looked adorably confused. "But... I just gave you a dollar twenty-five."

"I'll spot her." A big, burly guy pushed his way to the bar, a big grin on his face. He slapped two one-hundred-dollar bills on the bar. "You can start workin' it off once you get the first line done."

When she still looked confused, I knew me and Fury were about to challenge El Diablo's orders. Getting the girl and ourselves out without killing anyone might not be possible.

"Don't worry about orders," Fury said, taking off his jacket and laying it on the bar. "Just get the girl and get out. Otherwise, we die and she's fucked."

"Literally," I muttered.

As we shoved men out of our way, trying to get

across the bar to the girl, the biker grabbed her upper arm and was practically dragging her toward the door.

"What are you doing?" Her voice had gone even more high-pitched, and she was pulling against the biker.

"Takin' you to get the coke you asked for."

"Why is it back there? This is a bar, right? I just want something to drink!"

A roar of laughter went up at her proclamation, and the guy picked up the pace, now physically dragging the girl after him.

"Oh, I'll be givin' you somethin' to drink, all right."

"No!" She twisted her arm, trying to get free. There was real panic on her lovely face, and something inside me just snapped.

The crowd didn't try to keep me away, but the men just wouldn't get out of my way fast enough. Several of them were following the couple to the back, obviously thinking she'd be way more agreeable once she'd done a line or two of coke. I shoved several out of the way, which prompted them to retaliate. The next thing I knew, Fury was mowing people down left and right and the fight was on.

I kept the girl in my sights as I took out one guy after another. Her captor didn't seem to realize the chaos ensuing behind him or didn't care. Probably the latter. He'd just reached the door when I caught up to them.

"Please!" she pleaded. "You don't understand!"

"I understand I paid for a gram of coke for you. You're just paying me back in the currency of my choosing." He grinned at her, looking her up and down. The bulge in his jeans was obvious as he turned to the side to face the girl. Which was when I grabbed his head and smashed it into the door. The guy dropped like a stone.

She screamed, throwing her hands up, really panicking now. "Don't touch me!"

"Easy, girl. I'm the one getting your sweet ass outta here without you getting raped. Get me?" She screamed and ducked, her hands over her head. "I said I was getting --" Something slammed into me, knocking me into the same wall I'd smashed the other guy's head into. She screamed again, and the pain splitting my head from the sound was worse than the beating I was getting. "Would you --" *grunt, punch*, "-- shut the --" *kick, punch, grunt*, "-- fuck up!"

I finally got the upper hand on the guy and flipped him to his back. Wrapping my legs around his middle, I got him in a chokehold with my back to the wall, and just held him there. I was positioned where I could keep an eye on everything until the guy quit moving.

Some of the men in the bar sat along the wall laughing and betting on who'd win. About eight had joined in the fight. I'd taken a couple of them out trying to get to the girl, but Fury was taking care of the rest. Like I'd let him have all the fun.

"Come with me," I said, snagging her arm. She looked like she was in shock, but she didn't resist, following me right into the fray. I put her between me and the bar since the bartender had backed off and seemed to be on the side of watching and waiting. "Stay down." She ducked, and I jumped into the fight.

Fury was living up to his name. He laid into his enemy with fury and hate. Neither of us used a weapon, but Fury could kill just as easily with or without one. Three of the seven left were down. Fury threw himself at two of them. I took the other two. It was a short fight, but man, it felt good! One thing we never did was tear up a place if we got into a fight. It made things easier to get out of without involving the cops. Though the other guys weren't so discriminate, we managed to keep most of the damage under control.

I whooped and hollered as I beat the shit out of several of the pricks. This was better than street fighting because my opponents got in fewer hits, and I still got to beat the shit out of someone. I couldn't contain the laughter as I took on one after another of the men charging me. After I fought the last one off, I let my head fall back and let loose a howl of glee. Fury just gave me a "really?" look. I couldn't help it if I liked beating the fuck out of deserving men. Call it a character flaw.

One last guy came at me with a cue stick, swinging madly. Honestly, this was exactly what I needed. A good old-fashioned bar brawl.

"Little puke," I bit out as I ducked one swing, then lunged away from another. "Know when to fuckin' stop." When he lunged in again, I snagged the cue stick from him and swung at his head, landing a hard blow to his temple. Blood sprayed, and the guy went down hard. I looked up and met Fury's gaze on the other side of the room. He calmly pointed at me, his mouth open but not saying anything.

Then I heard a screech, a crash, and a thump. I turned around, and my little innocent kitten stood over the first guy, the one who'd dragged her off in the first place, with a broken cue stick in her hand and a fierce scowl on her pixie face.

"You're not a very nice man," she said, breathing hard. The little sundress she wore strained to contain her heaving tits. She glanced up at me, and I could see it in her face. The fight, much as she was trying to get a handle on it, turned her on mightily.

I grinned at her. "Nothin' like a good fight."

"I-I d-don't think f-fighting is the answer," she managed to get out. Her bottom lip trembled, but her face was flushed and before my avid gaze, her nipples hardened under the fabric of her dress.

"No," I agreed, then grinned at her. "But it sure is fun." I held out my hand to her, and she gave me a startled look.

"Are you crazy?"

"All kinds of, honey. Now come on. I promise you don't want to stay here."

"Where are you going to take me?"

I glanced around. Some of the guys were helping fallen comrades and eyeing me and Fury like they were considering taking a piece of us. Then Fury turned around and let everyone see his vest with the Black Reign colors on the back. More than one backed off, even left the bar completely. Murmuring all around suggested they wanted no part of us, even if we were outnumbered.

"Shoulda known the two'a you's gonna be trouble," the bartender said. Without a word, I reached over the bar, grabbed the man's head, and slammed his face into the bar.

"That's for not stepping in when you should've. You knew what she meant, and you just let it happen."

"You fucker!" The guy had his hands over his face where his nose was spewing blood. "You broke my fuckin' nose!" His words were muffled through his hands. Blood leaked through his fingers.

"Yup. I ought to break your fuckin' neck."

"Let's go, Shotgun," Fury said. "Break his neck next time we're here."

The second the guy dropped his hands to grab the rag he'd been wiping the bar down with, I slammed his face down twice more for good measure. The girl jumped and let out a little whimper. I forgot. She wasn't used to violence.

"Remember that next time you think about sellin' someone out, you fuckin' prick." The guy groaned and slumped to the floor. I turned to the girl. "What's your name, doll?"

"E-Esther," she stammered out. "Esther Ruth Haney."

I blinked. "Parents a bit Biblical, huh?"

"You could say that." She bit her lip, looking away. So, hard feelings there. Great. Just what I needed.

"Well, you can come with me or stay here. I don't recommend the second option."

"I-uh…" She cleared her throat. "I'd appreciate you taking me someplace safe, sir."

Fury let out a bark of laughter. The fucking man never did that unless he was around the girls at the clubhouse. Now, he tried to smother his reaction by pretending to cough. "Did she just fuckin' call you Sir?"

"I don't see how that's so fuckin' funny. I can be a Sir."

"Only in a dungeon, Shotgun. And we ain't in a dungeon."

"I can be Sir out of a dungeon." I grinned down at the girl. Yeah. I could see her kneeling before me, her legs spread wide, her hands resting palm up on her thighs. Ready to take my cock between those luscious lips.

"D-dungeon?" She looked so horrified I burst out laughing.

- 18 -

"Relax, doll. I ain't no Dom. I'm pretty sure you're a submissive, though. I can teach you if you want."

She blinked at me, then must have registered the snickering all around her. She bent and snagged a cue stick from the floor and swung at me. I chuckled as I dodged her, grabbing the stick from her hand.

"I didn't mean no harm, doll."

"Esther! My name is Esther!"

"Sorry," I said, trying to look appropriately contrite. I offered her my hand. "Come on, *Esther*. Let's get out of here before I have to fight more of these bastards for you." Surprisingly, she took my hand, if a little hesitantly. I hurried her out the door and handed her a helmet. When she just looked at it, I indicated the bike. "You'll have to put this on to ride behind me, Do-er... Esther."

"But, I have my own car."

"Where you parked?"

"Uh, over there..." Her voice trailed off when she pointed to a car currently in the process of having every removable part removed.

"I take it you're from out of town." I shook my head, sighing.

"How'd you know? And you've got to help me get them to stop!"

"Lady, they already took everything that matters. Those little fuckers there are just getting the rest of the shit. I know because if you'd had local tags, they'd've left you alone. Especially with a piece-of-shit car like that. They're scavenging it for parts or they'd have just driven off with it. Must not have been much worth taking."

"It might not be much but it's mine!" She looked like she was ready to cry as she spun around and started toward the remains of her car. I snagged her arm. "Uh-uh, baby. Helmet. Bike."

"But my car --"

"Is toast. I'll have some of the boys tow it to Red's garage and see if he can work some magic, but you ain't drivin' it now." She looked up at me, tears now pooling in her eyes. "Fuck this shit," I muttered.

I set the helmet on her head and lifted her bodily onto the back of my bike. Then I climbed on myself and started it up. Instead of telling her what to do, I reached behind me and found her hands, tugging them forward to wrap her arms around me. I revved the motor a couple of times, put it in gear, and took off. She didn't let go.

Chapter Two
Esther

If my dad could only see me now, I thought dryly. I was on the back of a motorcycle with a biker named Shotgun. Oh, *after* I'd nearly been raped and God only knew what else because I'd gone into a bar. *And* everyone had thought I wanted cocaine when I'd only wanted a Coca-Cola. Maybe my dad was right. I didn't know anything about my surroundings or even what was safe. I mean, it was a bar, sure, but it was in the middle of town. Maybe off the main drag a little, but I still thought I should have been safe. If it hadn't been for the man in front of me, there was no telling if I'd even be alive right now.

Now, I was on the back of his bike, my dress blowing in the wind, and I was afraid to let go to tuck it in. God only knew how many people I flashed. Thank goodness, the ride was only twenty minutes. But then he pulled into this big compound that looked like a ritzy resort.

"Woah..." I looked around in awe as we stopped. There were several buildings spread out within the fortress. All of it surrounded by a wall and gated. I'd never seen anything like it outside of a movie or magazine. And it most definitely was not what I was expecting in a motorcycle club.

His warm chuckle said he'd heard me. "Not what you were expecting?"

"Not sure what I was expecting."

He drove us through the gate and into the parking lot of the main building. There were several bikes parked, and the music coming from the building was every bit as loud and raucous as the bar. Only... more.

"Come on," he said, helping me down and removing my helmet. He grinned at me. "Let's go inside. I'll get you that Coke."

"The soft drink," I said hurriedly. "Not a drug. I don't do drugs."

"Not even the occasional joint?"

"No! I-I don't do any kind of drugs. Or alcohol."

He jerked as if I'd slapped him. "What do you mean, no alcohol?"

"I don't drink alcohol."

"You've got to be fuckin' kiddin' me." When I winced at his language, he snorted. "I take it you don't swear, either?"

"It's kind of frowned upon in church," I muttered.

"Well, doll, you ain't in church." He took my hand. "Come on. I'll get you a drink… err, a Coke, and we'll talk. What were you doin' in a bar if you don't drink?"

As he opened the door, the sound hit me like an explosion. The scent, too. I couldn't identify it all, but there was a bitter whang of alcohol and… something else. The second I stepped into the place, my mouth dropped open and I knew I'd forever link that unidentifiable, musky odor with what I saw.

Sex.

Lots and *lots* of sex.

How did sex even have a smell? I lasted all of five seconds before my knees gave way. Thankfully, Shotgun must have been expecting it, because his reflexes were positively catlike.

His warm chuckle at my ear sent my body into meltdown. Or something. Goose bumps erupted over me followed by a light sheen of sweat. I was light-headed and absolutely could not say a word. I looked up at him helplessly. But my stupid gaze drifted, and I was soon focused on the hedonistic Sodom and Gomorrah happening all around me.

"Oh, my..."

"Yeah, doll. That's a good way to describe it."

"I --" I swallowed. "I'm not doing that."

"Didn't expect you to," he said, handing me a glass. I sniffed. It didn't smell funny. "Relax. It's just a Coke. I swear. No alcohol or drugs."

"I shouldn't trust someone I just met," I said, inanely.

"Well, trust me or not, I saved your life today. If I'd been gonna take advantage of you, I coulda done it back at that bar."

He had a point. "Sorry," I muttered into my glass. I took a healthy pull. Plain Coca-Cola with ice.

"No sweat, doll."

"Esther." I yelled to be heard over the music and laughter and moans all around. I'd never seen anything like this. Sure, I'd heard tales, but this looked like an actual orgy taking place in the very room I was in!

"Yeah." He grinned. "I know. *Doll.*"

I narrowed my eyes, but that only made him laugh. Apparently, making people angry was a hobby for this guy.

"Just relax." He patted my shoulder and scooted my glass close to my hand. "Drink. Rycks will be here soon. Then we'll all have a sit-down."

"Who's Rycks?" I didn't like the idea of being alone with two strange men.

"He's... complicated. We just call him the Protector of Lost Female Souls."

That got my back up. "I am *not* lost! I'm a born-again Christian!"

Shotgun just shrugged. "Not what I'm talking about, doll. That's not my territory anyway." He tossed back a shot glass full of amber liquid. The way his throat moved as he swallowed fascinated me for some reason. Watching his Adam's apple bob made me swallow, myself, and my mouth went dry. Good thing I had that glass of soda.

"So, you gonna tell me what you were doin' in that bar? I mean. Since we established you don't drink."

How to answer that. "Well, I thought I might want a drink. Just one. But when I got inside…"

"The guys scare you off?"

"No. Not until later. I mean, I just…"

"Weren't sure if you were ready to throw all in and live dangerously?"

I blinked. "How did you know that?"

He shrugged. "Only two reasons a girl goes into a bar like that. First reason is to get laid. Which I don't see with you." I wanted to sputter and be all outraged by his language and insinuation that I could have gone there to have sex. I mean, did women actually do that? But he continued. "Second, because you wanted to go to a bar and have a drink, and you just picked something more than you could handle."

OK, this guy was too much. It was like he could see straight inside me. He didn't look like he was judging me, but I had so little experience with guys I wasn't sure. If he'd been Samuel, I'd have said he was definitely judging me. The man and his clique of seminary majors could be -- and often were -- the harshest judges in the campus church. They could cut a person to shreds for doing the exact same thing their group did at the same gathering and not bat an eyelash as they denied ever being there in the first place. This guy, however... I got the feeling he was just stating the facts as he saw them.

"So what if I did go there for a drink? There's nothing wrong with that. I'm twenty-one."

With a chuckle, Shotgun raised his hands in a defensive gesture. "Ain't nothin' wrong with you gettin' a drink, doll. In fact, if you want to try something while you're here, I'll be your protector. I'll watch over you so no one hits on you, and I'll make sure you get home safely. If you get too messed up, I'll make sure you have a safe place to sleep here at the compound. We have plenty of room."

"I'm not sure that's a good idea..." It was a perfect idea! But I didn't want to admit it to this guy. I wasn't sure why, but I just felt like giving him an inch would bring him crashing down on me, and he'd take over my life as sure as my father had.

"Come on. I ain't lookin' for nothin' from you but for you to have a good time. We already established I'm not gonna hurt you."

I thought for a moment. That was the reason I'd gone into that bar. A poor choice, to be sure, but I wanted to know what it felt like, darn it! What did alcohol taste like? How much was too much? I wasn't going to justify the whole thing by pretending to try to understand why someone would drink. I was simply curious.

Taking a deep breath, I asked, "What would you recommend?"

He grinned at me. "That's my girl." He motioned to the guy behind the bar. "Hand me the Captain," he said, taking my glass of soda out of my hand. He added a shot glass full of the amber liquid to my glass, snagged a straw from a pile, and stirred. Then he scooted it back to me and nodded. "Try it now."

I wasn't sure about this, but I thought I owed it to the guy to give it a try. Bringing it to my nose, I took a little sniff. Not too strong. It had just a hint of vanilla that intrigued me. I loved the shots of vanilla syrup from some of the fast-food restaurants. This kind of smelled like that.

I took a sip... and I was in love! "Ohmigosh, that's good!"

He chuckled. "Figured you like Captain and Coke. Drink up, then. You won't find this place so overwhelming if you do."

"I don't know about overwhelming, but it's definitely not what I'm used to."

"Most people can't survive in this kind of environment." Shotgun took a sip of his beer. "It's too raw. Too... honest."

That got my attention. "Honest?"

"Yeah. Everyone you see here is simply living their life the way they want. They don't care what other people think, and they don't pull any punches. That's how we live. By our own rules. No judgments."

"You mean, no one cares that there are people everywhere in this room having sex right out in the open." I meant for it to sound scoffing. I was pointing out a flaw in his logic. There was surely one person here with some decency besides me. Instead, it came out a little breathy.

Shotgun didn't bat an eyelash. "Nope. No one gives a flying fuck." I winced at his language. It wasn't the first time people had cussed around me. It was just the first time I felt like using such language was the accepted norm. I was dealing with a whole new class of society here, and I was floundering.

"I happen to appreciate honesty," I managed. "I mean, lying is a sin."

"True. but people do it every day."

"But not here." I figured I had him there. Now he wouldn't be so smug.

"Oh, all the time here. But not like you mean."

"I don't understand."

The smile he gave me was a little superior and a little indulgent. It set my teeth on edge because I just knew he thought he was better than me somehow. "Turn around," he said, taking my shoulders and gently turning me so I had to face all the naked and mostly naked people in the room. None of them cared even a little that I was fully clothed and watching. "Look at the room and tell me what you see."

So, maybe I wasn't really watching. I tried to look everywhere but at the writhing, naked bodies in various states of sexual activity. It was hard to miss, though. Women were on their knees in front of men -- or other women. I knew what they were doing, but I simply couldn't let my mind go there. Some were openly having sex either on couches, or the pool tables, or just standing up in the room. Others were doing it while their partner had a conversation with someone next to them. Sex was obviously a normal thing to these people when I'd been taught it was private and only between a married couple.

"I see people having sex," I finally said. "What else is there?"

"People acknowledging they enjoy sex in many different ways." He leaned in so that his breath brushed my ear as he spoke. "People getting turned-on by watching sex." I shivered. I didn't know what he was going for, but his words, his every touch, no matter how innocent, were turning me on. I might be a virgin, but I knew this feeling. I'd just never felt it this strongly before.

"What do you want from me?" I whispered, mesmerized by the blatant show going on before my eyes.

"Just for you to give me the same honesty I'm givin' you."

"I'm always honest, Shotgun," I said. Just saying his name seemed sinful to me. He inspired nothing but the forbidden. A devil whispering in my ear.

"Does the sight of people fuckin' turn you on?"

I jerked and turned to look at him over my shoulder. "What? NO!"

"Oh, really? Prove it to me."

"I -- what? How am I supposed to do that?"

"Show me your pussy isn't wet, and I'll believe you you're not turned-on. Because, lookin' at that little green sundress now... yeah. Your nipples are standin' up on those little tits somethin' fierce."

OK. This guy was out of his mind. But I crossed my arms over my chest anyway. "No. Not on your life."

He raised an eyebrow. "So you're lying, then. You *are* turned-on by what you're watching."

"I told you I wasn't. I don't have to prove anything to you."

He chuckled. "No. You don't. But we both know you're lying. And, as you said, lying is a sin. You'll feel much better if you just confess your sin and admit the truth."

I clenched my teeth. "You're so frustrating!" I wanted to turn away but doing so meant turning to face the orgy happening behind me. Except I caught a glimpse of everything in the mirror behind the bar and had to stifle a groan

"I'm honest, though." He grinned.

"Really. So you're not turned-on by what you're

seeing?"

"Honey, *I* didn't say that. *You* did."

"Well, I don't expect you'll actually admit you like it. Everyone always says this kind of behavior is bad. The women are promiscuous."

"Yeah? What about the men?"

"Well, they're... doing, uh, really bad things. No one should be doing this!" That got a hearty laugh from Shotgun. Which made me angry. "Why are you laughing at me?"

"Doll, I'm not laughing at you. I'm laughing at your, shall we say, unique view of how sex is in the real world. Which is why I say my MC is more honest than anything you're used to. Ain't no difference in men having sex or women having sex. They're all fuckin' each other's brains out and, most importantly, havin' a really fuckin' good time."

"That's it. I'm leaving."

"All right. All right." Shotgun raised his hands and backed away slightly, chuckling. "It's all in good fun. You don't have to do anything you don't want to do. Here." He motioned for the bartender to refill my glass. My chest felt warm inside already, and my head felt funny. Nothing horrible, just a little dizzy. I knew it was the alcohol, but I kind of liked the feeling. I also found my gaze wandering over the crowd of people having sex.

I sat in silence for a while. Just sipping my drink. The more I sipped, the more my head spun. My head was spinning, but I felt funny inside. Shotgun was right. I was getting turned-on. I squirmed on the barstool where I sat. The next thing I knew, Shotgun gently took the drink from my fingers.

"Think you've probably had enough of that for a while." He motioned for the bartender again, and another glass appeared. When I looked at it, then back up at Shotgun, he nodded at it, obviously wanting me to take it. "It's ice water, doll. Nothing else."

"I feel funny," I said inanely.

"Buzzing pretty good, are ya?"

I nodded. "I guess."

"Drink some water, doll." He grinned. In the back of my mind, I thought maybe I shouldn't, but did anyway. I was surprised at how thirsty I was. Hadn't I read somewhere that alcohol can dehydrate you? I hadn't drunk that much. But then, I wasn't exactly experienced in this sort of thing.

"I've never drank alcohol before," I said softly.

"Figured. You good?"

"My head is kind of spinning."

"Yeah. That's the buzz."

Looking up at him, I was struck by how handsome he was. It was obvious he was older than me, but just looking at him -- his face with his short beard, piercing green eyes, that little scar over his upper lip, and the crooked nose where it had probably been broken, not to mention all the tattoos on his heavily muscled arms, made me wonder what it would be like to see him every single day. Would I get tired of that brutally handsome mien? Would I grow to crave it?

"You're really hot." I have no idea why I said it, but the second I did, his lips turned up at the corner.

"I get that a lot. Can't say I expected it to come from you, though." The music blared all around us, a vigorous rhythm that more than one couple fucked in time to. I thought it odd, but with the bass beating through my chest and the state of arousal I found myself in made me appreciate their need. It was almost like a dance. And the pornographic dance fit the hard-driving music. "Come dance with me," he said, holding out his hand.

Looking around, I shook my head. "I can't dance like that," I said, indicating the writhing bodies.

"Sure you can." He grinned. "But that's not what we're going to do. You're drunk for the first time in your life, and I'm not the kind of man to take advantage of a woman in that way." He tugged me to my feet and into his arms. Oh, God! That felt wonderful! "What I will do is show you how a little play is healthy for the soul."

"I can't have sex with you," I blurted out.

"Not tonight, doll. Another night maybe." He pulled me so I was flush against him. I could feel him poking my belly where he was hard. Yeah, I knew the birds and the bees, but this was knowing on a whole other level. Instead of being horrified and pulling back, I stiffened and looked up at him with what I was sure were wide, too-innocent eyes. "You feel that?" He looked amused, but also something else I couldn't put my finger on. I nodded. "Good. I want you to feel it. Gonna rub against you while we dance. Gonna get you good and..." He paused, grinning as he leaned in against my ear and said, "Horny." I let out a little whimper as I looked up at him helplessly. "Don't worry, doll. Ain't gonna fuck you. Not tonight. Just gonna give you a good taste of what our life is like here. I think you'll like it if you give it a chance."

His hands rested lightly on my hips as he moved me the way he wanted. All the while, I watched the orgy going on all around me. Men and women laughed and drank. Sex was everywhere. There was a pool game going on, but it seemed to be more about getting a sex act performed for every ball they sank.

"This is... wow," I said. It was all I could

manage.

Shotgun spun me round, pulling me up against him so that his erection mashed against my belly. "Where you stayin', doll?"

"I --" I swallowed. "A little motel on the outskirts next to the beach. Beach Front Inn."

"Next to Tito's Diner?"

"You know it?"

"Know it's a shit-hole. Only saving grace is it's close to Tito's. Why you stayin' there?"

I shrugged. It wasn't his business, but I was feeling good enough not to care. "It's cheap? And I got a job at Tito's until I start school. Marge broke her wrist and needed time to recover."

"I'll get Rycks to give you a room here until you get settled. It's self-service, but it's safe, and you can rely on the door to keep people out if you lock it." He pulled me closer, reached behind him to snag the Captain and Coke I'd been drinking and brought it to my lips. "Also, if you stay here, you can drink as much as you want and not have to worry about being on your own tonight." I took a healthy gulp. I couldn't help it! The combination of the bitter rum and the sweet soda was perfect.

"Well, I suppose." Then a thought occurred to me. "But I'm not fu -- uh -- sleeping with you."

With a deep bellow of laughter, Shotgun pulled me in close, kissing my forehead. "No, doll. Ain't gonna fuck you. I told you that. Tonight is all about fun. Letting your hair down. Pushing your boundaries."

"My boundaries?"

"Yeah. Can you even say fuck?"

"Well, sure. I just choose not to." I totally couldn't say it. I couldn't even bring myself to think it!

"Uh-huh." He urged me to take another drink before setting the glass back on the bar. "Why?"

"Well, because it's not a nice word."

"Says who?"

This wasn't computing. "Says everybody." Why was he pushing my buttons? And why was I letting him get to me?

"Well, it's my favorite word. So not everybody says it's not a nice word. Doubt you'd get anyone here to say fuck ain't a nice word, or if they did agree with you, they still wouldn't give two shits if anyone said it." I couldn't help but wince. The turd-head picked up on it and snickered at me. "Got another word you don't like, huh?"

"Why are you being so mean?" He wasn't mean. He was just making me think, and I wasn't in any shape for that. I knew the alcohol was doing a number on me, and there was no way I could keep up with him.

With a soft chuckle, Shotgun wrapped his arms around me and lifted. Oh. My. Goodness. Being wrapped up in this man's arms... I could live here. It wasn't sexual, either. Well. Not *only* sexual. It was easy to imagine him feeling more for me than he did. Like his embrace was affectionate instead of a means to keep me off-balance. Before I realized it, I'd buried my face in his chest and inhaled deeply, taking him into my lungs. His scent gave me shivers. There were hints of wood, pine, and gasoline. All the men I knew cloyed themselves in aftershave. Not this man. He was exactly as he presented himself and made no apologies for it.

When he sat me on the barstool, I found myself still leaning into him. He'd relaxed his grip to let me go, but when he realized I hadn't sat up straight, he gave a little chuckle and tightened his arms back around me. I felt his chin on the top of my head, and one hand came up to cradle my face against him.

"You smell good," I murmured. "I like the way you smell."

"I like the way you smell too, little doll. Can you sit up for me?" With a disappointed sigh, I did. "Ahh." He grinned. "Don't go poutin' on me. I've got a game to teach you." There was a devilishly wicked gleam in his eyes.

I perked up even though I just knew it was going to be something to make me uncomfortable. "A game?"

"Yeah. Well, kind of. Have you ever done body shots?"

"Not sure what that is." I was beginning to see just how truly lacking my education was. In life.

"What was I thinking? If that was your first drink," he indicated my glass, "you've never done shots of any kind."

"You think I'm dumb, don't you?" Now I sounded sulky. I didn't mean to be but couldn't seem to keep a rein on my emotions.

"Sweetheart, you're not dumb. You've been sheltered. Think of this as broadening your education."

Well. When he put it that way. "Yeah. That's a great idea! That's what I came to Florida for in the first place."

"It is?"

"Yeah. I'm going to University of Miami in the spring. I'll have to pay for that semester, but in the fall, I'll have a full ride."

"What're you studying?"

"Oh! Computer Science. I'm gonna go into cyber security."

For some reason that got Shotgun's attention. He

straightened, and the playfulness disappeared from his face. He was all business now.

"You got experience in that shit?" Now he sounded a little growly.

"Not really. But..." I looked around me. No one seemed to be paying attention to us, so I figured I couldn't get into trouble. "Once, my last semester at BBC, I changed my attendance from ten absences to three so it wouldn't drop my letter grade." Then I hastily added, "But don't tell anybody. I was working to help pay for my first semester at University of Miami."

That got his lips to turn up on one side. "Living dangerously, huh?"

"I didn't want to ruin my GPA!" I hung my head. "It was still dishonest, though."

"Relax, doll. Ain't no one gonna harass you over that."

"It would get me expelled. Might get my degree revoked."

"Are you done with that school?"

"Well, yeah. But --"

"Then don't worry about it. You didn't hurt anyone, and you made the grade. You just spotted yourself the times you didn't go to class. To me, if you can get an A and still not go to class, who gives a fuck if you're sittin' there? Means you're fuckin' smart."

"Really?" A heat suffused my face, and I knew I looked way more pleased than I should but couldn't seem to stop myself.

"Absolutely. Now. Forget about all that." He got a look of intense concentration on his face. "I need you to concentrate on what I'm about to teach you. Now. And this is a serious question, Esther." He looked intently at me. "How drunk are you right now?"

I blinked up at him. "I-I don't think I'm drunk at all."

"Head a little fuzzy?"

"Maybe? Kinda, I guess."

"OK. So I'll give you one regular shot to get the hang of what we're doin'. Then I'm movin' you up to the semi-pros."

"Semi-pros? What's that?"

"It's not the big leagues, but one step under. Body shots can get pretty intricate once you're experienced at it."

"What do I have to do?"

Shotgun snapped his fingers. The bartender looked at me, then back at Shotgun. "You sure about this, Gun?"

"Yup. Hit us up."

"Little lady," the bartender looked at me, "I'll shoot Rycks a text. Don't like it when the responsible party drinks too."

"Relax, Loki. I'm only drinkin' enough to show her how to do it. Then she's on her own." Shotgun turned to look at me. "More or less."

"Still lettin' Rycks know. Don't want the little lady gettin' in trouble in the compound. El Diablo would have your balls."

"And my life," Shotgun said with a grin. "Don't worry. She's perfectly safe with me. We already discussed it. No sex until she's sober. Tonight is about fun."

I found myself nodding and grinning. OK, so maybe I was a little more tipsy than I'd first thought.

The bartender set up two shot glasses, a plate of lime wedges, and a shaker of... salt?

"What's this?"

"Tequila shots," Shotgun explained. "Let me

show you." He picked up the salt shaker and reached for my hand before hesitating. "I'll warn you now, this is a little more stout than the rum and Coke."

"I'll try it," I said, eager to see what he was going to do.

"OK. So. Body shots. We'll start out basic," he said. "Watch. You have to do it exactly, or it won't taste right.

"Gotcha," I said. My hand tingled where he held it. My belly was fluttering like mad and my heart pounding.

He pulled my hand closer for some stupid reason, which brought me closer. Getting nearer to him got me a hit of his scent, which just made me want to melt. Looking into my eyes, he took a long, wet lick of the back of my hand. I gasped and broke out into a sweat. Had I been standing, I'd have crumpled in a heap to the floor.

"Salt," he said, never taking his gaze from mine. He grabbed the saltshaker and shook a generous amount onto the back of my hand. Before I realized what he was doing, he took another long, slow lick of the salt, grabbed the shot glass with the tequila and downed it followed by biting into the lime wedge and sucking it hard. Then he gasped and let out a "whoo" before grinning at me.

I swallowed. Granted, my sexy experience was vastly limited, but if there was anything that sexy in the world, I couldn't imagine it. I glanced behind me at the orgy.

"Little more interesting now, isn't it?" I turned back to him and shook my head slightly, unable to actually voice the negative. Because what he'd said earlier made me ashamed to lie, but my ingrained modesty wouldn't let me admit it *did* turn me on.

Shotgun didn't push me. Instead he offered me his hand. "Your turn now."

I shivered. Could I actually... lick him? "If I lick it, it's mine," I said before I realized I was going to say it.

Shotgun burst out laughing, throwing his head back in his mirth. "Yeah, doll. If you lick it, it's yours. Keep that in mind if there's anything else of mine you want." He winked at me, and I knew he was teasing me, but I didn't get it.

Taking a deep breath, I brought his hand to my mouth and licked the back. I bit back a moan. Barely. Salt next, then (oh my God!) lick. My eyes closed in bliss, but he handed me the shot of tequila, and I tossed it back. Before I swallowed, Shotgun practically shoved the lime wedge into my mouth and instructed softly, "Bite and suck, doll." I did. My first instinct was to spew out the foul liquid, but sucking the lime kind of compelled me to swallow. Stuff burned all the way down, and I gasped before having a coughing fit.

Shotgun laughed heartily, pulling me into his arms in a warm embrace while I coughed with tears rolling down my eyes. He rubbed my back soothingly while he chuckled. Instantly, my lungs were filled with his scent once again, and I was certain this was where I wanted to be the rest of my life. I didn't know this guy other than he was everything I'd been taught to avoid in not only men, but people in general. In short, my father would kill me if he saw me with this guy. Which kind of made up my mind about Shotgun and how far I'd let this go. Basically, whatever he wanted to do, I was game.

"You good, doll?" He pulled back and looked into my upturned face. Tears were running down my face, but I grinned and nodded. I'd have said I was good, but I could barely breathe let alone talk. Instead, I gave him a thumbs-up along with my nod. He chuckled. "All right. Give it a minute, and we'll go again. Second shot won't be nearly as bad as the first." I wasn't so sure, but I was game.

"Come on. Let's dance a song or two."

The music was still blaring. I heard some of the guys complaining about it as Shotgun brought me to the center of a mass of bodies. Apparently, the club girls got to choose the music and tonight it was top forty. That surprised me as well. I'd never have thought anyone would have a say but the members. Wasn't that how it worked in the movies and shows? All I knew was the women here weren't weak, bowing to what their men wanted. At least, not in all things. I was sure there were times when there was no negotiation, but music wasn't one of them.

We didn't dance so much as sway. Shotgun held me to him, roaming his hands up and down my body at his leisure. He never strayed into forbidden territory except to give my ass a squeeze a few times. At first it shocked me, then I found myself anticipating it. Even wanting it. It made me brave enough to run my hands up his chest and shoulders. About halfway through the second song, I even slid my arms around his neck. When I did, he pulled me even closer to him. His, uh, penis was pressed against my belly, hard and proud. Who was I kidding? This man was way out of my league. I couldn't even think the word "cock" without stumbling over it! He probably thought I was pathetic. I ducked my head and dropped my hands back to his shoulders.

"Oh, no, doll." He caught my chin with his fingers and tilted my face up to his. "Get your arms back around my neck."

"I'm not, you know," I said. Did I sound sulky? That was even more stupid.

"You're not what, sweetheart?" I tried to look away, but he kept a firm grip on my chin. "Nope. You look at me. Now. You're not what?"

I closed my eyes, sighing heavily and trying to fight back tears. I wasn't usually so emotional. What was wrong with me?

Finally, I answered him. "Pathetic. I'm not pathetic because I don't know how to do body shots or because I can't drink or because I've never had sex. Or because I can't swear. I'm *not* pathetic!"

He sighed and pulled me closer, putting his mouth by my ear. "No, doll. You ain't pathetic. So let's talk about it." He urged me to look at him and kissed my forehead when I did. "I'm teaching you about body shots and drinkin'. Right?" I nodded. "You're learning about sex by watching everything here. Yes?"

"Yes, but I've still not actually done it."

"One thing at a time, doll. As to the swearing? Look at me and say 'fuck.'"

I started, shaking my head. "I'm not saying that."

"Fine. Something a little less harsh. How about 'hell?' That could even not be a swear word."

I thought about it a minute. He had a point. I could just pretend I was talking about the Biblical Hell. So, I nodded and said it.

"Good. Now try 'damn.'"

"Why are you doing this?" My head was swimming a little now. "If you're making fun of me --"

He put his hand over my mouth and gave me a stern look. "Not makin' fun of you, doll. Just tryin' to help you out. Teachin' you to stretch yourself. No one said you had to do any of it. You don't want to say damn, don't say it."

"No! I want to!" I took a breath. "Damn!"

Shotgun's grin was wide and triumphant. Just saying the forbidden word made me feel stronger. More in control. "Want to try another one?"

I nodded. "Shit! Piss!"

He laughed. "Now you're gettin' it." I soaked up his praise, tightening my arms around him. "You ever been kissed?" The question caught me off guard, and there went my stupid knees again. If he hadn't had a good hold on me, I'd have fallen. *Again*.

"I -- well. No. At least, not... I mean. Yes. I kissed a guy on the lips once."

"I'm talking besides a little chaste peck, doll." He grinned. "A real, open-mouthed kiss with lips, teeth, and tongue. You ever let a guy lick the inside of your mouth while he kissed you?"

Chapter Three
Shotgun

Yeah. I'm a bastard. But, fuck, it was fun pushing Esther's buttons! She had this sassy little mouth that was just made for kissing, and she same as told me she'd never been kissed. Which just put all kinds of dirty thoughts in my mind. I couldn't actually touch her or have sex with her (I'm not that big a bastard) but I could kiss her. And I wanted like fuck to kiss her. She was feeling the tequila, that was easy to tell. Loosening up was bound to happen.

"W-what?"

"I asked if you've --"

"I heard what you said!" she snapped. That was different. And damn, if it didn't make my cock pulse.

"Well?"

"No, OK? I've never... done that."

"Esther, when we go back to doing body shots, you're getting ready to be very drunk. Once you are, I can't kiss you like I want to. And make no mistake, Esther. I want to kiss you."

She sucked in a breath, her eyes going wide, her face flushed. That little light-green sundress had no hope of concealing her hardening nipples.

"You want to kiss me? Even knowing we can't have sex?"

There was no way not to grin at her innocence. "Doll, there is nothing I want more than to be the first man you've ever kissed. Been wantin' to kiss you since you first stepped foot inside that damned bar."

"Oh," she said, swallowing, obviously nervous. "Wha-what do I do?"

I chuckled, pulling her soft body closer to mine. "Just hang on to me. I'll take care of you, doll."

She whimpered as I lowered my mouth to hers, but the second our lips touched, she opened beautifully for me. And I wasn't sure how in the hell I was going to keep from fucking her.

Esther tasted like spring rain and wildflowers. She melted against me like she belonged in my arms alone. In that moment, she did.

I took her mouth and let her feel my hunger for her. My tongue slipped inside and coaxed hers onto mine, urging her to explore the same as I was exploring her. She clung to me, digging her little nails into my shoulders. The bite of pain both kept me centered and fed my lust. I'd never considered taking an inexperienced lover, but all kinds of naughty, delicious things ran through my mind at the thought of teaching her about sex.

But I couldn't. Not yet. Not tonight. And not if she decided she didn't want to in the morning when she was sober. I had to grin. She was going into this full throttle. She'd even managed to force herself out of her comfort zone. It might be partially the alcohol, but she was also really trying. I wasn't sure why, and I needed that information because I didn't want her hurt, but I wanted her to have whatever experiences she craved that had brought her to that fucking bar in the first fucking place.

Taking great care, I ended the kiss and stared down into her lovely, upturned face. Esther's eyes were closed, and there was a dreamy little smile on her face, her lips still parted. She looked like she was in utter bliss.

"Hey, doll," I said, stroking her cheek with the pad of my thumb. "You still with me?"

She looked up at me with an adorably confused look on her face. Then she frowned. "Why'd you stop?

More!"

Without waiting for an answer, she pulled me to her and continued the kiss. The girl was priceless in a very appealing way. She called to everything male inside me, and the more I tasted of her, the more I wanted to possess her.

I let her explore and play for long moments before I ended the kiss again. Again, she protested.

"Easy there, doll. There's lots more ahead. We've got some more shots to do. Yeah?"

"But --"

I silenced her with a hard kiss. "We've still got shots to finish."

"Shots," she said, a blank look in her eyes. I couldn't help but grin. No girl was this innocent. Except I knew Esther was. Innocence clung to her like a second skin. She was hesitant, but eager to learn things outside her comfort zone. Things I knew she'd never even considered doing before tonight.

"Yes. Body shot? Remember?"

Her brows knit together for a moment before she opened her eyes wide, a happy smile splitting her face. "Oh, yeah! Let's do that!"

She practically dragged me to the bar, then stood there, swaying slightly, looking up at me with a big smile on her face. Yeah. I might have created a monster.

"You ready?" I handed her the saltshaker, and she snagged it out of my hand.

"Absolutely!" When she reached for my hand, I pulled away.

"Uh-uh, doll. Not this time." She looked confused and maybe even a little hurt. I couldn't have that. She'd soon feel better, though. I pulled her close. "Lick my neck this time."

"Oh…" Her eyes widened. "Nuh-uh!"

"What? You don't like the idea of licking my neck? Want me to do you first? I hadn't planned on it since I'm supposed to be the sober one, but if you insist…"

I bent to her slowly, giving her plenty of time to back out. With one hand I pulled her hair out of the way while I grabbed the saltshaker with the other. I urged her head to the side, and she went willingly. The pulse at the side of her neck was thumping like mad, and she was practically hyperventilating. When I was sure she wasn't going to balk, I took a long, slow lick up the side of her neck. Esther squealed and clung to me. She quivered in my arms when I shook the salt onto her neck and licked again. Then I pulled back to catch her gaze as I shot the tequila and sucked the lime. Esther watched me avidly, her whole body now shaking. God, I wanted to shove my hand up her skirt and see just exactly how wet she was. I'd bet my last dollar she'd soaked her panties and had moisture dripping down her inner thighs.

"Now." I handed her the salt. "Your turn."

She took it with trembling fingers. "D-do I g-get to ch-choose where I lick?"

I grinned. "Anywhere you want, doll."

For a long, long time, Esther just looked up at me. I could see the internal debate going on in her head. Truth be told, I was as anxious as she looked, just wondering where she'd choose to lick.

"If I lick it," she said softly, "it's mine." As she spoke, Esther's gaze drifted over my chest, her fingers bunching the material of my T-shirt.

"Only if you're brave enough to take it, little doll."

That must have been the exact right thing to say

because she tugged my shirt from my pants and shoved it up my belly and chest, struggling to get it off me. With a laugh, I helped her, pulling it over my head and tossing the material down on the bar.

"Oh, wow," she said, a look of awe on her face.

I knew I looked good. Ripped with muscle and inked all over, I'd had more than one woman worship my body. This woman, however, appreciated what she saw more than all the others combined. And, Lord help me, I appreciated her appreciation. My cock was harder than it had ever been, and she hadn't even touched it. *And* I had no hope of getting her to ease it.

"Well?" I asked. "What are you going to lick, doll?"

She ran her hand over my chest and abs as if trying to decide. Finally, she settled on my chest, just over my heart. I suspected she wanted to go lower but chickened out. Which didn't matter much. It just meant I needed to give her a little more time.

Esther licked, mimicking the way I licked her. Slow. Leisurely. Then she salted the area and licked again. She moaned before shooting the tequila. The sight was so erotic, I nearly forgot to feed her the lime. This time, she barely grimaced. Which meant she'd had enough.

She looked up at me with wonder in her eyes, and my heart melted a little. "Wow," she said. "You taste… really, *really* good." There was a silly little grin on her face, but her eyes didn't seem as focused as they had been.

"You like it?"

"Oh, yeah," she said. "Can I taste more?"

I chuckled again. "Yeah, doll. Just not tonight. But, after you sober up a little, you still want another taste, I'll be happy to let you taste anywhere you want." When she grinned, I added, "Provided you let me taste you."

Her hand went to her neck, rubbing the spot I'd licked. "You can lick me anywhere you want, Shotgun."

"Oh, that could get very, very interesting," I said, watching as she flushed a lovely shade of pink. Her little hand went out and touched the spot on my chest where she'd licked.

"I want to do it again," she said.

"Lick me?"

She didn't quite meet my gaze but nodded. I reached for her and she came willingly, pressing her face against my chest and kissing lightly. Experimentally. "Do I have to drink the tequila if I lick you?"

"No, baby. In fact, I have to insist you not shoot another. You're not used to it, and I think two shots was probably at least one too many."

She'd just stepped between my legs and snuggled into my bare chest when I heard a woman calling out to her.

"Esther! Hey! Esther!"

I turned to see Eden approaching. Her older brother was our vice president, Sampson, and she could be hell on wheels if she chose. "Esther! How'd you get in here?"

Esther grinned, patting my chest. She didn't straighten, just stayed cuddled into me. "I came with Shotgun. He let me lick him. Now he's mine."

Strangely, Eden frowned. "Yours? Shotgun?"

"Yeah. I licked him. So he's mine."

"Esther, honey. Are you drunk?"

Esther nodded at the same time she said, "No! Not at all!"

Eden glanced at me. "Do you know what you're doing?"

"Mostly," I said truthfully. "Went a little further than I intended, but she's safe."

"Is she? Because she's not like everyone here."

"Yeah," I said. "Figured that one out before I brought her here. She needs a place to stay tonight. Stayin' by herself isn't a good idea, and the place she told me she was renting is shit."

"She works at Tito's. It's just across the street from there, so it's convenient."

"Yeah. She told me she was workin' there. You know if she works tomorrow?"

"Don't think so. We were supposed to go house hunting for her, but I'm guessing she's going to be a little hungover."

I shrugged. "Maybe. I'll make sure she drinks some Gatorade and gets some ibuprofen down before she goes to bed. If she's not feeling well in the morning, I'll have Fury check her out to see if she needs something else."

Eden glared at me. "She's a good girl, Shotgun, but she's not part of Black Reign. Does Samson know she's here?"

Something dark crawled into my good mood. "Why would Samson need to know if she's here?"

"Hello? Because he's vice president and likes knowing everything?"

"I'm sure he knows if he wants to know. But she's here with me. Under my protection and my responsibility. Not Samson's."

"Look. I just don't want her hurt. She's… different."

"Yeah. I know about her differences. I'm teaching her to stretch herself."

"Considering she's cuddled into your chest with a big, dreamy smile on her face, yeah. I'd say she was stretching herself." Eden shook her head and sighed. "Don't hurt her, Shotgun. She might not understand the kind of player you are."

"I won't hurt her, Eden. I swear."

"Do you know Eden?" I was beginning to think Esther had dozed off. "She's my best friend in the whole wide world."

"Hey, honey," Eden said, stroking hair gently from Esther's face. "You good?"

"Better'n good," she said, slurring her words a little. "The best!" She inhaled deeply, her eyes sliding shut as she did. She looked like she was in heaven.

"Yeah, I can see that. Maybe you should come home with me."

"But…" She looked up at me with those big brown eyes of hers. The hurt plain to see. "I thought I was staying with you?"

"You are if you want to, doll. Eden's just lookin' out for you."

Esther straightened, lost her balance and fell back against me before righting herself. I steadied her with my hands at her waist. "I'm good, Eden," she said. "I really like Shotgun. Besides, I licked him." She giggled.

"You licked him." Esther blinked, looking a touch confused. Then she glared at me as realization dawned. "She licked you. So you're hers." When I just shrugged, Eden slapped at me. "You asshole. Don't put ideas like that in her head. I told you she doesn't understand shit like that! She'll think you mean it and will end up hurt!"

"Hey, no one's getting hurt." Eden amused me, but I knew she was right. Much as I was enjoying myself, this was one night. Trying to coax a little virgin into my world would only amuse me so long. Then she'd get to be tiring. "I promise, once she's sobered up, I'll let her down gently. You'll see. We'll be great friends." I gave Eden my best smile, but I was sure the girl saw right through me.

"You know Rycks will kick your ass when he finds out about this."

"There's nothing to find out about. Besides, I couldn't leave her where she was. She walked into Crank like she owned the place. By the time we got out of there, not only had Fury and me rearranged a few faces, but the neighborhood kids had stripped her car. I didn't want to take her back to her place and risk her coming back on her own. Best to distract her until she's thinking more clearly, and I can come up with a plan for her to get another car."

"You? You'll come up with a plan?"

"Well, no. I just mean, she'll need a car." I winced. Maybe the alcohol was getting to me too. I didn't come up with any plans regarding women unless it was getting them horizontal in my bed.

"Uh-huh. I'm telling Rycks. He'll take care of her, and you can move the fuck on."

"Be reasonable Eden. We're here now. It's late. I've already got her a room. Even I'm not a big enough dick to take advantage of a drunk woman. Not unless she gets that way for me on purpose." I couldn't help goading Eden a little. "I'll take care of her tonight. Take her home tomorrow. The end."

She regarded me for long moments. Meanwhile, Esther snuggled closer, turning her face up to me and burying her nose in my neck, taking a long breath in. She sighed happily and murmured, "You smell so good. If I say fuck, will you kiss me again?"

I kissed the top of her head. "Yeah, baby. You say

that, and I'll definitely kiss you again."

Esther giggled but promptly passed out again.

"How much did you give her to drink?"

"She had a couple Captain and Cokes and two shots of tequila. That's it."

"Yeah, she's probably never had a drink in her life. She's schnozzled."

"How'd you meet her, anyway?"

"At Tito's. I'd come by to help Marge, but they'd hired Esther. We hit it off. She's a good kid, just extremely sheltered."

"That's something I'm trying to remedy."

"This isn't the way, Shotgun. She'll be angry tomorrow."

"I'll soothe her," I said confidently. "She won't be mad at me long."

"Not at you, Gun," Eden said, holding my gaze. "At herself."

"Huh?"

"She'll see this as weakness on her part. Did you know her father forbade her to come down here? He made Miami sound like one step away from Hell."

I shrugged. "He ain't wrong."

"Gun! Would you just listen? She's been brought up to believe all this --" She waved her hand around to include everyone and everything in the clubhouse. "-- Is a sin. Something she should never be a part of. Sure, she's trying to break out of her shell, and she's not as naive as you might think, but a club party is a lot to take in. She's gonna have second thoughts. Especially when she wakes up with a fucking hangover."

I sighed, pulling Esther close when she snuggled deeper into my chest. She was totally passed out. "You're right." That must have surprised Eden, because she just started at me. "What? I'm not totally unreasonable."

"No, but you don't typically admit you're wrong."

"Ain't too proud to admit I might be in over my head with this one." I looked down at Esther and couldn't suppress my smile. "I like her spunk."

"Just don't lead her on. You've probably already got her under your spell." Eden tried to look stern, but I could see the grin tugging at her lips.

Was I leading her on? I knew in my heart kissing her and pushing her sexually wasn't the smart thing to do. Any virgin was bound to latch on to the first guy they fucked. To say I didn't want or need that kind of complication in my life was a vast understatement. If I had any sense, I'd pass her off to Rycks for safekeeping. But, A, I didn't want my ass kicked, and B, I didn't really want another man looking after my little innocent. So what to do?

As if I'd summoned the man, I saw Rycks approaching us. He had his gaze firmly on Esther as he stalked toward me, and there was a heavy scowl on his face.

"What the fuck, Gun? Since when do you party with someone as innocent-looking as that one?"

"Why is everyone suddenly interested in my choice of women?"

"Since you busted up a biker bar and put three members of other clubs in the hospital."

I winced. "Heard about that, did you?"

"Uh-huh. So did El Diablo. Only reason he didn't send El Segador to teach you a lesson is because he also heard about that one." He indicated Esther. Who was currently snoring softly against my chest. I grinned and just lifted her up onto my lap. She adjusted her arms around my neck and rooted her face into my neck, then continued to snore.

"Well, I have a witness this time. Fury was with me. He can tell you there was no way to avoid the incident. And, to be fair, we didn't destroy the place. All that was the other bikers."

"Yep. Heard that too." Again, he nodded at Esther. "What'er you gonna do with her?"

I shrugged. "I intended on findin' her a room here. You have a problem with that?"

"Not at all. Was gonna insist on it. You don't own a cage, and she's in no shape to ride a bike. *And* you've been drinking."

"Hey, brother. Relax. I'm not stupid."

"No," Rycks said. "You're not. Just don't hurt Little Bit there. She's probably not gonna handle the alcohol too well."

"Don't worry. I'll take care of her. I led her into this mess, I'll make sure she gets out OK."

Rycks nodded crisply. "See that you do. There are several rooms open in the East wing if you want to take her there. I'll get you a key."

I thought a minute. "No. Takin' her to my room. I can watch her there. Make sure she's not alone if she gets sick."

"Your room. You sure you don't want me to get her own? You can stay with her there without taking a woman to your private area."

Irritated, I rolled my eyes at him. "If I hadn't wanted to bring her to my private space, I wouldn't have suggested otherwise."

Rycks raised his hands. "No one's judging, brother. I was just giving you an alternative. You've never been one to invite a woman to your suite. Didn't figure you'd start now."

"Well, I am. Don't read too much into it. I just

happen to like this one."

Rycks stepped closer and brushed a lock of hair off Esther's forehead gently. "She does seem to be special. Did she fill you in on her background?"

"Enough. Eden told me more. So before you say it, I understand how she's different. I don't want to break her."

"Good. Just so we understand each other." Rycks gave me a hard look. "I'll be keeping an eye on you both."

"Fucker," I muttered.

Chapter Four
Esther

Oh, my God. I'd never hurt this bad in my life. And I was gonna puke. Right here.

I kicked off the covers and stumbled to the floor. My ears *roared*, and my head spun when I stood up. But I didn't have a choice. Either I made it to the bathroom or I was gonna hurl on the floor or in my bed.

Strong arms slid around my middle. "Easy, doll. I've got you." The guy picked me up and hurried several steps across the room. My eyes felt like a thousand hot needles were poking my eyeballs when he turned on the light. He set me down in front of the toilet just before I started vomiting violently. The sour scent of alcohol only made the problem worse and before I knew it, I was gagging with every breath I took. If I breathed through my nose, I smelled liquor vomit. If I breathed through my mouth, I tasted it.

"Oh, God," I groaned, coughing and gagging yet again. Someone flushed the toilet and handed me a cool, wet washcloth. That was when I realized someone was also holding my hair out of the way.

"Just try to breathe, doll." A bottle of water appeared in front of me. "Here. Take a couple of sips. Rinse out your mouth."

I did, swishing and spitting into the toilet. Then I took a couple more sips. That's when I realized it was a lemon-lime sports drink. *And it tasted heavenly!*

"Easy. Just take it slow."

That voice was familiar. The nickname "doll" was, too. But where…

"Sh-Shotgun?"

"I'm here, doll. Just take a few more sips. Do you

hurt anywhere?"

"My head." I was embarrassed by the weak whimper, but it was all I could manage. "I'm so sorry."

"For what?" He didn't sound like he was making fun of me, but I was in no state to analyze at the moment.

"For whatever this is. I can't believe you watched me barf all over the place!"

"Ain't the first time I helped someone hungover. Won't be the last. Been there a few times myself." He chuckled. "Glad I could help out. Can you swallow a couple of pills for me?"

"Pills?"

"Just some ibuprofen. Will help your head. That and the Gatorade."

If I'd been in any other situation, I'd probably have balked at taking pills from a strange man, but how much more trouble could I possibly get into at this point? Besides, he wasn't exactly a stranger, was he? As the events of the night started rolling back inside my brain, I groaned. I'd had this man's tongue down my throat! And had begged for more! I wanted to cry, but it was a little too late to put that horse back in the barn.

"Did we have sex last night?" That was a question I never thought I'd utter.

He brushed my hair off my forehead and took the washcloth from my hands. With slow, comforting strokes, he washed my face lightly. "No, doll. I'd never do that to any woman, much less someone like you."

"What does that mean? Someone like me?"

"You're as innocent as a newborn lamb. You had no idea what you were getting into with any of what happened last night. Starting from the moment I found you at Crank. Ain't never met a woman like you. I'd certainly never have sex with you while you were drinking. Not even if we'd planned it ahead of time as a way to help ease you into it."

"You've done that before?"

"Not exactly," he said. "I've had sex with drunk women before, but it was always with an established partner, and it was always something we'd discussed beforehand. You said you'd never drunk before last night. I took you at your word. I tried to let you have the experience without having to worry about someone taking advantage of you. Yeah, we fooled around a little, but that was it. Besides, even if I'd had it in mind to be that kind of bastard, you had people watching out for you, doll. Not just me."

He wasn't making any sense. At least, not to my befuddled brain. I just wanted to go lie down and close my eyes.

"Come on. Finish that bottle and I'll get you back to bed. You need to piss?"

I groaned, muttering, "Well, I didn't."

He chuckled. "Can you stand, doll?"

"I'll manage."

Instead of leaving me, Shotgun helped me stand. He hesitated. "I don't want you falling and hurting yourself, but I know you want privacy. I'm leaving the door open and will be right outside. Don't try to stand if you get dizzy. You call for me."

"Are you always so bossy?"

"Pretty much, yeah."

I'm not sure how I made it, but I managed to pee without falling off the toilet or leaning against the counter next to the toilet and just dozing off. Somehow, I managed to clean myself and right my clothing before flushing and washing my hands. The second the water was off, Shotgun came through the door and scooped me up. I should have protested, but it felt too good to be in his arms. Also, I wasn't sure I could have walked to the bed.

Which was when I noticed I wasn't in my own little motel apartment. "Where am I?"

"Do you remember anything, baby?" I got the impression Shotgun was fishing, but I wasn't sure what for.

"I remember making out," I said with a snort. "Hard to forget that."

"I must have been pretty good, then." The man sounded entirely too pleased with himself.

"Don't flatter yourself. It was my first real kiss. And I was drunk off my butt."

"Ass, doll."

"Not saying that."

He smirked. "You said more than that last night."

The memory came rolling back, and I groaned. "Well, I wasn't myself."

"No, I guess not." He chuckled. "The important part is that you remember me kissing you. If you hadn't, I'd have been crushed." How could a man look so boyishly desirable when talking about wicked things? Because I had no doubt in my mind that what he and I had done together last night had been more than a little naughty. I'd say sinful, but my mind just stumbled over the word. If it was sinful, then I wasn't the good girl I'd always thought I was. Because I wanted to do more with this man. Much, much more.

I steeled myself as I got to my feet. Shotgun helped me stand, then put an arm around me to steady me. "You good, doll?"

"Yeah. My head still hurts."

"Give the pills time to work." He walked me to

the bed and urged me to sit. Then he handed me the bottle again. "Drink some more. It will help more than the pills."

I did. Small sips until I was sure my stomach was settling. Then I took larger drinks. Before long, I'd drunk the whole bottle.

"Good," he said, setting the bottle on the nightstand. He urged me back under the cover. "Sleep for a while longer."

I protested weakly, but he managed to get me covered up and tucked in. "I think I'd better go home," I said.

"I'll take you home first thing in the morning. But I've drunk a bit my own self. You wouldn't want me drivin' you home drunk, would you?" He turned off the bathroom light and shut the door, then snapped off the bedside light, plunging the room into the darkness of very early morning.

"I guess not." I sighed as I snuggled down into the pillow. "This is a good pillow." It smelled like him. Shotgun.

"Yeah. I think so, too." Was there amusement in his voice?

There was silence for a while. I waited, thinking he'd try to get in bed with me or get handsy, but he didn't. I had no idea where he actually was, but there was absolute silence.

"Shotgun?"

"Yeah, baby?" He was close.

"Are you... are you sleeping on the floor?"

"I am now. Was in the chair, but thought I'd stretch out for a bit."

"Why would you do that? It's your bed. Why would you not sleep here?" I started to get up, but a big hand fell to my shoulder and pushed me gently back onto the pillow.

"Because you need the bed more than me. And I've never climbed into a woman's bed who didn't invite me in."

I sighed. Honestly, how could he know the exact right thing to say to put me at ease with the situation? Shotgun wasn't a bad person, and he wasn't going to take advantage of me. He'd had plenty of opportunities to do that long before now.

"Get in the bed. Plenty of room on the other side. It's huge."

I expected him to laugh or something, but instead he was silent a long moment, as if debating with himself. "You sure? I won't touch you or anything. I swear."

"If I'd thought you would, I wouldn't offer."

He moved around the bed, and I felt the mattress dip as he slid in beside me. I could tell he was on top of the covers because of the way they resisted when I turned over. Not uncomfortable. Just a reminder he was being the gentleman others never would have.

"Thanks," he muttered. "Floor really wasn't comfortable."

"Didn't figure."

I was still buzzing, but the headache had eased off. This feeling wasn't so bad. I could easily understand wanting to keep this feeling going. As I thought about the evening I'd spent with Shotgun and all I'd done with him, I became aroused. Sure, I'd been in this situation last night, but nothing like this. This was all me. He wasn't whispering wickedly in my ear or coaxing me to do naughty things. I was lying beside him. He was asleep as far as I knew -- he hadn't moved since he'd lain down. And my sex was *aching*!

"You good, doll?"

Had I groaned aloud? That was so embarrassing! "Um, yep. I'm good."

"Still buzzing?"

"How'd you know?"

I felt him turn over beside me. "You're squirming." When I didn't say anything else, he asked, "Thinkin' about everything you did tonight?"

"Oh, my, God! Can we not talk about it?"

He chuckled. "As you wish, doll. Try to get some sleep. If your head spins too much, put one foot on the floor. It will ground you."

Yeah. I'd try anything at this point. Though I wasn't really disoriented or bothered by the buzzing of my poor head, I let my leg dangle off the bed to touch my toes to the floor. Amazingly, it helped.

"Thanks," I muttered.

"Any time, honey. Get some sleep. I'll take you home tomorrow."

"Shotgun?"

"Yeah."

"I'm sorry if I gave you the impression I didn't appreciate all you did for me. I know I was in trouble in that bar. Thanks for getting me out. And thanks for the experiences tonight. I probably won't repeat them, but I needed and enjoyed them."

He reached over and found my hand on the mattress and squeezed. "Any time, honey."

He didn't let go of my hand. I didn't mind because, for some reason, I drifted off to sleep easily.

* * *

I have no idea how I was still buzzing, but I was. I didn't mention it to Shotgun because I was afraid he wouldn't take me home. And I desperately needed to get home. For one, I felt gritty, and I smelled like a brewery. Thankfully, I made it the twenty-minute ride on the back of Shotgun's bike with no problems. Unfortunately, I then stumbled and nearly fell when I got off. If Shotgun hadn't caught me, I'd probably have face-planted.

"Easy there. You good?"

"Yes," I said softly. "Sorry."

"Nothin' to be sorry for. You still buzzin'?"

I glanced up at him. There was real concern in his face. And he smelled good. And his arms around me were strong. I wanted to just close my eyes and stay right here for the rest of my life.

"Doll?"

"Uh, yeah," I managed, pushing at his chest to at least make an effort to step away from him. He wasn't having it. "Maybe a little."

"Shouldn't have pushed you to do the tequila."

"It wasn't your fault," I said softly. "I was so enthralled by you and everything around me I was willing to do anything."

"Yeah, well, don't make it right." He kept an arm around me but urged me to walk toward the motel. "Which one's yours?"

I showed him and took out my swipe card. He led me to the door. Just as I was about to swipe myself in, he plucked the card from my fingers and did it himself, entering first and walking quickly through the small room and bathroom.

"Looks safe. Anything seem to be missing?"

"Not that I know of. Did you expect a break-in?"

"Never know in this place. It's not the safest place for you to be. Why not pack your shit and come back to the Black Reign compound with me? There's room to spare, you know."

"Thanks, but I can't. This is my place until I start school. After that, I'll probably live on campus."

"When does school start?"

"A couple of weeks."

"Ain't you got your shit line out yet? Don't they usually have you a dorm assignment by now?"

"Well, I'm a little behind with payment. My classes and books are all paid for, but I'm having trouble with the room and board part."

"If you ain't got that locked down now, you ain't gonna."

"I guess not," I said softly. "It's not a far commute, though. With the money I'm making at Tito's I should be all right."

"Until Marge comes back from her injury. They indicate that was a permanent job?"

"Not exactly. They were expecting me to move on when school started." I sighed. I couldn't think right now. "Look. I know it doesn't seem like it right now, but I'll be all right. I just need to sleep this off."

He nodded at me. "Yeah. I get that." He scrubbed a hand over his face. "Look. Go take a shower. You'll feel better. Then you can sleep."

"Good idea. I need clean clothes. I can still smell the tequila."

"All part of being hungover, doll." He grinned. "Go. I'll stay here for a while. If you get dizzy, call for me. I promise I won't look."

"Right. I believe that."

He laughed. "Go on. Make it long and hot. You really will feel better."

Yeah. I wasn't so sure. I glanced at my phone. It was only seven in the morning. Not even a full twelve hours after my wild night out. I groaned. Yeah. Not sure the wild life was for me.

I did as Shotgun suggested, letting the hot water pour over me. He was right. I felt incredible. I slid down the shower wall to sit in the bathtub with the water streaming over my side. *Heaven*!

I closed my eyes… And I was out…

Chapter Five
Shotgun

When Esther didn't come out of the bathroom after twenty-five minutes, I started getting a little concerned. I knocked lightly. "Esther? You good?"

No answer.

"Esther?" Nothing. "Esther!"

Fuck it. I opened the door and walked into a bathroom full of steam. It was telling to me that she hadn't locked the door. First to how tired she was. Second to the fact that she must trust me at least a little bit.

"Esther, honey?" I heard her snore softly and pulled back the curtain just a little. She was curled in a little ball in the bathtub, her body propped against the back of the tub. Water sprayed over her naked form just out of her face.

I sighed. Yeah, the sight made me hard as fuck, but it also made something protective and possessive rise inside me that never had before. Up to this point, I'd been playing with her. It had been fun and, though I had no intention of hurting her, I'd had no intention of seeing her beyond this encounter, either. Now, I wasn't so sure. There was just something about the little pixie that intrigued me. It wasn't just her innocence, though I wanted to explore that with her and see just how far I could push her. It was the quiet confidence she had even in the face of something so foreign and alien to her as that club party. Most girls like her would have run screaming. To say nothing of being at Crank in the first place. Crank was the roughest biker bar in the area and definitely not for the likes of Esther.

I crouched down and laid a hand on her

shoulder. "Esther, honey. Can you wake up for me?" She murmured something and seemed to push back into my hand like she wanted my touch. Fuck. She was so beguiling. I couldn't decide if I wanted to fuck her or wrap her in bubble wrap and put her on a pedestal.

There was no way I was getting her out of that shower without getting soaked, and I didn't have a change of clothes with me. I grinned. No, I couldn't do anything naughty with her right now, but I could have fun teasing her.

Stripping off to my briefs, I got in the shower with her, lifting her into my arms. She clung to me as she woke slowly. I let her feet touch the shower floor in case she needed her freedom once she realized where she was.

Esther opened her eyes and looked up at me. "Why are you in here with me?" It was a simple question. Not a demand that I leave or explain myself. I tried to smother my grin but wasn't sure I managed it.

"You fell asleep, doll. Didn't look like you'd done much other than let the water pour over you. So, I thought I'd finish washing you, then help you out."

She blinked, then looked away. Not in shame or anything -- which I'd never allow -- but like she was deciding what to do.

"You really mean to help wash me?"

"Yes, doll. Now's not the time for anything else."

"Fine," she said. "But I'm not usually helpless. You seem to be seeing me at my worst."

"Seeing you at your best, as far as I can see," I insisted. "You're willing to allow someone to help when you need it and have pushed yourself beyond your comfort zone. Most people aren't brave enough to do either. You have more courage than you give yourself credit for. And that's seeing you at your best." I brushed a stray lock of damp hair off her cheek. Esther looked up at me, her eyes wide.

"You really see me that way?"

"Absolutely. Anyone who doesn't hasn't taken time to see your worth. You're a strong woman, Esther. One any man would be proud to call his own."

Instantly, her neck and face went red. As did the tops of her breasts. I looked down, then grinned when I met her eyes again.

She scowled at me, trying to cover those luscious tits with her arms. "You said that just to make me blush!"

"No, doll," I chuckled. "Honest. You blushin' is just an added bonus. One thing you'll learn about me is that I never say anything I don't mean. Lyin's too much effort to keep straight when people start askin' questions."

She was silent for a long while. I snagged the shower gel sitting on the edge of the tub and squirted a generous amount down her back. Using my hands I smoothed it over her skin, everywhere I could reach including the cheeks of her ass. I didn't delve any deeper or do more than trail my hands over the sides of her breasts. Hooking one of her legs over my hip, I trailed my hand over her thigh and calf before giving the same treatment to the other leg. All the while she clung to me, mashing those tits of hers against my chest. Occasionally, she shivered, and I had to think it was from fear or maybe desire. I was betting on desire, but I wasn't taking any chances.

"You afraid?"

"What? No! I mean, no. You've given me no reason to fear you and every reason to trust you'll do exactly what you say."

"Then, you cold?"

"No. Water's hot."

"So, why you shivering?"

She looked up at me, her eyes confused and so sweet it nearly hurt to look at her. I couldn't help but place a gentle kiss on her mouth. She sighed and opened her mouth to me, accepting me like she'd been kissing me for years. It struck me how she hadn't protested this time. She just accepted and followed where I led.

My dick was pointing due north now, pulsing between us. She gasped, and I slid my tongue a little deeper. Esther just melted against me, taking everything I wanted to give her without backing down. She didn't shy away from my hard-on or try to ignore it. In fact, unless I was mistaken, she was rubbing against it deliberately now.

I ended the kiss gently, urging her to look at me. I caressed her cheek, rubbing my thumb over her bottom lip. When she opened her mouth and darted her tongue out to draw my thumb into her mouth and suck, I thought I might come right there.

"You're playing with fire, doll," I whispered. "You feel how hard I am?"

She nodded, not saying anything, but pulling stronger at my thumb.

"You wantin' to suck on somethin' else?"

She shivered again, moaning around my thumb, her eyes closed. She let it slide out long enough to whisper, "I don't know how. I've never done it before."

"You're welcome to practice all you want on me, doll, but -- I can't believe I'm saying this -- not now."

Esther started like I'd smacked her, looking very hurt. "You don't want me to do that for you?"

"Oh, I definitely want you to do that for me, doll.

But you're still about half drunk. You sober up, then we'll do more than just you giving me head."

She closed her eyes and sighed, resting her chin on my chest so her face was upturned to mine. "I've never wanted to have sex so badly in my life," she said softly before opening her eyes. "Why is it a sin to want it so much?"

I shrugged. "I wasn't raised that way, but my mother was very religious. Even she always said it seemed wrong for such emphasis to be on the woman's purity with none on the man's. Me? I think people are just jealous when the young are enjoying themselves. They remember when they were young and there wasn't as much freedom as there is today. So, you just have to decide for yourself what's right for you. I ain't gonna push you. And I won't pursue you. But you come on to me, I'll be there to teach you and let you experience anything you want. Just understand that there are no strings. It's all in fun."

She frowned at that and lowered her face. Seemed little Esther didn't like that. For some reason, the thought of her moving on from me to one of my brothers didn't sit well with me either. I was saved from having to analyze that by a loud knock at her door. She stiffened in my arms.

"You expecting someone?"

"No one has my address except Tito. Even Eden doesn't know which room I'm in."

"Come on," I said, helping her out of the shower. I tossed her a towel and wrapped one around my waist. "Wait here. I'll check it out, then call for you when it's safe."

"Why wouldn't it be safe?" She looked puzzled.

"Are you kidding me?" I must have looked irritated, because she narrowed her eyes at me.

"I have no enemies here, Shotgun."

"That you know of. Trust me. You should always check before answering the door. Even if you're expecting someone."

She nodded, but didn't shut the door after me. Instead, she stuck her head out and watched as I stalked across the room. I snagged my gun where I'd lain it at the foot of her bed. I chambered a round in the Sig Sauer. Pulling back the drapes slightly, I glanced out the window to see who was currently pounding on her door.

Then I saw fucking *red*.

I undid the chain and the deadbolt, then threw the door open, cocking my Sig as I raised it to the bastard's face.

"What the fuck?" He backed away, raising his hands.

"I could ask you the same Goddamned question. What'er you doin' here, and how did you find out where she lives?"

"Bitch owes me a hundred dollars. I came to collect."

"You can collect from that bastard at Crank. She didn't use anything you paid for. You want your fuckin' money back, here's not the place." I was wearing a towel around my waist, and no shoes, but I advanced on the bastard from the bar like I had on fucking armor.

"No refunds, man. You get me?" He lowered his voice, as if afraid someone might hear. "Look. I got no problems sharin' the bitch. I'll even take sloppy seconds if you --"

I pulled the trigger, shooting a round over his shoulder at an upward angle before bringing it back to a bead between his eyes. Not the safest thing to do and could cause some blowback with the city police, but I wanted to get my point across.

"You even think about touchin' her and I'll fuckin' kill you, you son of a bitch. She's property of Black Reign now. You come after her at your own peril."

"Black Reign?" The guy swallowed. "Are you fuckin' kiddin' me? She wasn't with you last night. Not until you left with her."

"Don't matter. She is now. Which is why you're still alive. Now you know. You don't get a second chance."

I backed back into the room and slammed the door shut. I didn't put the chain or deadbolt on but stared out the peephole to see if he left. Dumbass just looked around for a minute, then walked off.

I dressed quickly, firing off a text to Fury. Thankfully the man answered almost instantly.

Had company this am. You at the clubhouse?
Nope. Watching your company leave.
Taking Esther back.
Good plan. Got brothers on the way.
ETA?
10.

"Esther, honey. Get dressed and pack anything you don't want to leave here."

"Why?"

"It's not safe here. I'm takin' you back to the clubhouse. Rycks will get you a room, and I'll arrange transport for you to and from work."

"Wait. Stop. What's going on? Did you shoot someone?"

I shrugged. "Shot around someone. If I'd'a shot at him, I'd'a killed him. Then El Diablo would'a had my head."

"El Diablo. Isn't that Spanish for the Devil?" She pulled the shirt she held in her hand up to her chest as if it were some kind of shield. "Who are you people?"

"El Diablo's our president. He's also the one who keeps us all in line. His word is law, and he said not to kill anyone unless it was absolutely necessary. While I personally feel like that guy deserved killin', I don't get to make that decision."

"So, you're more afraid of making your president angry than you are of actually killing someone?"

I sighed. "Look. I can explain it all later. Right now, we need to go. That guy is with another club -- ain't sure who -- but the point is he's not alone. He'll come for you and with his brothers. I have no doubt I can protect you against however many they send, but why put both of us through that when we can get the hell outta Dodge now and save the trouble?"

"We just came from the clubhouse."

"So?"

"Won't everyone think I'm a wuss or something?" Esther looked more vulnerable than I'd ever seen her. Even when faced with a common room full of sex-hungry bikers, or with the possibility she was getting ready to be raped.

"Look at me, doll." When she did, I framed her face with my hands. "No one is gonna give you a hard time. Not about that. Ain't sayin' the club girls won't test you, but that's just life. They will try their best to embarrass you because they know that's your weakness."

"How do they know I'm embarrassed easily?"

I couldn't help but grin. "Because you've got it written all over you. You're too damned innocent for a place like that."

"Then why take me back? Won't I just be in your

way?"

"Never, doll. Never in a million years. Now, get dressed. Pack your shit. You got more than one suitcase?"

"Not really. Everything fit in my hiking backpack."

"Good. Pack it and sit it by the door. One of the guys will pick it up and follow us."

"I can carry it on my back. It's kind of bulky but not too bad."

"You think you can balance on the back of my bike with it? 'Cause I'm bettin' you can't. You're new to riding, and I'd like to put some distance between here and us."

She shook her head. "Good. Do what I told you. I'll be outside the door. Knock before you exit so I know you're comin'. Wait for me to tell you before you open the door."

I could tell she thought it seemed a bit excessive, but I could also see she would do whatever I told her to.

"If you think it's best."

I leaned in and kissed her mouth lightly before I left the room. If I knew Fury, he had the brothers coming in force. Just as I stepped outside, I heard the rumbling of pipes. Around the corner, Samson and Hardcase pulled into the parking lot next to Fury's bike and revved their engines. I knew from experience they'd sped ahead of the main pack to get to us as quickly as possible. I nodded, acknowledging their presence as Fury pulled up beside them on my bike, everything ready to go. I texted Rycks about Esther's backpack just as she knocked on the door.

"Come on out, doll. Where'd you leave your things?"

"On the side of the bed next to the wall in the corner."

"Good." I relayed Rycks the information, then grabbed her hand. "Let's go."

When we got to my bike, I handed her the helmet. Once she had it on, I helped her onto the back and the five of us took off. At intervals down the road, one Black Reign brother after another met and joined us. By the time we got to the clubhouse, ten other bikes surrounded us as we pulled into the compound.

Those are my brothers. Always there when another brother is in need.

Chapter Six
Esther

I couldn't believe I was back in what amounted to Shotgun's home. Sure, he was just trying to help me, but I couldn't help but want what he was dangling there in front of me. He'd made it abundantly clear any kind of relationship we had wouldn't be an exclusive one. We could have fun, he could introduce me to things gently and safely, but we wouldn't actually be together. While I wasn't sure if I wanted that exactly, I knew I wanted Shotgun. I was completely and totally infatuated with the man. He was the classic bad boy. The one you never wanted to bring home to meet Daddy. In fact, I think my dad would faint dead away if he knew I was with Shotgun even knowing he was trying to protect me. He'd see the whole place as evil and sinful, no matter what good they did.

Speaking of sinful, as I entered the common room, that same scent of sex and alcohol hit me as it had the night before. Deja vu. Only this time, I drew more stares than before. Not from the men. From the women. They seemed to smirk at me, as if they knew how uncomfortable I was. Guess Shotgun was right.

Instead of ducking my head or looking away, I threw my shoulders back and met gazes boldly. It didn't seem to help. They just held my gaze as they sucked a guy off (I couldn't believe I could even think those words!) or had sex with a guy (or three). I remembered what Shotgun said, about them being able to tell how innocent I was about this stuff. I decided to just pretend none of it bothered me. Fat lot of that. It bothered me, all right. It was turning me on again, and I had no idea what to do about it.

"You good, doll?" Shotgun's mouth was right by

my ear. There wasn't the blaring music from the night before, so it was quieter, but the sounds of sex were much more amplified.

"I'm good." I shrugged. "Can't say this is completely comfortable, but I think I'll be able to keep my eyeballs in my head this time."

His warm chuckle sent shivers through me. God, I wanted him to kiss me again! I shouldn't, but I did. That and much more. "You just stick with me. I won't leave you alone with anyone you're not comfortable with."

"Would anyone here hurt me?"

"No. Rycks and El Diablo would have their hide. Like I said, club girls like to test newbies out. See where they are in the pecking order. You just stick with me, and you'll be fine."

He held out a hand for me, and I took it eagerly. Not only did I want to stick close to him, but I just liked the feel of his big hand holding mine. Even though I'd resolved not to, I found myself looking around the room in a kind of captive awe. These women were so free with their sexuality. Proud of it. They seemed to love showing off their bodies. Some were perfect. Some less so, but to a woman, they all looked like they were in the throes of ecstasy, loving every single second of what they were doing.

"I got you a room next to mine, doll. You ready?"

"What? Oh. Yes. Will someone be bringing my backpack?"

"Yes. Iron says he has it and is getting your schedule from Tito's. We'll get this all taken care of, and everything will be fine. Come on."

Shotgun led me to the room next to his but hesitated. "How are you feeling?"

"Actually, I feel much better now. The shower

and the excitement afterward seemed to have cleared the last of the cobwebs away." I smiled at him.

"Good." He opened the door and led me inside. The room was made up much like a hotel room might be, only this was much nicer than my little crappy motel room near the diner. "Our doors adjoin," he said, showing me what he meant. Sure enough, a door opened up, separating our two rooms. "I'll leave it open. You want to shut it, go ahead. Otherwise, it'll be like we're roommates." He grinned.

I figured it was now or never. "Look, I need something."

Instantly, he was all business. This intense gaze of his was sexy as everything else about him. "Name it, doll."

"How to word this," I muttered. "I know you said earlier that I was still drunk, but I swear to you I'm not."

He stiffened, his face closing down. "I can't, Esther. Not now."

"Why not? Shotgun, you've opened up a whole new world to me. I'm not sure I'm ready for everything, but I know one thing for sure. I don't want to have my first time be with a guy who doesn't know what he's doing. I don't want it to hurt, and I want to feel pleasure."

"You don't know me, Esther. Sure, I could do what you want, but I'm a bastard when it comes to relationships. You need someone who can promise you more than an hour. That ain't me."

"I don't want promises. I just want this ache inside me eased! Do you have any idea what it's like to have your body so out of control and you can't get any relief?"

He narrowed his eyes. "You've never

masturbated, have you? Never orgasmed."

"Shotgun, I've not touched myself more than a couple of times like that and never got any relief. I might have felt some pleasure, but I've never felt anything like what I felt last night and today. In the shower with you. Watching the scene in the common room. I just... I don't know what to do about it. And I want to do more than just m-mas --" I took a breath. All in. I had to be all in or he'd never do this with me. "Masturbate. I want to have sex. With you."

He stared at me a long moment. I had no idea if he was finding me lacking or just trying to make up his mind about what to do.

"I know I'm not that pretty. My boobs are small, and I'm built like a boy, but I promise I'll make up for it with enthusiasm. Isn't enthusiasm supposed to trump experience?"

"Honey, it's not that. You're a walking, talking wet dream as far as I'm concerned. I just don't want you to regret this."

"I'm not going to, Shotgun. Please, this is hard enough for me to ask as it is. If you make me beg for it... I'm... I'm not sure I could do that."

"Fuck," he said, reaching for me and pulling me into his arms. "Fine. But we do this my way. You understand?"

"Since I don't have my own way, I'm good to follow any lead you lay down."

"OK," he said. Without anything further, he lifted me, urging my legs around his waist, carrying me to his room to set me on my feet beside his bed. "Let's get you naked."

"What about you?"

"I'm getting naked too," he said with a grin.

If I'd been a good girl, I'd have been shy about

getting naked. Sure, I was probably as red as a lobster, but I didn't hesitate to do what he asked. I stripped myself bare. Was I self-conscious? Absolutely! But I was determined. I could do this. Once he started, this would be easier. I just had to do what he said, and Shotgun would take care of me.

It didn't take long for him to be naked before me, all that gloriously tattooed skin and muscled body looming over me. He seemed to tower above me, larger than life. I was in complete awe of him. This man was soon going to be working my body with his. Giving me pleasure. Taking my innocence. If I was going to back out…

No. I was grabbing on with both hands and taking anything he wanted to give me.

* * *

Shotgun

I was going to hell. I mean, there was no way to come away from this with my soul intact. In fact, I was pretty certain that, once I took Esther's virginity, some part of me would always belong to her, and I wasn't sure how I felt about it. It might be a punishment, but I was almost sure it would feel like salvation. Coming home to this girl every night with those big brown eyes and soft, silky skin… Yeah. No way I deserved a woman like this. Not in this life or the next. But, Goddammit, I wasn't made of stone. She was giving herself to me. Handing me her innocence on a fucking platter, and there was no way I couldn't take what she was offering.

My dick was hard as steel as I stalked toward her. She met my gaze and held it, reaching out to touch me when I was close enough. Her hands ran lightly over my chest and shoulders, like she was starved for the feel of my skin under her soft hands.

"You get nervous, we take a time-out and talk about why. You get me? Ain't goin' forward unless you swear to me you won't just push through it. You're uncomfortable, I want to know it and to know why."

"I hear you," she said softly, never taking her eyes from my chest. "You're so beautiful..."

I chuckled. "I think that's my line, doll."

Her gaze flew to mine. "But it's true! All the tattoos seem to accent your muscles. I've never seen a guy so built and cut before. You look like a professional athlete or a model or something."

"I'm just a hard-workin' guy. I work out some. But only because my brothers would call me a pussy if I let myself go."

She grinned. "Somehow, I doubt anyone would ever call you a... er... that."

"You can say pussy, you know. In fact..." I stepped into her space and lifted her. She put her legs around my waist automatically, and it filled me with so much pleasure, I was sure I smirked at her. I laid her on the bed before pushing myself off her. The temptation to just slide my dick inside her and start the day off right was tempting, but that would come later. I intended to spend hours with her. If I was doing this, I was doing it right.

I stood on the floor and pulled her body to the edge of the bed. She squealed a little and tried to close her legs, but I hooked an arm around each thigh and parted them gently. "Legs open." When she held them there without protest, I leaned in to trail my lips gently along her neck.

"Oh!" Her hands flew to my head, and she clutched at my hair. She didn't push me away, just held on. Her breathing was erratic as she adjusted to the sensation of my lips, teeth, and beard. She shivered beneath my touch with each inch as I slid down to her breast. I kissed each peak, and she cried out, jerking beneath me.

"You good?"

"I -- Yes! D-don't s-stop!"

I took one nipple in my mouth and sucked gently, rolling my tongue around the peak several times. Then I did the same to the other nipple. Esther was wide-eyed, her face flushed. Her hands clutched my hair in a death grip, so I looked up at her, meeting her gaze just as I ran my tongue over her erect nipple. At once, she groaned and let her head fall back onto the mattress.

"You still good?"

"Yes," she breathed.

"Want more?"

Instantly, she brought her head up, her eyes wild and her expression fierce. "Yes!"

I chuckled as I gently pried her fingers from my hair, kissing her hands. Then I slid down her belly to her mound where I placed a gentle kiss just above the dark patch of curls I found there.

"Tomorrow, you still want me fuckin' you, we'll get rid of this." I ran my finger through the downy thatch. "It will make you more sensitive. You'll love it."

She looked adorably confused. "Get rid of it?"

"Yeah, baby. I'll shave it off for you. The top and all around your little pussy."

Tensing, she asked, "Should I already have done it?"

I shrugged. "No right or wrong answer to that, doll. Some women do. Some don't. Most I know do because they like the feel of it."

She seemed to think about that for a minute. I wanted to taste her, to take her mind off it, but I also didn't want to rush her. "Like the first time I shaved my legs. It felt kind of odd, but good at the same time."

I trailed my fingertip through the downy hair to find her clit. She was dripping wet, the moisture beading at her opening. I didn't push my finger inside her but found her clit and circled it lightly. She gasped and jerked her pelvis, apparently unsure if she liked the sensation or not.

"Just imagine how that will feel if there were nothing to buffer the sensation."

"Oh, God!" she cried out when I did it again. "I'll never survive that!"

"Oh, yeah, you will, doll. You'll love every fuckin' second of it."

I spread her lips, looking at her. She was so beautiful, her lips pink and flushed with desire. Her little clit stood out from its hood, just begging for my lips and tongue. With a growl, I dove in. Esther tasted every bit as sweet as I'd known she would. Her cries were loud in my room. The air was scented with her arousal and the clean smell of her sweat when it erupted all over her body.

"Yeah. I think you'll love having this little pussy shaved."

"Shotgun!"

"Talk to me, honey. Tell me what you feel." I took another swipe. Her body jerked beneath mine.

"I -- I don't know! There's something..."

"Just out of reach?"

"Yes!"

"Think it'll feel good when you catch it?"

"I know it will! It's just... it's right there! What's

happening to me?"

I took her to the edge several times, but she was never quite able to fall over. When I could tell she was about to go, she'd tense up. Trying too hard.

"Just relax, baby," I coaxed her. "Let it happen on its own."

"What's wrong with me, Shotgun?" She was sounding desperate.

"You're overstimulated, honey. Trying too hard. Do you want to continue, or wait until you've calmed down? Then we can start over."

She sobbed then, tears rolling streaking down her temple. Shaking her head, she said, "No! Please don't stop!" She reached for me, pulling me over her.

"Fuck," I swore, scooting her up the bed so I could climb on top of her. "Are you fuckin' sure, Esther? I'm not gonna be mad. I just don't want to hurt you, honey."

"No," she whispered. "D-don't stop." I could barely hear her, but her body language was clear. She wanted this. More, she wanted to come. I knew she was on the verge but how to help her relax so she could get the relief she needed?

I lowered my weight on top of her, letting her feel my body pressing her into the bed. She wrapped her arms and legs around me instinctively, holding me to her with all her strength. She thrust her pelvis at me, rubbing her clit over my dick. I thought that might do it, but it didn't. Girl was just too worked up. Wanting it too much.

When she sobbed into my neck, I pulled back long enough to frame her face with my hands and lower my mouth to hers, kissing her gently. I needed to calm her down, then bring her back up softly. Fuck! I'd never taken a virgin before, and it was showing. Sure, I could take her with minimal pain, but making it good for her was proving to be a challenge.

"Just relax, honey. I've got you. Not goin' anywhere. We'll just take it slow --" I drew in a sharp breath when she reached between us and found my cock with her soft fingers. She had a determined look on her face as she guided me to her entrance, tucking my cock against her cunt and engulfing the head. "What the fuck'er you doin', girl?"

"Need you inside me," she whimpered.

"Baby, we're not ready --"

She hissed at me. Then clutched my buttocks and arched her back as she impaled herself on my cock. I could tell the moment she realized it was too much. Her eyes widened in panic, and she winced. There was no help for it now. I was fucking halfway inside her.

"Just relax, doll. I know it's uncomfortable. You can take the rest of me."

Nodding, she gritted her teeth and pulled my ass closer to her until I was in as deep as I could go. She squirmed under me but didn't complain even a little bit. I knew she wasn't as turned-on as I was. Instead of her discomfort making her reset her arousal, however, it just made her that much more determined to come. And I wasn't altogether sure I could fucking hold off to come with her. I mean, maybe if she'd stay still. But she wiggled on my cock, writhed and bucked. She'd stopped whimpering and making all those little noises, but she was still moving. Trying to get me to go deeper. Move faster. God! How was I supposed to survive this?

"Sh-Shotgun…"

"I'm here, doll. Just hold still and adjust."

"No! I need this!" Then she demanded, "MOVE!"

That was all I could stand. I'd reached the limit

of my control. "Goddammit, Esther!"

I started to ride her, surging forward hard only to pull back. Her breath caught and her eyes widened as she clung to my ass. She continued to pull me to her, hooking her heels around the backs of my thighs.

I kissed her again, hard and deep this time. Her cunt spasmed around my dick, and I felt the wet rush of her heat all around me. Which was when I remembered I hadn't used a condom. Which was what triggered my fucking orgasm.

With a brutal shout, I pulled back. To my complete and utter surprise, little Esther had wrapped me up so tight, I didn't have room to pull out. When I tried to, her body just moved with mine. I raised myself off her only to find her clinging to me so tightly, I was holding her entire weight off the bed. Cum erupted in an explosive rush, filling her to overflowing. She let out an anguished cry as she must have realized I'd come without her, but her body didn't relax. It tightened around me even more. The little sprite must have been determined not to let me go until she was done.

I could never remember a time when I'd unintentionally come before a woman. There were times I just didn't give a fuck, but, anytime I'd set out to pleasure a woman, she never left my arms less than satisfied. This time would be no different.

"Shh," I soothed as I settled my weight back on top of her. I smoothed back the damp hair from her face. "We're not done, Esther. Far from it."

"What's wrong with me?" The little sob in her voice shamed me. I was a selfish bastard, as evidenced by the fact that I'd just fucked the most innocent virgin in the fucking world. But I wasn't letting her think for one moment this was her fault.

"Nothing's wrong with you, baby," I said, kissing her lips and cheeks, her eyes, then back to her mouth. "This is my fault all the way around. I'm the one who couldn't last long enough to get you off."

"But I was right there!" she cried. "I could feel it, but I couldn't reach it!"

"I know, honey. I know. I could see you trying with all your might to reach it." I kept kissing her. When I caught the first tear, I thought I might have to beat my own ass.

I pried her arms from around me and slid down her body. I couldn't believe I was getting ready to do this, but I was not leaving her like this. Not even to cuddle until we were ready to start again.

Before I could think about it too much, I flicked her clit with my tongue and thrust two fingers into her pussy. She screamed, arching her back and flailing her head from side to side. Her whole body tensed, and she gasped in a breath only to scream again when I continued flicking her clit with my tongue. Her pussy gushed with the combination of my cum and her own. Sweat erupted over her body, and her breaths came in little gasps.

When she finally stilled, her eyes drowsy and a little stunned expression on her face, I sat up slowly. "I'll be right back, doll. Don't move, OK?"

She nodded and I left to get a wet washcloth from the bathroom. When I came back, she was in the same position I'd left her in, her legs spread wide, my cum dripping from her pussy. Thank God we were on top of the covers and on one end. I cleaned her up before turning down the bed and carrying her to the other side. I helped her in, then followed behind her, pulling her firmly against my body and wrapping my arms around her.

"This is nice," she murmured. "Is it always like this after sex?"

"No, honey. Don't usually sleep with a woman."

"Why are you now? I can go back to my bed if you want me to."

"You do and I'll follow," I growled before I realized what I'd said. Then I just tightened my arms around her. "Rest, honey. We've got all the time in the world."

"You promise you'll be here when I wake up?"

"I'll be right here. Ain't goin' nowhere. Besides. You don't get to sleep long. I'll be wantin' more before morning."

She giggled sleepily, then rolled over to lay her head on my chest. I think she went to sleep directly after she stilled. Me? I lay awake a long time. For the first time in my life, I'd come inside a woman. And it hadn't even registered until it was far, far too late to do any Goddamned thing about it. Worse? Esther still hadn't realized it.

Yeah. I was going to hell. I was *so* fucking fucked.

* * *

Esther

There was a soft glow all around me. It took several moments to realize it was the sun filtering through the sheer curtains over the windows. I stretched and became aware of the warm, male body wrapped around mine.

The previous night came tumbling into my mind. The sex. The first orgasm of my life. Shotgun coaxing and praising me through it all. I looked up to find him smiling down at me. I couldn't help it. I burst into giggles, ducking to hide my head in his chest.

"Someone's in a good mood this morning."

"Well, I'm not hungover, for one thing," I said, snuggling closer and taking a deep breath. The extra hit of his scent made me sigh with happiness.

"That's always a plus." His voice was deep and husky. And guarded. Which made me push through the surface to the deeper meaning beneath. Last night had been awesome, but it wasn't reality. I looked up at him again. Though he smiled at me, that smile didn't reach his eyes. Which was when the rest of it fought its way through my happiness.

Shotgun wasn't exactly happy about last night. Or, more accurately, the fact that I was in his bed. I knew it like I knew my own name. Still, I couldn't stop the next question out of my mouth.

"What's wrong?"

Instead of answering, he nodded at the clock. "Don't you have to work today?"

I whipped my head to the bedside clock. Eight in the morning. I was supposed to be at work at the diner by nine!

"Oh, shoot!" I jumped up and ran to the bathroom. Shotgun's chuckle followed me, though I knew he wasn't in a laughing mood. He was anything but pleased about waking up with me in his bed. Oh, well. No time to worry about it now.

After I used the bathroom, I dashed out and into my own room. My things were there, which meant my clothes and my toothbrush. Essentials. I dug frantically through my bag until I found the plain white cotton panties I owned. I happened to glance over my shoulder and saw Shotgun standing there watching me. I groaned in embarrassment.

"What's wrong, doll?" The corners of his mouth twitched.

"Look," I said, still rummaging through my bag until I found the sports bra I always wore. "I'm not fancy. I don't have fancy things. Underwear is meant to be serviceable. Not... seductive."

"Never thought I'd find granny drawers sexy, but I might have to rethink that notion," he muttered.

"Would you go in the other room? I'm trying to get ready for work!"

"Nah. I'm good. Like the view too much."

"Ugh!" I would have tossed something at him, except the only thing I had was the shirt I was putting on. Since I didn't have time for a shower, I hurriedly ran a brush through my hair and braided it into one long braid, then wrapped it up in a bun at the back of my head. It would have to do.

"Finish up, doll. I'll take you to work."

I paused in pulling up my jeans, remembering I didn't have a car. And I was in a strange place. What were the rules here? Was I allowed to come and go as I pleased?

"You don't have to do that. I can call a cab."

"No way. I got you."

"Really. I'm good."

"I know you are. Ain't got nothing better to do today. I'll drop you off, then pick you up." He snapped his fingers. "Hurry up. Time's a-wastin'."

Bossy man. Still, I was thrilled at the thought of spending even this little bit more time with him. His smile was genuine now. Maybe I was overthinking things. As long as I remembered this was a temporary situation, I'd be fine. I could enjoy what he was offering and guard my heart. Even if I knew with everything in me, I wanted Shotgun for my own.

* * *

Shotgun

How the fuck was I still in the fucking diner sitting in the corner drinking coffee while Esther waited tables? I'd intended to drop her off and get back to doing something fun. Instead, I'd seen a couple bikers from another club enter just ahead of Esther. Which meant I had to go make sure they didn't hit on her. I might have growled once or twice before Elena shoved a cup of coffee in front of me, giving me a stern look. I muttered an apology and drank that cup and four more.

Tito had Esther bring me my favorite lunch along with a beer.

"You keep growling at my customers, you'll pay double," Elena called from the back when Esther set the plate down in front of me. Esther ducked her head but not before I saw the grin she tried to hide. Just to see what she'd do, I growled at her. She giggled, which got more than one man in the diner to smile. That sound could truly light up the world.

"You keep pushin' me, I'll kiss the hell outta you right here."

"Don't you dare," she said, backing up a step. She tried to look serious, but the smile on her face wouldn't be fought down. "You lose me my job and I'll never forgive you."

"Ain't like you're not startin' school in a couple of weeks."

"True, but I'm going to work here on the weekends and the days I'm off. Marge will be back part time by my first day of school. We're working on a schedule that benefits us both."

"You sure you can work that much? You don't want to let your grades slip."

To my surprise, she giggled again. "You sound

like an old man. In case you didn't know, you're not my daddy."

"Just what the hell does that mean?" I wasn't sure if I should be offended or not. Had a feeling I should.

"She means you're freakin' old, Gun," Tito supplied cheerily as he waved a spatula at me from the safety of the counter where he was cooking. "You just proved her right with that statement."

"Don't need your help, Tito," I growled. He just grinned even bigger, and Esther laughed. Yeah. I was fucked.

"I think you both need to get back to work before I hire my brother and sister-in-law to replace you," Elena called from the back.

"Uh-oh," Tito said with a wink at Esther. "I think we just got in trouble."

"I think you're right," Esther said.

Tito mouthed, "Worth it!" And Esther gave him a thumbs-up.

The rest of the day, I had a lot of time to think. And watch as Esther went about her job with grace and a smile for every customer. The more I saw, the more I wanted her. It was more than just a sexual thing, though I couldn't help recalling the night with her. She'd been so giving and willing to follow where I led. Until she wanted more than I was letting her have. Then she was as aggressive as any experienced club girl, taking instead of asking. Just thinking about it got me hard.

Then there was the little matter of us not using protection. I needed to ask her if she was on the pill. If not, I'd take her to get Plan B or whatever she wanted. But I was hesitant to mention it. I mean, Esther was a smart girl. She knew about the birds and the bees. As she smiled and patted an older gentleman on the shoulder, I imagined her turning to the side and her belly sticking out, full with the child she was carrying. My child. Rather, my children. 'Cause if I'd knocked her up, I was sure it would be twins. The thought made me grin and puff out my chest at the same time. Why the fuck did the thought of me knocking her up fill me with such satisfaction? I wasn't a one-woman man. Never had been. Never would be.

Would I?

No. I couldn't promise her a relationship. I'd take care of her and any kid of mine, but that was all I could give her.

As if she realized I was staring at her, Esther glanced my way and gave me a soft smile. I raised my coffee mug to her and took a drink. Then she went about her work while I kept a silent vigil in the corner. Tito smirked at me. I just flipped him off.

Chapter Seven
Shotgun

What the fuck was going on with my fucking life?

My day consisted of either taking Esther to work and sitting in the fucking corner like a fucking stalker, or taking Esther to school. And waiting outside each of her fucking classes. *Like a fucking stalker.* It was beginning to feel suspiciously like I was in a fucking relationship.

It had been two months since I'd met Esther, and I seemed to be growing more protective of her. Not less. Today, I sat in my usual spot in the corner of the diner with my usual fucking cup of coffee. Two bikers from across town were monopolizing Esther's time with their endless need for refills or additions to their order. One of them even asked for a fucking glass of water. What the fuck?

"Better settle down, boys," Tito called from his cooking station. He threw a grin over his shoulder at the pair. "That one's got a very overprotective man. He don't take kindly to other men flirting with his girl."

One of them snorted. "Yeah. Heard all about Gun over there." He nodded my way. "Ain't comin' here to steal your girl. Heard about the new help Tito had hired for Marge and came to see for ourselves."

"Rumors didn't do her justice," the other one said.

"You askin' to be fucked up?" I bit out the question. "'Cause I'll totally fuck you up."

"Hey," Tito said sharply. "Language. My Elena is a good Catholic girl, and she doesn't like it in public."

"So she lets you swear at home, Tito?" the first biker asked. His colors said he was Iron Riders. They were more of a recreational club. Good guys who helped with charity events in the community and not much else other than the occasional ride across the state. They definitely weren't into the kind of shit Black Reign or even Salvation's Bane were into, and they weren't one-percenters. It was the only reason I let them live.

"Only in the bedroom." Tito grinned as he flipped a burger.

"I heard that, Tito. Keep it up and you'll be on the couch by yourself."

They all laughed. My lips tugged at the corners. Esther grinned at me, her cheeks flushing becomingly. Was she embarrassed? If so, I had to make a note to tease her lightly. That flush was a good look for her. Then again, I could put that same look on her face in bed.

I smirked at her. The blush deepened. Yep. She had something naughty on her mind.

"None of that," Elena said. I hadn't even realized the woman was out in the diner. She usually stayed in the back doing managerial stuff. Sometimes she helped with the cooking, and did all the baking. "You're having naughty thoughts about my girl. She's working, Shotgun. You can't keep your thoughts to yourself, you can go sit on your bike outside."

Even Esther laughed wholeheartedly at that.

"Laugh it up, guys. She's on the back of my bike."

"Fully aware of that," the second guy said. "Don't mean a man can't enjoy looking at a beautiful woman."

"Does if he wants to keep his eyeballs," I muttered.

"Shotgun!" Elena scolded.

"What? I was bein' nice!"

"You're horrible," Esther said as she approached me with the coffee pot. She topped me off, then bent to kiss my cheek. I grabbed the back of her neck and kissed her full on the mouth. A hot, lingering kiss.

The bikers whistled and cat-called while Tito laughed and Elena tsked in exasperation. Esther looked a little shell-shocked but had a grin on her face just the same.

"You should go easy on the man," Tito said through a chuckle. "You get him wrapped around your little finger and he'll have to turn over his man card."

"He won't turn over his man card, little lady, come see me. I'll gladly give you mine." Biker One winked at her.

"Me, too. Besides," the other one said, "I saw her first."

"The hell you did. Bozo did."

"She won't like Bozo. Too much a ladies' man. She'd see right through him."

"Hey," I said, snapping my fingers to get their attention. "I saw her first. An…" I looked at Esther and grinned. "I licked her. Means she's mine."

They both groaned while Tito just laughed. I thought I heard Elena chuckling from the back but couldn't be sure.

"Shotgun," Esther said softly. "Don't get me fired."

"Honey, Tito's not gonna fire you. Not for something I did."

"Still, maybe you should leave. I don't want to be a problem."

"You're no problem, child," Tito said gently with a soft smile in her direction as he flipped another burger. "Anyone's a problem, it's Gun there. But Elena likes him for some reason, so I let him stay."

"Ain't leavin' anyway, doll. You're stuck with me."

She sighed and shook her head, a look of bemusement on her lovely face. So I winked at her.

"You're crazy," she said with a little nervous giggle. I couldn't really blame her. That was the first time I'd kissed her in a public setting *not* a club party. It felt too much like I'd just staked a claim on her, and I wasn't as torn up about it as I should have been.

"Never claimed to be sane, doll. Now, you better get back to work before Tito thinks you've quit him."

"I'm *not* quitting, Tito," she said, turning to look at the older man.

"I know you ain't, sweet girl."

She gave me a reproachful look before going back to her customers. I just grinned. God, she was fun! When was the last time I'd just had fun with a woman? Everywhere she went she made others smile. And it wasn't just her beauty. She didn't flirt except with men over eighty. Unfortunately, she had about thirteen octogenarians hot on her heels that I could do nothing about. She just genuinely seemed to love what she was doing and threw her whole heart into it. People noticed and appreciated it.

"May have to find a way to keep little Esther even when Marge is back full time. She's meant for greater things, but me and Elena love the way she brings joy everywhere she goes." Tito set down a burger and fries at my table before scooting into the booth across from me. It was only half an hour before closing, and Elena and Esther were wiping down tables in preparation for closing.

"Not sure what to do about her, Tito," I said quietly. "She's got me tied up in knots."

"Pfft." Tito waved his hand dismissively. "Easy." He leaned forward and motioned me to do the same. "You put a ring on her finger and your cut on her back. You mark my words, that one's a keeper."

"Ain't no family man. She'll get tired of me always bein' gone with the club."

Tito snorted. "Like you are now? How much time you spend away from your girl there? 'Cause I'm bettin' it ain't much."

I scowled at him. "None of your damn business, old man."

"That's what I thought."

Tito was just about to go back behind the counter to finish his cleaning when the door opened. I saw Esther's reaction before I saw the man entering. That same fucking bastard from Crank. The one who'd come to collect at Esther's motel room.

"Fucker's gettin' ready to have himself an accident," I muttered. Before I could get my gun from the holster at the small of my back and shoot the fucker, Tito approached him.

"Sorry. We're closing early. Family emergency."

I sat back in the booth, lounging lazily, gun under the table at the ready. The guy swept his gaze around the room until it landed on me. I just smirked at him.

"Just wanted a cup of coffee to go. Surely you can manage that."

"Already cleaned the coffee pot," Elena said. "I'm not making a whole pot even for a large cup. I'm sorry. I was just putting up the *Closed* sign."

Everyone was silent for long moments. Elena pulled Esther behind the counter, putting some protection between her and the biker.

Finally, the guy's gaze found Esther, and he

smiled at her. "I'll be seein' you around, honey."

"No, you won't," I said, laying my Sig on the table.

"Why does he get to stay if you're throwing me out?" the biker asked. He spoke in a mild tone. Any other time, the question might have come out sounding whiny, but this guy made it seem like it was really just a question he wanted the answer to.

"'Cause he's the lady's bodyguard," Tito supplied. "Seems she ran into a bit of trouble and needed some protection. I hired the best there is for her because she's my sweet girl." I didn't miss the look of surprise on Esther's face. Did she truly not realize how many friends she had here?

He snorted. "We'll see, old man." He pointed a finger at Esther. "You too, little girl."

Esther shivered and shrank in on herself, moving toward the back of the diner. I stood, bringing my gun to bear on the fucker, but he raised his hands and backed out the door. Tito immediately locked it and turned over the *Closed* sign. Then he and Elena closed all the blinds.

"I have a bad feelin' about that one, Gun," Tito said. "You make sure you protect our girl. Don't be too proud to call in reinforcements. Did you see the tattoo on his forearm?"

"Yeah," I said. "Don't know how I missed it the first two times."

"He's Kiss of Death," Tito said softly.

"I'll get Fury and Samson to escort us back," I said. "Ain't like the fucker's're doin' anything anyway."

* * *

Esther

I'd never been so scared in my life. It was terrifying at that bar when the guy had basically dragged me across the room, headed to rape me. But the fact that he knew where I lived and worked really unnerved me. I wanted to curl up in a little ball and retreat into myself. I wanted to hide where no one could find me. The only thing that kept me from it was not wanting to disappoint Shotgun.

He definitely wasn't in the running for boyfriend of the year (mainly because he wasn't really my boyfriend), but he had a protective streak where I was concerned. I knew he had one foot out the door and couldn't quite commit to taking the other step, but it was only a matter of time. At least, until this guy had started stalking me. Which wasn't fair at all. If it hadn't been for that guy, Shotgun would have probably been long gone. Just the look on his face now made me shiver. It was equal parts angry, dangerous, and possessive. I wasn't certain which turned me on the most.

As much as I wanted to cling to Shotgun, I couldn't help but remember my dad's warning. *This life is leading you into sin, and that sin might lead you into more trouble than you can defend yourself from.* Shotgun was my only defense now. But how long would he stay? Wouldn't he get tired of always fighting my battles for me? Was this what my father had meant?

While I hurried about my task readying the diner for opening in the morning, I reflected on all I'd accomplished.

I'd almost finished my first semester at University of Miami and was doing really well so far. I loved the school and my classes and was learning so much. I'd found a good part-time job with flexible hours so I could work and continue to go to school and made some really amazing friends in doing so.

I'd met a guy. Sure, I was having sex out of wedlock -- *incredible* sex out of wedlock -- but surely the way he made me feel couldn't be that much of a sin. I was truly happy for the first time in my life and was having trouble reconciling the fact that my father would see all of this, the new life I was so happy with, as something bad. How could something that felt so good, that built my self-esteem so much, with a man who made me happy and protected me like this, be a sin? It wasn't like I was having sex with everything that moved.

But there was that party. And the things I'd allowed Shotgun to coax me into watching at that party. And the way he'd made me feel while I'd watched...

And I hadn't been using any kind of birth control at any time during our sexual encounters. Not the night of the party. Not since.

The second that realization hit me, my knees went weak and the tray full of dishes I'd been carrying slid from the tray to the floor to crash all around my feet. I barely registered it.

"Esther?" Elena's voice seemed to come from down a long tunnel. My ears rang, and I couldn't seem to catch my breath. "Esther! What's wrong?"

I sat down. Right on the floor. I felt light-headed and dizzy. And why not? There was a very good possibility I was pregnant. *Pregnant*! Not only would my father disown me, but my mother was probably turning over in her grave.

"Esther, honey. Talk to me." That was Shotgun. Was he kneeling beside me? No. He was gathering me up in his arms. "Did you cut yourself? Esther, talk to me."

I looked up at him helplessly. "I-I need to..." I was going to puke. No doubt about it. I struggled from his grip and beat feet to the bathroom. I barely made it to the toilet before everything in my stomach came back up in force.

I had no idea how much time passed, but when I finally stopped heaving, Elena was kneeling beside me, brushing loose strands of hair out of my face and dabbing a cool cloth over my forehead.

"There, there, sweetheart. It's passing." She handed me a second cool cloth while she continued to dab at my face and my neck. "It's all over, *bebe*. You're all better. Just breathe for me."

"Elena," I sobbed, looking up at the older woman. Then I dissolved into tears.

"*Miel*, talk to me. I can't help you if you don't tell me what's wrong."

"Me and Shotgun..." I swallowed, wincing as I closed my eyes. Finally, I managed to get out, "I... What if I'm pregnant?"

Elena stilled. "Is that what all this is about, *pequeño*?"

"You're Catholic. Isn't this bad?"

"*Bebe*, life is never bad. But why do you believe you're pregnant? Have you taken a test?"

"No. I just... We didn't use protection. And I'm not on birth control."

"This just happened today?" The other woman seemed so perplexed I realized how stupid I sounded.

"No," I whispered. "Over the last several weeks. I just... It never occurred to me..."

"Child, were you innocent before Shotgun made you his?"

"I'm *not* his! That's the problem! At least, that's part of the problem."

She grinned at me. "So you think it would be more acceptable for you to be pregnant if he'd made a commitment to you?"

"Yes. No! Oh, God! I don't know!"

"Esther, sweet girl, look at me." I wiped my eyes with the washcloth but did as she told me. "Why are you so freaked out? Is it that you don't want a child or that you don't know how to care for one? Or maybe that you were so caught up in all these new experiences that you didn't even think about protecting yourself?"

Could this get any more humiliating? "This is the first time it even occurred to me that I might get pregnant. Not one time during these weeks with him."

"What about him? Do you think he forgot?"

That brought me up short. "Well, he must have."

Elena gave a merry laugh. "*Bebe*, men like him don't forget things like that. So, now you need to figure out what you're doing about this. Because I guarantee you he's just waiting for you to realize what you've done."

I thought for a minute. "Well, I guess I need to figure out if I am."

"That would be a great start. Now. Go wash your face and get your wits about you. Shotgun's going to want to know what's wrong."

"Why would he? Yes, we're sleeping together, but he made it pretty clear this was temporary. I thought that first morning when we woke up that he regretted everything."

"Yet he kept bringing you back to his bed?"

I groaned. "Why are men so much trouble?"

"When you figure that one out, be sure to let me know. Believe me, the only thing that gets better about the trouble they cause is the sex when they're making it up to you."

That got a surprised laugh out of me. Which must have been what the other woman intended, because she beamed at me. "Now. You need to look appropriately angry with him. Give him the cold shoulder for a few days until you figure out if you're pregnant. That should be enough time for him to break down and ask you what's wrong."

"You think that's a good idea? I mean, won't he get tired of me quicker?"

"Just trust me on this."

She helped me to my feet, and I did as instructed. As I looked in the mirror, I winced. I was definitely a mess. Red eyes, dark circles under them, my cheeks splotchy red, and my hair was sticking out all over the place. With a sigh, I washed my hands and tried to prepare myself to face Shotgun. This was going to be the hardest thing I'd ever done in my life.

When we exited the bathroom, both Tito and Shotgun were just inside the main diner close to the hall that led to the bathroom. Tito looked at Elena first, then me. Something seemed to pass between the older couple. The longer they looked at each other, the more irritated Tito looked. Finally, he head-slapped Shotgun and moved back across the diner to turn out the lights. Elena gave Shotgun the stink-eye, but the infuriating man merely shrugged before his gaze landed on me.

Those penetrating blue eyes nearly knocked the breath out of me. It also told me Elena was right. The rat turd knew. He'd realized all this time, and he'd still not used a condom. Why would he do that? That was so mean! Now, I was near tears. I turned away before I gave too much away, needing to get out of here and away from Shotgun. Unfortunately, there was still the ride home. I no longer had a car, and I was living in a room adjoining his. Yeah. Not the best of situations.

"I need to stop by the pharmacy on the way home," I said softly.

"We can do that," he said. "My brothers are on the way. Just a couple more minutes and we can leave."

It didn't take that long. Several bikes pulled into the parking lot, half pulling next to Tito's truck. The other half went to Shotgun's bike. Apparently, the club wasn't taking any chances with the older couple either. Again, it surprised me how thoroughly this group protected those they considered theirs. It was clear they all respected Tito, Elena, and Marge, but I never thought they'd go this far. Hadn't my church back home done much the same for vulnerable people in our community? How were these people any different? What made them bad other than their lack of reverence or modesty? That was something for a later time. I had more pressing problems, and there was no way I could wrap my head around philosophical questions right now.

Shotgun snagged my hand, pulling me along with him. He made sure I put on my helmet, then helped me onto the bike. He did exactly as promised, taking me to the pharmacy. Instead of me going in, however, he instructed me to stay with his brothers and he went. When he came back, he opened his jacket, and I could see the little blue box in an inner pocket. Without a word, he started his bike up, and we rolled on to the compound.

I felt like I was in a daze as he kept holding my hand and took me back to our rooms. I wanted to be alone, but Shotgun would have none of it. It was hard, and I struggled, but held on to what Elena told me. I just needed to keep my distance from him for a few days. It would help me get my head straight. And let me decide what I wanted to do.

"We gonna talk about this?" he asked once the door was closed and locked.

"Not much to talk about. *Now*."

"Look, I figured if you weren't on the pill or had an IUD, you'd have said something."

"It wasn't something I ever thought about. I hadn't planned on having sex until I was married. I was just too caught up in how much fun I was having to think about the consequences. I'm not even sure when my... uh... my cycle..." I floundered a moment before rallying. "You said I'd be safe with you! Why would you do this?"

"I get it." He crossed his arms over that massive chest of his as he leaned against the wall. "You have every right to be angry, and I don't blame you. You've got those tests. Take one. We'll discuss what happens next once we actually know what's going on."

I shook my head. "Not now. I can't do it now."

"Fine. Then take a bath and come to bed. In fact, I'll take one with you. We can relax together."

"No! No way! Not tonight, Shotgun." I was sure Elena hadn't meant I was supposed to completely pull away from him, but in that moment, I absolutely needed some space.

"Why the hell not? I'm the same person I was this morning. So are you."

"I wasn't as raw emotionally this morning as I am now. I need some space. Alone."

"You're pale and sweating, Esther. I get you need some room, but I'm not leaving you like this."

"You had your chance to make your choice. You don't get a choice right now. I'm going to my room alone. I don't want you near me for a while. I need to think and get myself under control."

"Leave the door between our rooms unlocked," he said steadily. How could he sound so rational when I was a complete wreck? Did he not care if this changed my life forever? Probably not, since it wouldn't have an effect on him unless he chose for it to.

"No. If I need something I'll reach out to Eden."

He straightened in a quick motion, swearing softly. "Dammit, Esther. Don't shut me out. I'm trying to be there for you if you need me."

"I'll be fine. Just leave me alone for a while."

For a moment, I thought Shotgun might continue his protests. Then he relented. "Fine. But I will be in this room all night. You need me, I expect you to open the door and tell me."

No way I was promising that. Instead, I just shut the door between our rooms and locked it. I thought I heard him lean against the door or touch it or something, but I wasn't sure and didn't intend to find out.

For a long, long while, I lay on the bed. I was numb inside. I wanted to cry, but the tears wouldn't come. My belly was twisted in knots, and I was still trembling, but my heart had slowed down, and I no longer felt like I was going to be sick. Maybe I'd feel better after a bath. Yes. A long soak in the tub with some bubbles, and I'd feel more like myself. Then, maybe I'd get up the courage to take that test.

Instead of the bath, I picked up the box that contained the pregnancy test. There were two in the box. It said morning urine was the best, but the test could be taken at any time. I thought about it but quickly decided there was no way I could wait until morning. If the first one was negative, I'd take the second one in the morning.

The box said to wait the full time before reading the test, but I sat on the toilet and watched as the urine saturation made its way across the testing field. The control line popped up bright pink. I had to force myself to breathe as the test continued to creep its way across the test area. When it reached the spot for the test line, it immediately lit up. Bright pink.

"Don't panic. Don't panic." I chanted the mantra to myself as I sat there. Ten minutes later, the line was still bright pink. So I took the second one, watching with a growing sense of dread as it was a repeat of the first one.

So yeah. I was pregnant.

Now what?

I knew one thing. I wanted to go to Shotgun and let him hold me, to let him tell me it would be all right. That he'd always be there to support me. Not with money or material things. But emotionally and physically. I didn't want to do this alone. But I knew that was nothing more than a foolish dream. Shotgun didn't do relationships.

Taking a deep, shuddering breath, I washed up and sat on the edge of the bed, trying to figure out what to do next. All of a sudden, the room seemed to close in around me. I needed to get out. Get some air to clear my muddled head.

It was nearly midnight. I knew people would still be up even during the week. If I took a walk, I wouldn't be bothering anyone. Maybe that's what I needed.

Chapter Eight
Shotgun

Yeah, it was a dick move on my part not to say something the second I realized what I'd done two months ago. But I didn't. And I kept doing it. And I wasn't sorry for it. I guess it was the Neanderthal in me, but I liked knowing there was a good possibility she was carrying my kid. I didn't even want a kid! Yet, the thought of seeing her growing round and heavy with my child made my dick hard as a pole. So what the fuck was I going to do if she was pregnant? And, frankly, I'd been fucking her every day for two months. Unless she had female issues, there was every probability she was pregnant.

When I heard her leave her room, I followed. At a distance and silently, but I followed. At first, she didn't seem to have a particular direction in mind. I thought she might go to Eden, but she only paused at the other woman's door before moving on. She looked lost. Maybe a little frightened. Everything protective inside me wanted to go to her, but now wasn't the time. I'd just keep an eye on her, stay close, and wait. I'd stalked enough prey to know when it was time to strike.

She went through the common room. Several of the club girls gave her a hard time, but most realized she wasn't in the mood. I watched as Eden crossed the length of the room to go to her. It was clear the other woman knew something was wrong. Esther just smiled and reassured Eden before leaving the party out the back door. Which was when Eden spotted me. Her brows knitted together. She was headed in my direction, but I shook my head and followed Esther out the door.

***

Esther

I needed to snap out of this funk. Feeling sorry for myself wasn't cutting it and wouldn't fix anything. So, OK. I was pregnant. Now what?

I'd made my way to the pool. It was lit by soft underwater lights. A few floodlights pointed at other areas of the compound gave off some indirect light, but it was mostly dark. Dangling my feet in the water warmed from the sun that day. A soft breeze blew in from the ocean, the occasional streak of lightning dancing in the clouds over the sea.

I'm pregnant. What now?

Supposing I was two months along, I'd have seven months before the baby came. This was the end of October. I had two months before the end of this semester, which left five months or so. Then another four months for the end of the Spring semester, which got me to about eight-and-a-half months. I couldn't do the summer -- even the four-week short summer session was too long. Maybe. OK. So I needed to go to the doc to get precise numbers before I could decide about that. I'd definitely have to take the Fall semester off. If I'd counted right, I should deliver in June or July. Maybe I could do some online classes in the Fall, then I could return to full time in the Spring.

But who would keep the baby? How much would it cost? I'd have to talk to Eden and see if she had ideas.

Insurance. I'd need insurance, too. If I was still working at the diner, maybe I could ask Tito if he could help me. But I'd have to figure out how to stay full time and care for a baby. And that was all assuming Marge still needed me that much.

And the really hard question -- would Shotgun be in the picture? Would he want to be part of our lives? Maybe not after I'd acted like a spoiled brat on him tonight. He was doing his best to protect me from someone he saw as a threat, and I'd effectively shut him out. Sure, Elena had said it would be fine, but had it been the right thing to do. Maybe it was time I found him. Talked about this with him. It was the only sure way to know what he was thinking. Shotgun might be a lot of things, but he wouldn't lead me on about something like this. And he wasn't the kind of man to promise a woman something he had no intention of following through with. He'd be more likely to tell me I was on my own than that he'd be there with me.

Resolved to not put this off any longer, I stood to go find Shotgun. The sooner we got this talked out, the better I'd feel. It might not be the outcome I wanted, but at least there'd be no uncertainty.

As I neared the door, I saw a familiar figure leaning lazily against the door frame, blocking anyone from exiting, but also blocking me from entering unless he allowed it. We looked at each other for a long time. I wanted to just run into his arms but that wasn't an option. Not this time.

Shotgun made the first move. He straightened and silently held out his hand. Without a word, I took it. He led me back to our suite of rooms, to his room.

Once there he pulled me into his arms, giving me time to pull back if I wanted. I didn't. Then the dam broke. I sobbed into his chest. Shotgun picked me up and sat with me on his lap in the bed. I had no idea how long we sat there, but he just let me cry, stroking my hair and murmuring to me.

When the storm had passed and all my tears stopped, Shotgun tilted my face up to his and looked at me for long, long moments.

"You're beautiful, Esther. Perfect."

"Shotgun, I --"

He silenced me with a gentle kiss that I didn't resist. "I know, baby. I promise you won't be alone. Never alone."

"I'm not going to be beautiful for long, you know."

"Why?"

"I'll be fat."

"Honey, even if you weighed four hundred pounds and grew a wart on your nose, you'd still be the most beautiful woman I've ever seen."

"You're just saying that."

"You know I'd never just say something, doll. I never say anything I don't mean. Especially something as serious as this. Now, we'll work this out. But we'll do it together."

I nodded. "OK."

"Good. Now, no worries the rest of the night. We'll start fresh tomorrow."

Before I could agree, Shotgun kissed me again, this time rolling us over so I was underneath him. His kisses were hot, but soft and sweet. Each sweep of his tongue or nip of his teeth made me sigh in pleasure.

He stripped us both, taking care to kiss every inch of my skin he exposed. I hadn't known he could be this breathtakingly gentle. When he got to my belly, he kissed and licked and rubbed his bearded face against the gentle swell below my abdomen.

"Seeing your body growing with my child will be the sexiest thing imaginable. Did you know that? We'll have to make sure it's OK for you to have sex. When we go to the doctor I'll be sure to ask."

I stiffened. "You mean you're not going --"

He covered my mouth with his hand and chuckled as he kissed his way back up my body. He paused at my nipple and swirled his tongue around it before he covered his mouth with mine. "Of course, I'm gonna," he said between kisses. "But I'm also gonna ask the doc how long and how safe it is for us to do this. Don't worry, though, doll. If I can't fuck you, I'll find plenty of different ways to satisfy you."

Then he made love to me. It was slow and sweet, but no less intense than it ever had been. When he entered me, he was careful to use measured thrusts. I had no idea why, because it was only last night he'd been just as rough and wild as I'd seen some of the guys be during parties. The thought turned me on even more. I knew what it felt like to be taken that hard. I knew how much pleasure those women felt when their men fucked them so hard. It felt wonderful. And I'd learned to love it when Shotgun fucked me. But I also loved it when he took his time and made love to me like this. The sensations were just as acute and powerful, but different.

Finally he settled his weight fully on top of me, pressing me deep into the mattress. His fingers threaded through mine as he worked my body with his. He continued to praise me, to praise my body's response to his. Never once did he promise me the happy ever after I craved, but he swore he'd always do right by me and any child who came along. It wasn't everything I wanted, but it was enough to know I could rely on him. Count on him when I needed him.

The only thing I couldn't get out of my mind was a future where Shotgun was with a woman other than me. I knew he'd never be a monk. He was too sexual a man for that. But when he moved on from me, when I had to see him because we had a child together, seeing him with another woman would break me. Because I'd know what it felt like to be kissed so possessively. To be held in his arms after sex. To submit to that magnificent body when he was in the mood to fuck. I knew seeing him with someone else would completely break me.

Then I could do nothing other than surrender to the pleasure he was building inside me. When he angled himself to give me the friction I needed so my orgasm exploded through me, I clung to him, sobbing out his name as I came helplessly under his body.

When my pleasure was done, he kissed me over and over until I met his gaze. Then he moved faster and faster, never taking his eyes from mine. His face hardened as he bared his teeth slightly. Then he shuddered and grunted above me. I felt his seed explode deep inside me. He'd done that deliberately, staking a claim he dared me to deny. No matter how much I knew it would only lead to heartache, I couldn't deny that blatant claim. All I could do was cling to him and sob into his neck as he brought me down slowly, kissing me tenderly before rolling off me and sliding off the bed.

He returned with a wet cloth, washing me gently as he'd done so many times over the last few months. What would I do when this was no longer my reality? Was I already so wrapped up in Shotgun I couldn't imagine my life without him? Maybe. But I couldn't confide in him, couldn't tell him how I felt about this. Not now. Too much too soon might make it seem like I was pressuring him for something he simply wasn't capable of giving.

Shotgun's arms securely around me, his lips in my hair, I clung as tightly as I dared. Then I drifted off to sleep.

Shotgun

This was getting complicated. Not only was I still taking Esther to class, but I'd started taking my own classes again. Online crash course. With fucking Giovanni Romano. I was beginning to hate that man with a passion, but I couldn't deny he knew what the fuck he was doing. I remember how, right before I met Esther, I'd wanted no part of this shit. Now I needed it like I needed my right fucking hand.

I'd managed to find the motherfucker stalking Esther. His name was Donovon Carter, also known as Money and a prospect with Kiss of Death. I was basically at a standstill with Money. Other than him belonging to the wrong fucking club, there was nothing on the man. It was possible he was mentally unstable and had fixated on Esther, but that wasn't what was really bothering me right now. I could shut that shit down if I had to. I wanted to know about Esther's background. Her parents in particular.

Turns out, that fucker Giovanni was right about everything he'd taught me. It took less than an hour to find everything I wanted to know about the gaps in Esther's childhood. Or, rather, her parent's pasts. Seemed her father had been in the Army. Did a stint in logistics during the war in Iraq before being discharged after a year and a half for misappropriating firearms and selling them in the U.S. on the black market. His lawyer had worked out some horseshit to keep him from doing time, but he'd been dishonorably discharged from the service.

Back home, he'd been unable to find work and found himself again working on the wrong side of the law. This time selling and distributing drugs. Would have probably ended up dead that time except he ran into a club called Iron Warriors. That MC had been a haven for vets in Missouri at the time. Stephen Haney had happily called the Iron Warriors family for four years. Until he'd met Ruth Green. Ruth was the daughter of the pastor of a very large church in Springfield. The same church Stephen now served as pastor. It was at her insistence he left the Warriors because Ruth had been convinced they were nothing more than a gang. Stephen apparently had never bothered to explain to her how they'd basically saved his life. Hell, the prick was probably too stupid to realize it.

In any event, he'd left, never looking back at that life. I had to wonder if anyone in his life, other than his wife, knew his secret? Given Esther's lack of mentioning it when she was so forthcoming with everything else, I doubted it. Oh well. It was something I'd file away for later. If push came to shove, I'd force him to reveal it to Esther.

Esther never complained, but I could tell she was feeling the pregnancy now. I'd even gone to the fucking doctor's appointment with her. Saw the little gummy-bear-looking parasite inside her belly. She'd gasped in horror at me calling our child that, but she'd been so nervous I had to take her mind off the actual exam and everything it meant. She must have seen my lips twitch. Or maybe it was the doc's sudden bark of laughter that did it, but she gave me a wry grin and slapped my stomach with the back of her hand. I had immediately snagged her fingers and brought them to my lips. Yeah. Didn't plan on telling that story to the brothers. Turned out she was nine weeks along. Which meant she'd gotten pregnant right away when we'd started having sex. I couldn't help the grin now as I watched her move around the diner.

"You can just wipe that grin off your face, Shotgun," she said, pointing a finger at me from across the room. She'd grown more comfortable with my presence at the diner. Tito and Elena had congratulated me for not being an ass about the pregnancy, and I'd responded with a scowl and a grumble as expected.

"Can't help it," I replied. "I tend to get that look when I catch a glimpse of that little baby bump." Esther sputtered, trying to look appropriately put out, but I saw the grin she tried to hide.

"You keepin' that girl, *amigo*?" Tito grinned as he sat in the booth across from me.

Good Goddamned question. "Ain't gettin' rid of her," I murmured. "Who knows how long we'll be together?"

The other man didn't like that answer at all. "Not sure what that means, Gun. You might want to explain."

"You ain't her daddy, old man. Don't got to justify myself to you."

"Someone has to look out for her. Thought it would be you."

"It is."

Tito sighed. "You're fixin' to get yourself in trouble. What will happen if she gets tired of all the non-commitment and leaves your sorry ass?"

"I'll go after her and bring her back." No hesitation on my part. There was no question what I wanted. I just wasn't sure I was capable of it. I knew she was scared. I'd spent the better part of a week trying to ease her fears, but commitment was the one thing I couldn't give her. No one knew what the future held. Fuck. Maybe I was going about this the wrong way.

"How long were you and Elena together before you proposed to her?"

"I proposed to her the day I met her. Took me a year to convince her I was serious."

I chuckled. "You know, that actually makes sense. That woman has you wrapped around her little finger."

"She does." Tito grinned. "And she's the best thing that's ever happened to me."

I snorted. "Not afraid people think she took your man card?" I was throwing his words back at him, trying to get the reaction I wanted. I thought I wanted him to tell me she only thought she had his man card, that he was the head of the house or some horseshit so I wouldn't feel like I was less of a man if I committed to Esther in such a short time. I mean, having a baby wasn't a reason to get married or anything. It usually just made things worse.

"Everyone knows Elena is the love of my life. Without her, I'd never be whole. If that means I'm less of a man for it, I'm willing to accept it. Which, of course, makes me more of a man for being willing to let others think as they will. I know where my heart is." He pointed to his wife as she brought in a freshly baked apple pie and put it in the display case. "That woman... She's everything to me. I'd give anything if it meant I'd get to spend a very long life with her at my side."

Fuck. I was so in over my head. Because, fuck it. That was how I felt about Esther.

A couple hours later, the diner clean, closed, and ready for the next day, Esther came to me and held out her hand. "Take me riding tonight?" Girl loved riding. Especially at night when the sun was down and the breeze coming off the sea was a balmy caress.

I took her hand. "Anything to keep a smile on your face, doll." Esther gave me the smile I was hoping for. Tito snorted in laughter. Elena smacked Tito on the back of the head.

"You two be careful," Marge called as she came in from the back kitchen. She still worked, but mostly helped Elena in the back because it was less taxing on her wrist than carrying food-laden trays all day. "And you, young man. You be good to that girl. She's my angel."

"Do my best, Marge. She's my angel, too."

As we walked out the door and I helped Esther onto my bike, four Harleys rolled into the parking lot, surrounding us. Something felt off. I turned to look back at the diner. We could get back inside, but it would take time. Tito and the women were in the back locking up and always came out that way.

"Text Elena to stay inside."

"What's going on? Who is that?"

"Not sure, doll. Get your helmet on, and whatever happens, do not get off this bike unless I say otherwise, or I fall. Then, you get in the diner and call for help." A moment later, when they rolled close to us so the lights from the parking lot hit them, I found out. "Money," I called. "State your business." That same fucking biker now had three backups. This was likely to turn bad quickly.

"You know my business. The bitch. I want her."

"Not happenin'."

"The four of us say otherwise." Money indicated his buddies. All of them climbed off their bikes. I had no choice but to follow suit.

"Not unless you get past me," I said, preparing for battle.

"Oh, we'll get past you, all right," Money

continued. "Once we do, we'll take the bitch and teach her how a real club whore is supposed to act. You Black Reign types are too soft on the bitches. Once all of us fuck her, the whole of Kiss of Death will have a go. We'll take that pussy and ass and break them in nicely."

"Or just break 'em," one of the other bikers said. The rest of them chuckled.

"Bitch owes me, Gun," Money said. "I always collect the debts owed me.

"Think real hard before you commit to this," I said. "It's the only warnin' you're gonna get."

"Oh, yeah? It's four on one, and we're just as armed as you are."

"So you're committed." I sighed. "Fine."

I charged straight into the middle of the pack. I always carried my Sig at the small of my back, but I didn't want to start a gun fight with Esther in the crossfire.

The first guy went down hard, and I smashed his face against the pavement with a satisfying *crack*. If he wasn't dead, he likely had a bad skull fracture for his loyalty to this motherfucker. Money tried to dance away from me, but I dove over his bike and tackled him to the ground. One of the other guys pulled me off and landed two punches to my side. I snapped my elbow back and caught his chin before grabbing his head and flipping him over my shoulder right into Money.

The fourth guy pulled out his gun, but I saw it and managed to kick out. The gun went flying, and I heard something snap where I'd kicked him. Hopefully his wrist so it would be difficult for him to use the fucking gun if he found it.

Money came at me with a roar, a knife in his

hand. I snagged his wrist and twisted hard, snapping the bones with another satisfying *crack*. Money screamed but came at me with another blade. This time, I used his momentum against him, side-stepping his lunge and shoving his arm back into his own body. The blade sank into his right thigh as he rotated his body instead of hitting anything vital. Though, if the blood spurting from the wound was any indication, I might have gotten his femoral artery.

"Fucking motherfucker!" Money spouted. "I'll fuckin' kill you!"

"Heard that one before. Ain't worked out yet."

The one guy who was uninjured pulled out a gun and aimed it at Esther. There was no other choice. Before he could get off a shot, I pulled my own gun and fired three rounds. Two went into his chest, making him stagger back. The third round went between his eyes. Esther screamed. Money and his one man left climbed on their bikes and started them up with a roar.

Just as they started to leave, five more bikes sped into the parking lot, blocking the exit. Money wheeled his bike around and took off on the grass beside the diner, over a parking tie, and into the back lot of the nearby gas station. His buddy tried to follow suit, but his bike bottomed out as it tried to go over the big slab of concrete and tore shit loose. His bike died. The man jumped up and ran. The only thing that saved him was the fact that the bikers in question weren't Black Reign, but Salvation's Bane.

When they shut down their bikes, Thorn, the president, approached me, still watching the guy on foot. "Heard there was some trouble."

"Yeah. Guy named Money from Kiss of Death started some trouble. Wants my woman for some sick reason." I indicated the bodies in the parking lot. "I finished it. Well, part of it."

"Blood, contact El Diablo and tell him this one's on us. You and your men got this?"

"Place will be clean as a baby's freshly washed bottom before anyone gets here." He held out his hand to me. "Take your woman and go. They never do well with violence."

"This one likely worse than most." I took his hand. "Appreciate the assist."

Thorn nodded, then turned back to his men. Tito emerged from the diner and went straight to Esther. It was easy to see she was in tears and trembling. Tito spoke quietly to her while I approached them.

"Get her home, Gun," he said urgently. "She's in shock."

"Yeah. Figured." I turned to Esther. "Doll, you good?"

She just looked at me, her eyes wide and wild. "Y-you killed those men."

"It was them or me, honey. If they killed me, you were next. You heard them."

"Y-yes, b-but --"

"We'll talk about it at the clubhouse. I promise." I swung a leg over the bike and started it up. "Hold on tight, doll. We'll be home in no time."

"What about those men?"

"Thorn's people will take care of it. By the time they're done, no one will be able to tell anything happened."

"But they're dead!"

"Yeah, they are," I snapped. "Now wrap your arms around me tight. We're gettin' the fuck outta here."

Chapter Nine
Esther

I only thought I'd been scared in the bar when that man was dragging me off to get raped. Shotgun had just killed not one, but two men! Right in front of me. To make matters worse, the only thing he seemed concerned about was getting rid of the evidence. As I held on for dear life while he navigated the streets of Palm Beach down to Fort Worth, I couldn't help but question the choices I'd made these last two months in a huge way. I might be able to convince myself that the sex and the way Shotgun made me feel wasn't a bad thing, but how did I reconcile this? Killing was a sin. Period. There was no way around it. I couldn't just ignore what happened. But what did I do about it? Because I seriously doubted his club would let me go to the police. And I wasn't really sure I was ready to see Shotgun go to prison. Or to the electric chair.

Once we got to the compound, Shotgun helped me take my helmet off. He tried to brush my hair out of my face where it clung to the damp skin, but I flinched back.

"What?"

"I-I just need to think."

He gave me a puzzled look. "I understand that was pretty violent, but I protected you. You're not hurt. Are you?"

"I -- no. No one touched me."

"OK, then. Come on." He reached out a hand, but I was hesitant to take it. Exasperated, he simply grabbed mine and marched to our rooms.

Once inside he closed and locked the doors. "Come here, doll. Talk to me."

"I don't know what to say." I was feeling a little

desperate. All I could see when I closed my eyes was the macabre way that man had jerked when Shotgun had shot him. "You killed those men."

"Yeah," he said, looking angrier than I'd ever seen him. Angry and... hurt? "Did you hear what they wanted to do to you?"

"That didn't mean they had to die! Are you kidding me? I'm not more important than anyone else!"

"What the hell is this? As far as I'm concerned, it would have been worse to let them live and hurt you, or even Tito and Elena, and Marge! Did you think about them?"

"You don't know they would have come after anyone else. They were there for me."

"So what was I supposed to do, huh? Just back off and say, 'Here she is! Have at her!'"

"No! I mean, we could have gone inside the diner and waited until those other people got there."

"Honey, I had no idea anyone would be there that quick. Thorn and his men are from another club. They aren't affiliated with us, and sometimes we're rivals. El Diablo tries to make us allies, but things don't always work out like that. I had hoped someone from Reign would get here eventually, but it's a good twenty-minute ride."

I shook my head, unsure what to say or do. "I just don't understand why they had to die. Why couldn't you have just, I don't know, wounded them or something?"

"Are you for fuckin' real?" Shotgun looked like I'd just slapped him. "It was four against one! They told me they were armed! One of them actually got his gun pulled out and had a bead on you!" He turned and paced across the room, scrubbing his hands through his hair. "I was protecting you! You and the baby! My family! Wounding a man when you're outnumbered four to one just means there's a chance he comes back to kill you later. It's fuckin' suicide!"

"But --"

Shotgun threw up his hands. "Just stop." We stared at each other for a very long time, neither of us giving an inch. Finally he nodded his head. "I need to do something. I'll be back later."

"Where are you going?"

"You don't get to ask me that, doll," he said bitterly. "I need space."

"So, I'm just supposed to sit here like a good little girl and wait on you?"

"No. You've got free rein of the compound. You always have. I just think it's best if I'm not here for a while."

Then he left, closing the door behind him.

* * *

Shotgun

I found El Diablo in his office. As expected, he knew everything that had transpired. Including how upset Esther was.

"You spyin' on us?"

"What? Like cameras in your room and such? No. But I think you know that. You're trying to pick a fight so you can avoid your feelings regarding Esther. Tito called to tell me Esther was a bit taken aback by what she witnessed. I asked him the same question I'm about to ask you. Do you think she'll go to the police?"

Not two hours ago, if someone had presented me with this same scenario, I'd have said a resounding "No." Now I wasn't so sure. "You're guess is as good as mine. We all have our own moral code. Mine just isn't up to her standards." There was no way to keep the bitterness out of my voice.

"Blood informed me all was taken care of. The bodies disposed of. The parking lot and security feeds all secured."

"I'll double-check it to make sure. Because I learned how from that prick Giovanni," I laughed. It sounded a touch hysterical. "Learned all that because I was trying to track down her stalker to keep her safe. Look where it got me."

"Give her time. She'll work it out."

"She's already worked it out. And I'm the bad guy." When El Diablo would have said more, I just waved him off. "It doesn't matter. All that matters is that she's safe. At least for now. That son of a bitch Money is still out there. It's too soon to go after him."

"Agreed. I've taken care of that, though. Donovan Carter, aka Money, will soon be taken care of along with the other rider with him."

I nodded in satisfaction. "At least that's something. One less thing she'll have to worry about." One more stain against my character with her.

"Go talk to Archangel. Maybe he can offer you some peace."

"Don't need peace. I've had peace. Believe me, it's fuckin' overrated. When it leaves, all you're left with is emptiness. And rage."

I left El Diablo's office feeling every ounce of that rage. I needed to strike out, but the only person I could strike at was myself. Maybe that was what I needed. To punish myself. I headed to the gym. Maybe a couple of hours on the bag would take away some of the pain.

How the fuck had I let myself get into this situation, anyway? When did the opinion of a little slip of a preachy tight-ass matter so much to me? Maybe since I went and fell in love with Esther. She was definitely too good for me, and I had my doubts if I could ever be what she needed me to be. I was too old for her anyway. There was more than ten years difference in our age. Before, it hadn't mattered. I'd never given it more than a passing thought. Now... It was just one more thing I couldn't fix. Esther and I were worlds apart morally. And I wasn't sure I wanted to bend myself to her version of morality.

* * *

Esther

I sat on the couch in my room, quietly looking out the window at lights from the harbor off in the distance. What a mess. Somewhere in my mind, I knew after that first bar brawl that Shotgun had it in him to do great violence. I'd been appalled then, telling him violence wasn't the answer. Of course, that message had been blunted because I'd just whacked a guy over the head with a pool stick. Then, as now, he'd done it for me. At least, that was what he said. But did I truly believe it? He'd said he'd been protecting his family, but he'd never given me any reason to think he saw me as family. Maybe he was referring to his child growing inside me.

Ugg! This was maddening.

A knock at the door brought me out of my musings. I opened the door to find Lyric, Celeste, and a man I didn't know. Lyric smiled warmly at me. Celeste looked equal parts happy to see me and worried.

"This is Archangel," Lyric said. "He's a counselor of sorts. The club's spiritual advisor."

That brought me up short. "Wasn't expecting that," I said softly. "Spiritual advisor?"

Archangel smiled slightly. He seemed very

reserved but didn't have the hardness about him the others had. Sure, he sported the beard and the ink, but there was something serene about him I couldn't resist.

"I am, little one."

"What denomination?"

"None," he replied. "I merely offer advice when life gets to be too much to deal with."

I stepped aside. "Please. Come in."

We sat in the little living area off the kitchen, next to the door leading to Shotgun's room. Lyric and Celeste sat on the couch while Archangel and I both sat in plush chairs opposite each other. I glanced at the door with longing. I wanted to talk this out with Shotgun, but had the feeling we'd reached an impasse. It felt like when I was arguing with my dad. Only this time, Shotgun was me. I was my dad.

"El Diablo said you might have some issues with Shotgun now," Lyric said. "He thought we might be able to help you work through them if you knew our stories."

That shocked me. "You know what happened?"

Celeste nodded. "The whole club knows. Hard to keep something like that a secret around here. We all look out for each other. If the cops come around, we'll all cover for Shotgun as best we can."

"Why would you do that? He killed two people." I tried not to sound harsh, but was pretty sure I did.

"He did it to protect you," Celeste said softly. "And your baby. Assuming he's like Wrath and Rycks, he'd do it again in a heartbeat if he had to."

"How can you accept this so easily?" I wasn't sure what surprised me more. That it hadn't been more than an afterthought to Shotgun, or that it wasn't much more to these three. Indeed, if they were to be believed -- and I had no doubt they were telling the truth -- the entire club could give two shits that Shotgun had killed.

"How can you not?" Archangel asked. He had a perplexed look on his face, but that didn't fool me. He got how I felt. I could see it in his eyes. But there was more. He also approved of what Shotgun had done.

"I don't believe you should ever kill someone. It's a commandment."

"Even to save your child?"

I sighed. "I don't know," I said, my gaze drifting back to the door where Shotgun should have been. I needed him, but at the same time, I knew now wasn't the time. My head wasn't in the right space.

"My daughter has leukemia," Celeste said in what I thought was a sudden change of topic. "When I first met Wrath, I was a paid escort for a law firm looking to schmooze a bunch of recruits. Wrath included. It took everything in me to sell myself like I did. But I was willing to do it if it meant keeping Holly in treatment. Wrath was the man who picked me that night. Even though it went against everything I thought I knew was right, I did it to keep my daughter alive. Looking back," she shook her head fiercely, "I'd do it again. In a heartbeat."

"That's not killing someone, though."

"No. It's not. But wait until you have that baby inside you in your arms. You'll understand then. It's not about right and wrong. It's about giving your child what she needs to survive or to be safe and free from the threat of harm. There's not a single man in this club who wouldn't hesitate to kill to protect his family. For the single ones, that means this club. We're all family."

"Rycks taught me that," Lyric said softly. "He brought me from a really dark place to this compound. He killed, too. To get Bella away from those monsters, he had to. And you know what? Though I hated he had to do it himself, I'm not sorry those men are dead. In fact, I'm glad of it. After what they did to so many women and children, to say nothing of what they had planned for Bella, it's no more than they deserved."

"I hear you," I said. "I really do. I'm just having trouble thinking about it like that."

"How about this, then?" Lyric persisted. "Here, with Shotgun and the rest of Black Reign, you're safe from the outside world. You never have to leave this compound if you don't want. Shotgun will pamper you for the rest of your life. If not him, every other man in Black Reign will. They may not be overly obvious about it, but they have their ways. In here, with all of us, you're protected from everything. All the women are. They may find it hard to form emotional attachments sometimes, but they have a strong sense of family, and all of them are over-the-top protective."

I looked down at my hands, unable to find the words Lyric wanted to hear.

Finally, Celeste sighed. "I'm sorry, Esther. I hope you can find some peace with this." She stood, taking Lyric with her. "We'll leave you to your thoughts," she said. Then she and Lyric left my room.

Archangel, however, just sat with one ankle crossed over the opposite knee, leaning against the arm of the chair.

"Tell me something, Esther," he finally said. "Why is it you find what Shotgun did objectionable? You realize that, without his aid, you'd likely be begging for death now. Right? Not to mention that your child would likely not have survived to be born."

"I get it. I just don't think it's right to trade one life for another."

"You said that before. Are you telling me you

wouldn't sacrifice yourself for your unborn child?"

"I would," she said immediately. "But that would be my choice."

"And you don't think those men made their choice when they chose to target you?"

"They didn't choose to die."

"No, but they knew the reputation Black Reign has. We are a ruthless bunch."

"That doesn't mean it's right." Now I just sounded belligerent. What Archangel and the women had said made sense to me. I just couldn't seem to let it go.

"You know. Shotgun did more than just randomly kill two men. He did more than just save you and your child. He risked his life to take the fight to those four."

"That's what I don't understand," I said immediately. "Why didn't he retreat? Why not go back to the diner and wait?"

"You know the answer to that," he said softly. "He had no expectation of help arriving in time, and he would be putting others at risk besides you. Did Tito and Elena and Marge deserve to be put in danger, then? Did Tito and Elena deserve to have their property severely damaged by the attack, or, worse, destroyed in the retaliation?"

"No."

"And did you consider the risk Shotgun took for himself? If he's found out, he'll go to prison. Rycks has a ward. Her name is Mae. She found her mate in a man from Salvation's Bane. His name is Justice. Mae got him freed from prison after he'd served seven years. If you think it's a small thing to be in prison for that length of time, have Lyric introduce you. He'll be happy to tell you anything you want to know. I suspect, though, even if he glossed over some of the more graphic parts, you'd still find it repulsive. Shotgun took that risk rather than see you harmed."

I knew all this. At least, what Shotgun had risked. I knew it, and still, my mind clung stubbornly to something I wasn't sure even my dad would question. He might have been harsh the last time I'd talked to him, but I still remember how he was with me. Always wanting to protect me. Even that last day, he'd still been trying to protect me. He just went about it the wrong way.

Maybe I was thinking about this in a two-dimensional perspective. There were always shades of gray. Very few things in this world were black and white. If there were, life would be a whole lot easier.

Then I thought of something else. "If he goes to prison, that would leave me and the baby alone. Why would he risk leaving us alone if he did all that just to protect us?"

"You'd never be alone. Shotgun knows that. You're as much a part of Black Reign now as anyone. If he was unable to watch over you, there would always be someone from the club doing his job in that regard. It's the way we work."

"But we're not married."

"Doesn't matter. You're carrying his child. For all intents and purposes, you're his woman. He's not publicly claimed you, but I suspect that's more due to him trying to protect you from himself than that he doesn't want you. El Diablo knows. The club knows. If something happens to Shotgun, the club will be your protector until you find someone to fill that role. Even if you did, we'd likely still watch over you. Shotgun knew all this before he made the decision to stand and fight rather than barricade all of you inside the diner.

He chose the safer path for you. The path where he eliminated the threat to you instead of it always looming over your happiness. Perhaps you should consider this sacrifice of Shotgun's. His freedom. His very soul. He put it all on the line to do what he thought had the highest likelihood of getting you out of danger. If he'd put three more lives at risk, would that have been the best choice, do you think?"

That was a question that would haunt me for a while. Because, deep in my soul, I knew the answer was *no*.

Instead of acknowledging that, however, I fired off with my own question. It was so reflexive, I knew it was an answer I'd been trained to give. Not so much an answer to a specific question, but an answer to all those philosophical debates. You turn it around. "Was it the best choice for the loved ones of those men he killed? I'm sure they didn't ask for it any more than the rest of us."

Archangel sat up straight then, his face going from serene to disgusted in a heartbeat. "Those men made their own decisions. They are the ones their loved ones should blame. If they hadn't been trying to kidnap you to use in vastly more sexually perverted ways than you could ever possibly imagine, they wouldn't have put Shotgun in the position of having to defend you. Would it be better for you if they killed Shotgun and raped you for days on end? Would that satisfy your delicate conscience?"

He let the silence drag on for a moment, then added. "So, the question becomes, whose life is more important to you? Shotgun's and your unborn child's? Or the men who would have taken both from you?"

Again, I responded automatically, though it was barely above a whisper. "All life is important."

He stood then, shaking his head in both sadness and disgust. "I guess we all misjudged you, then. You, my dear Esther, are not nearly worthy of our brother."

Chapter Ten
Esther

I watched Archangel leave my room with a gnawing pain in my belly. Everything I'd said, all my arguments, had been automatic. And none of them remotely true. There had been a time in my life when I'd believed things like what I'd said with all my heart. Everything had been in black and white. Good and bad.

In my foolishness, there was a time when I might have answered with every conviction that I'd put the life of myself and my child above someone else. It was what good Christians did. Right? Hadn't Abraham been willing to sacrifice his only son, Isaac, at the commandment of God? At least, hadn't I been taught that Abraham's willingness to follow God's orders was what saved his son in the first place?

Now, as I rested my hand on my growing belly, I wasn't so sure. No. I was sure. I'd never willingly sacrifice my child for someone else. If that made me a bad person, I was willing to accept it. This situation was different. Those men were evil. Evil didn't deserve to win. Maybe what I needed to think about was something more like this.

Shotgun stood between me and pure evil. He was a warrior through and through. If God hadn't made men like him to stand between the rest of the world and the evil in it, evil would surely win. I might not have it in me to kill, but Shotgun did. To save those he cared about, he absolutely did.

Instead of defending him as hard as he'd defended me, I'd let him down. Judged him harshly and found him lacking. Archangel hadn't been wrong. Those men made their choices. Shotgun had just delivered the consequences.

And there was something else. The men and women of Black Reign -- not to mention Tito, Elena, and Marge -- had taken me in. Given me a new, if unconventional, family. I'd repaid them with my judgmental attitude. From the very beginning I'd judged them for who I thought they were without ever bothering to see who they really were.

I needed Shotgun. I needed to apologize and see if he could find it in him to forgive me. If I were honest with myself, if I were in his shoes, I'm not sure I could forgive so easily.

I found him by the pool. The same place he'd found me the night I'd found out I was pregnant. He had a bottle of whisky in his fist, sipping on it occasionally. I knew he heard me approach, but he didn't move. Didn't acknowledge me in the least. Just kept taking pulls from that bottle.

Sitting beside him, I hoped he'd look at me. Or at least acknowledge my presence. He didn't. I laid my hand on his shoulder, but he just stared out into the night.

Finally, he said, "You know. I've been over and over it in my mind. What I did was reflexive. If put in the same situation, I'd gladly do the same thing again. Only I'd get all four of the fuckers instead of just two."

"I know," I said softly.

"I can't move past this, Esther. I'll always be your protector. Yours and the baby's. Any threat to the two of you, I remove. Permanently. It's who I am. Ingrained into my soul." He shook his head and closed his eyes briefly before speaking again. "I've always been used to the ill opinions of others. They look at the ink and the colors on my back and assume the worst. It never bothered me. Until you." He turned his head to look at me for the first time then. "I'll always be there for you, but if you can't accept who I am, then we never had a chance to begin with."

I swallowed a lump in my throat. This man hurt more deeply than he wanted to admit. The thought of losing him cut me to the bone, but I was willing to bet he shared my pain. I was about to apologize when we were interrupted.

"Ah, little Esther. I've been looking all over for you." I turned to see El Diablo standing in the doorway. "I'm sorry to interrupt, but it's time for you to go. I've arranged for you a ride home." My father stepped around him to face me. He looked dazed and more than a little shocked. El Diablo had come from the front of the estate, so I could only assume he'd brought my dad through the common room. And all the club girls putting on a show for the newcomer. The thought actually threatened to make me giggle.

"Come with me, Esther. We're going home."

"I am home, Daddy."

Beside me, Shotgun snorted but said nothing, preferring instead to take another pull from his bottle.

"Do you know what happened tonight?" I asked my father, unsure how much I could tell him if he didn't know the full extent of the situation.

"El Diablo filled me in." My father glanced at El Diablo. "He told me because I understand what it means to be MC. I know you don't rat out your brothers. I also know that Black Reign have taken you in as one of them. What I need to know is if *you* fully understand what happened."

"I didn't. At first. But I talked with Archangel, and he made me look at things from a different perspective. I realize that, had Shotgun not acted as he had, he'd be dead. Maybe even Tito, Elena, and Marge too. I'd be in the hands of some very evil men." I expected my father to reaffirm his last words to me. That I was headed into sin. To my shock, my father agreed with me. "El Diablo told me you used to be part of an MC. He said Mom didn't approve." I shook my head. "I never pegged you to be like these guys."

To my shock, my dad just grinned. "Iron Riders weren't like most MCs. Yeah, they were rough around the edges, but they weren't into the parties and stuff. We mostly banded together to do things for the community."

"No parties? At all?" I raised an eyebrow. And yeah. Dad actually blushed.

"Well, maybe some. But nothing like this." He waved his hand, obviously eager to change the subject. "Anyway, I also had a chance to really think about how I'd directed your life. I realized that I'd made a mistake in that. This is your life. Not mine. Not your mother's. I've been trying to hold onto your mother by making you into what I thought she would have wanted. Instead, I only succeeded in driving you away from me."

Taking a deep breath, I reached for Shotgun's hand and placed it over my gently swelling abdomen. "I'm pregnant," I said without preamble. "Shotgun's the father."

My father looked at Shotgun. His gaze was steady but resigned. "Do you plan on being in their lives?"

"Just try and stop me," Shotgun said with such vehemence it sent a thrill through me. Maybe I hadn't lost him after all.

"I take it this means you don't want to come home with me."

"I told you. This is home. Not just Shotgun,

though he's a huge part of it. But this whole crazy club. They're devoted to each other. I want a chance to earn that devotion as well."

I stood and hugged my father. "Are you sure this is what you want, sweetheart?"

"I'm sure. I have a lot to make up to Shotgun, but I want the chance to prove I'm not a complete bitch." I winced, but my dad didn't. He just grinned. "I have the feeling he'll come around. I was once part of something like this. One day, when we can sit down and really talk, I'll tell you all about it. It might explain some of why I tried to shelter you. I know what goes on in clubs like this." He glanced back at El Diablo. "Despite the sharp reminder on the way in that I wasn't prepared for."

I grinned. "The exterior doesn't prepare you for the interior."

"It's certainly not the typical MC clubhouse. At least, not like the ones I was exposed to."

"You sure you can't stay a while?" I said, reluctant for him to leave even though I needed to get back to Shotgun. I had a lot to apologize for, and I hoped it would take a very long time.

"I'm sure, sweetie. I'll keep in touch, though. And when you have the baby, I'll be waiting with the other anxious grandpas out there." With one last hug and a kiss to my cheek, my dad reached out a hand to Shotgun. Surprisingly, Shotgun took it. "Take care of my daughter, Moses."

Shotgun winced, but didn't say anything. "That's the one thing I can promise you, sir."

"His protective streak isn't a curse, or a sin, you know," my dad said, looking at me again. "It's the biggest blessing you could have. Embrace it. Accept it. From what I've found out from El Diablo, he's a good man." That surprised me. My dad wasn't one to take anything someone said at face value. He always checked it out. Something must have been really compelling. Though, I had to admit, everyone at Black Reign I'd met could be very persuasive. Mainly because they told the truth from the beginning, no matter how harsh. I respected that. My dad would, too.

Dad left with El Diablo. As they went back inside the building, I heard my dad ask if there was possibly another exit. El Diablo just laughed.

"So, your real name is Moses?"

"Yeah. Moses Blackstone. Long line of law and military men in my family. Guess you needed to know that. You know. My real name."

"I appreciate you telling me."

He turned his head and waved me off. Yeah. I got it. "I'm sorry," I said. "You're absolutely right in what you did. The world isn't black and white, and if it were, good people wouldn't have a chance. Sometimes, it takes brave people, people like you who are willing to do anything they have to protect those they care about."

"Not just care about, Esther. Love." He shook his head. "I can't change who I am. Not even for you. Not about this."

"And I don't want you to," I said quickly. "I know I'm not worthy of you. Archangel was right about that. But I'm willing to work at it, to prove I can make myself worthy."

He blinked down at me, surprise on his face. "All right. Wasn't expecting that."

I winced. "I'm really sorry. I have no excuse. Just know that I'll do better. I'll see things in more than just black-and-white."

He pulled me into his arms. "I'm not sorry I

killed those fuckers. Only sorry I didn't kill the other two. You sure you can accept that?"

"I can. Wholeheartedly. After I thought about it, how I'd feel if I'd lost the baby because of this."

"Doll, I wasn't even thinking about the baby. All I was concerned about was keeping you safe. I see you growing, but the baby isn't something I can process in that kind of a situation. I was protecting you."

"I know," I said softly. "After I got off my high horse, I realized how stupid I was being. You were absolutely right to do what you did. I'm glad you had the courage to do what needed to be done. I'm just ashamed I didn't have the courage to see the situation like you did." I took a breath, fighting back tears. "I realized something else, too. I'm thankful, not only for the life of my child, but for my own life. If I'd died, I'd have missed out on so much of life. Things I'm hoping you'll be willing to teach me."

He kissed me then. A slow, lingering kiss. "I will. I don't know how, but I managed to fall in love with you when I wasn't looking." He gave me a wry grin.

"I'm glad. Because I love you right back." I grinned at him, something in my chest easing. "You could try to leave me, but I'd follow. And I'd be ruthless about finding and keeping you."

He raised his eyebrows in surprise. "Ruthless, huh?"

"Oh, definitely. You'll find I'm opening my mind up to new possibilities. Nothing is out of the question. As long as I'm with you."

"Is that so? Because I have a long and raunchy list of things I want to show you." He raised a challenging eyebrow at me.

"Lead the way. I'm ready to try it all." I grinned, knowing I would probably eat those words. In fact, I was hoping I would.

I didn't have to wait long. Like he'd been starving for the taste of me, Shotgun kissed me deeply, sweeping his tongue inside my mouth in long, teasing strokes. His fingers threaded through my hair, angling my head exactly where he wanted it. I followed where he led willingly, knowing he'd see to the pleasure of both of us, without exception.

In a move that left me breathless, he stripped off my shirt and bra, pushing me back on the concrete to take off my jeans and panties. Then he did something unexpected. Instead of continuing with the erotic, demanding interlude, he picked me up and tossed me in the pool.

I came up sputtering, wiping water from my eyes. "What the heck?" I was very aware I'd just said heck. Especially when Shotgun guffawed at my delicate use of language.

"Thought for sure that would have garnered even a delicate swear word, doll."

"Oh, really? Well, here's one for you. Asshole!"

"Better, but I think you can get more creative."

"Baby steps, Shotgun…"

He laughed, relenting far easier than I was afraid he would. "Fine. But before this night is out, I'm going to get you to beg me to fuck you. Using exactly that language. You have to say, 'Fuck me.'"

"Why do I have a feeling this is going to be a baptism-by-fire kind of thing? "

"It's not so hard. It's just words. You'll find yourself a lot more comfortable with the language here if you can at least say the words when we're alone. Besides, getting you to tell me to eat your pussy, or that you want to suck my cock, or that you want me to fuck your ass… yeah. That will be hot as fuck."

I thought my face was going to boil the pool water. "I'm not saying any of that."

He gave me a wicked smile. "We'll see." Then he stripped off his clothes and dove in after me.

I managed to get to the shallow end before he caught me, wrapping his arms around my body. The second he did, a feeling of safety and warmth sparked inside me. I knew I'd always feel like this. There was just something about my rough biker that made me feel safe. Ever since the first day I'd met him. He'd protected me then, and I knew he always would.

"Well," I said. "You have me. What are you going to do with me?"

"Oh, now, little doll. That's a simple question." He kissed me again, hard and demanding. His hand swept down my belly to my sex. My pussy. Then he glazed two fingers over my lips, coaxing them apart. His finger grazed my clit, but I still jumped.

No matter how many times he did it, I was always sensitive to him. I thought I always would be. He seemed to know exactly how to touch me.

"I'm gettin' ready to fuck this sweet little pussy. Gonna put my dick in there and fill it full of my cum. You good with that?"

"Better than good," I said, turning around to face him in the water." Feeling bold, I dipped my head to his nipple, laving the hard little nub with the flat of my tongue. He grunted, his body stiffening before squeezing one cheek of my ass.

"Hmm," he said. "Maybe I've created a monster."

I looked up at him solemnly. "I meant what I said. I'm going all in with this. My take on it is going to be what two people who love each other do together isn't wrong. Maybe the main thing is that you have a moral code and keep to it. I realize now that my dad doesn't have all the answers. Neither do I. Maybe the best a person can do is to just try to help people more than harm them. And showing you with my body how much I love you isn't wrong. Not by a long shot."

"Couldn't have said it better myself."

With a wicked smile, I ducked under the water, sinking low and wrapping my legs around his. Then, I gripped his hips and sucked the head of his cock into my mouth. The water muffled any sound from above, but I thought I heard him grunt. His hand jerked to my hair and fisted there while I sucked hard. I couldn't keep it up for long. The pressure and the lack of oxygen guaranteed that, but I pushed myself as long as I could.

He released his hold and pulled me to the surface when I unwound my legs from his. I gasped for air, and Shotgun took advantage, kissing me deeply. I wrapped my legs around his waist this time, guiding his cock inside me. He thrust home in one sure stroke, moving us to the edge of the pool as he held me tightly against him.

"Brace yourself on the edge of the pool," he said. "Tell me if you can't hold yourself. I don't want to hurt you accidentally."

I leaned back, unsure exactly what he wanted me to do. I reached behind me until I had the concrete edge on my palms. I gripped it with my fingers, straightening my arms to hold my weight. It wasn't much, as the lower half of my body was in the water. Shotgun adjusted his hold on me so he gripped my waist in his big hands. Once he was satisfied I was good, he started to move.

It was a whole other world of sensation! Water sloshed all around us in more and more violent waves as his intensity increased. I just hung on for dear life, loving every second of this new adventure. Water was everywhere. I giggled as it broke into fizzing bubbles all around us. It was like a turbulent sea, though it wasn't angry. It was filled with the pleasurable cries of both Shotgun and myself. His masculine, mine all too feminine.

Over and over he fucked me, riding me hard until I shook my head and reached for him with one hand. He stopped instantly, just like I knew he would. I just wrapped myself around him while he stepped out of the pool on the shallow end, taking us to one of the many chairs around the patio. He lay down on one, settling me over him, encouraging me to sit up.

It took some doing, but I finally settled with my feet on the ground as I straddled his hips. His cock pulsed inside me.

"Ride me, doll. Ride me 'til I come."

It was all the encouragement I needed. I rose and lowered myself, hesitantly at first, then with more confidence. I impaled myself on his cock over and over. Shotgun ran his hands up and down my body from my knees to my breasts. He stopped and squeezed my breasts, kneading them in his big hands.

"You have the most beautiful tits I've ever seen," he rumbled. "Bit small, but I imagine they'll be gettin' bigger very soon."

I gasped. "Shotgun!'

"What? I imagine they'll be good and full of milk after the baby's born. Might have to sample some for myself." He gave me that wicked look that always made me blush. For once, I was determined to meet his wickedness with some of my own.

"Well, I've heard some mothers taste everything their baby eats beforehand. I think it's only fair the father participates in that."

His grin widened. "Now you're talking. Maybe I'll sample every time the baby eats. It could be my mid-day snack."

"You'd do that?" I was getting worked up and more turned-on by the second. "You'd suck milk from my t-tits?"

"You're adorable when you try to talk dirty. Makes me hard as a motherfucker."

"I'm not sure adorable was what I was going for."

"It's hot as hell, baby. Knowing it was me to corrupt you, and that I'll be the only one to ever hear it."

"Well, that's a good thing. I could never say stuff like that if anyone was listening."

I'd slowed my movements, but Shotgun wanted more. I did too. He sat up, urging me off him, turning me away from him so I had one foot on each side of the lounge chair. Then he pushed my upper body down, so I rested my chest on the edge of the chair. I ended up with one knee on the chair and the other foot on the ground. Then Shotgun was behind me, guiding his thick cock inside my weeping pussy.

"That's it, doll," he murmured. "Let me inside. Let me fuck you 'til neither of us can stand."

I rocked back with him, meeting his thrusts until he gradually built the speed and force he needed. It was a new position for me and let his cock slip deeper inside me. It was nearly painful in its intensity, but oh so good! His balls slapped against my pussy with every thrust. Occasionally, he slapped my ass so that I cried out sharply.

In the back of my mind, I realized we were out in the open. The club girls came out here occasionally to skinny-dip in the moonlight. We could and probably would be seen by many people. But I found that I didn't really care. In fact, I thought I might want them to see. It would show every single one of them Shotgun was mine.

"Gun!" I screamed. "Fuck!"

"Now, that's what I like to hear," he growled at my ear. "Fuckin' let me hear you scream!"

His words triggered my orgasm, and there was no way to suppress my cries. I thought I might have screamed some more obscenities, but I wasn't sure. All I knew was that I came harder than ever before. My body seemed to have a life of its own. The harder he fucked me, the better it felt.

Finally, I felt his cock swell inside me just as my body started to spasm around his once more. We both cried out. His brutal yell was like howling at the moon, mine not far from it. He ejaculated deep inside me, his hot cum filling me to overflowing. I felt it trickle down my thighs in a warm slide.

When he was still above me, he wrapped his arms around my waist, resting his head on my back. "Fuck me," he said, his voice hoarse with his shout of completion.

"Think I already did that," I said, giggling.

He chuckled but slapped my ass all the same. "Sassy little thing. I can see I'm going to have to keep an eye on you."

I shrugged. "Might be in your best interest."

He stood, pulling me with him. It surprised me that there wasn't an audience watching us. But then, after all, what we did by the pool was tame in comparison to what was likely going on in the party room.

Shotgun carried me to our room without so

much as breaking a sweat. Then he cleaned me gently in the shower, inspecting my body thoroughly.

"I got too rough with you," he said. "Have to be careful with the mommy-to-be."

"Not that careful," I countered. "And you weren't that rough."

He set me on the vanity in the bathroom, my legs spread wide at his insistence. My baby bump was on full display. To my amazement, Shotgun knelt and placed a gentle kiss on my belly.

"Don't worry, li'l bit. I'll be more careful from now on. You're mama's one sexy little woman, though. Hard to keep my hands to myself."

"You better not try," I scolded. "I'll be greatly disappointed if you do."

"You don't have much to worry 'bout on that account, doll. Only reason I leave you alone is if the doc says I have to. Otherwise, I'll be makin' love to you until this baby is born."

He helped me brush and braid my hair. It was damp, but nothing that would be too uncomfortable. As he pulled me into his arms, I couldn't help but think to myself, "There is no place in this world I'd rather be right now than in your arms." I was dead tired, but I might have said it out loud. I knew I did when he gave a soft chuckle and kissed the top of my head.

"Yeah, doll. Me too."

"Will you still be here with me in the morning?"

"I will. Tomorrow and every morning after that for the rest of my life."

"I love you. But I'm not calling you Moses."

He gave a little startled laugh. "I can accept that. Shotgun or Gun is perfectly acceptable."

"Do you love me too?"

"I do, doll. Love you so fuckin' much it hurts."

I yawned, snuggling against his chest. "Don't want you to hurt."

"As long as you can take me on, baby, I'll never hurt again."

Fury (Black Reign MC 4)
Marteeka Karland

Noelle: I had dreams. Goals. That all changed when my baby brother suffered a traumatic brain injury. Now Jonas is my responsibility, and I can't let him down, even if he's his own worst enemy. I still have goals -- I'm a fighter. As in MMA. Mixed Martial Arts. I want to be the best -- fighting in the UFC. To be the best I need the best trainer. That's Fury. The toughest man I've ever met. He doesn't know it, but he's also the man I'm in love with. But when Jonas gets in trouble, the only way I can save him is to go underground -- illegal fights. I can't tell Fury. He'd kill me himself. Or worse. Disown me. But Jonas' life is on the line. I have to fight. And I have to win. No matter the cost.

Fury: I spent seven years in the Army -- the time it took to pay back my obligation for earning my medical degree free of student loans. After that the Army and I both decided I'd be better off putting my skills to use somewhere else. Now I put bikers back together for Black Reign MC. I'm damn good at what I do. I'm even better at taking anyone who gets in my way apart. Lately I've been passing those skills on the smartest, most street savvy kid I've ever trained. Now she's gotten herself in a boatload of trouble. If she tries to fight Shadow, he's going to kill her. How do I choose one life over another? It was hard enough as a doctor in the field. Now it's so much worse... because I did the stupidest thing I could have done -- I went and fell in love.

Chapter One
Noelle

"You drop that fuckin' shoulder one more time, girl, and I'm gonna take the opening and kick your fuckin' ass. Woman or not."

That was my training partner. Fury was a good guy, but he had zero tolerance for what he saw as lazy shit in the ring. I wasn't lazy, but I'd gone past my endurance range. I just was too stubborn to admit it.

It wasn't four moves later, I dropped my fucking shoulder. True to his word, Fury took advantage, catching me with a powerful right to my head. I managed to dodge him, but he got in enough it stunned me. The next thing I knew, he had tackled me to the mat, where he proceeded to pound the shit outta me.

"What the fuck, Fury! Lay the fuck off! Can't you see she's ain't got no gas in the fuckin' tank?" Larry, the gym owner, was quick to break that shit up, but the damage had been done. And the lesson learned.

"Yep. Was her job to say she was tapped. She didn't."

I lay in a heap on the mat. I wasn't sure there was any part of my body that didn't hurt. It took every ounce of willpower I possessed not to turn over and puke. I looked up at Fury. The massive man stood over me like a conquering gladiator without an ounce of compassion in him.

"You're bleedin' all over the fuckin' mat, Brawler. Get up and hit the fuckin' showers." He didn't offer me a hand up, but then, he never did. This was one time I might have taken it had he offered. Fury wasn't mean or anything. In fact, he was perfectly cordial to the other women he trained with. Just not with me. He said it was because I was gonna make it to the big time in the MMA. Unless he went easy on me. Oh. And he called me Brawler because with my fair skin and bright red hair, he said I looked like an Irish brawler.

I groaned. "Fucker."

"Yeah? Bet you won't drop your fuckin' shoulder again no matter how tired you get, huh?"

"You're still a fucker." I stumbled to my feet, noting the cut on my lip. I wasn't actually bleeding on the mat, but I was bleeding. "Good thing I didn't have a hot date lined up tonight," I groused. "You ruined my pretty face." I was lying. No way I was pretty. My nose had been broken more than once, and I had numerous scars all over my body, including my face. With my hair in braids and pinned tightly to my head, every bruise and cut and scar stood out. The only thing I didn't sport was a fucking cauliflower ear. Thank God.

"You ain't got time to date," Fury snapped. "You want sex, buy some fuckin' toys. Now hit the fuckin' showers. I'll take you home."

Taking me home was the only kind thing Fury did for me. After training, I was always too weak to do much of anything. He'd noticed I put in my all and reacted accordingly. Thus, he picked me up to go to the gym, then took me home. Though I liked knowing someone had my back if there was trouble and I was too weak to defend myself, Fury kept it all very impersonal. Which was fine with me. It kept things simple. At this stage in my life, I had enough personal shit going on without adding a romantic relationship. With my trainer, no less. It didn't matter the man was sin and sex. I didn't care. Much. Hardly any at all. Besides, my brother was hard enough to care for without that kind of entanglement. Besides, no one understood Jonas or why I still felt the need to care for him instead of just living my own life now that our parents were gone.

After my shower, Fury walked with me to his truck. He never left the gym without me. More than once, I'd stumbled and would have fallen hard if he hadn't been there. Most of the time, I even had to sit down in the stupid shower. It just depended on how hard I'd had to work my legs on any given day. Today? Yeah. I could barely put one foot in front of the other without tripping.

Fury helped me into the truck, then slid behind the wheel. Instead of taking off immediately, he sat there, looking out the windshield. I was hesitant to break his brooding silence because he looked pissed as fuck. If I'd done something, I needed to apologize. I needed him as a training partner way more than he needed me.

"You would have not only lost the match, but might have gotten seriously hurt if you'd dropped your shoulder like that even once in the big leagues, Brawler. You do it again, I'll cut you loose faster 'n you can say scat. You hear me?"

"Yeah," I said, trying to sound appropriately contrite. "Shoulda called it five minutes before you grounded and pounded me."

"No," he barked, looking sharply at me. "You shoulda called it a fuckin' hour before I pounded you! You ain't fuckin' Superwoman, Noelle. You want to win? You've got to finish the fuckin' match. You can't do that if you overtrain and injure yourself. I ain't worked this hard with you to see you fail before you even reach the big time."

"I hear you. I won't do it again." I held up three

fingers. "Scout's honor."

He snorted. "I know you won't. Mainly cause this is the only warnin' you get. You do it again, I'm done."

He meant it, too. Fury never said anything he didn't mean. Everything about MMA he took seriously. He couldn't fight professionally or manage a fighter himself, so he tried to teach others. How to win. How to not fuck up like he did.

"Do the ice bath thing, then get some rest," he growled. "And don't come to the gym tomorrow. Take a run instead."

I wanted to grouse, but he was right. I was overtraining. I didn't have a match planned or anything, but I'd been stressed about Jonas lately and tended to push myself harder than I was supposed to in order to forget my problems. It wasn't healthy, but Jonas could be a handful sometimes.

Fury sped off after I got out of the beat-up Ford, not waiting for an answer from me. I sighed. I wish the man gave a good Goddamn about something other than fighting. Because I could really use some adult support. Problem was, if he did show more interest in me than just fighting, I'd fall head over heels for him and Fury was *not* that man. He had a different woman every week. Sometimes more than one.

Jonas was my younger brother. He was special needs as well as some serious PTSD after being involved in the wreck that killed our parents. Most days, he functioned pretty well. But, even before the wreck, he'd sometimes retreat into himself, and it was hard to get through to him. He also had no concept of his limitations, fighting as hard as I did. Instead of fighting in the ring, though, he was fighting to be a normal person. To get his old life back. It sometimes landed him in trouble. Our mom had usually been able to keep him in line, but since she and Dad had been taken from us, I was struggling.

The second I unlocked the door and walked into the house, I knew something was very wrong. The house stank of weed and alcohol. I heard male voices in the living room. Laughter. And one higher-pitched voice that sounded like it was in pain. And terrified.

"You listen to me, you little shit. You'll get me the money for that coke, or I'll take it out of your hide. You get me?"

"B-but I never h-had it. Th-the guy who n-normal-ly drops it n-never sh-showed." That was Jonas. Some of his stutter was terror, some was his natural speech pattern since the injury.

"You're lying, you little bastard!" There was the unmistakable sound of Jonas being slapped. I glanced over my shoulder outside. There was no sign of even Fury's taillights in the distance. I could have called him, I suppose, but I wasn't sure I could take it if he told me to suck it up and deal with it. Though, if he thought I would get hurt, he might come back. If for no other reason than to keep me from wasting all his time with me.

When the hits continued, I decided I just had to dig deep. It was like a big match. I'd be completely wiped, but I had to find that little bit extra. I could do this.

I put down my gear so my hands were free, then walked to the doorway of the living room. "What's the problem here?" I tried to look like a badass, not like I was wiped from the gym.

"Oh! This big sis?" One of the three men surrounding Jonas asked the question. "Heard you some badass MMA wannabe." He sneered at me.

"Heard about you types. From the looks a' ya, you just come from the gym. Bet you one tired bitch." The others looked me up and down in that superior, blatantly sexual way. Like they were just waiting for the right time to jump on me and take whatever they wanted.

"Yeah. I am," I said in an irritated voice. "And the last thing I wanted to do tonight was beat the fuckin' shit outta some wannabe gangster. Get the fuck outta my house!"

One of them pulled a gun, his face a mask of fury. He appeared to be the leader. They all wore black vests with the close-up nose and mouth of a skull with flames behind it. The name said Southern Discomfort MC.

"Yeah, bitch? You gonna make me?"

I wanted to pound the little fucker, but even the best MMA fighter in the world was no match for a gun. He held it sideways, gangster style. What was with this guy? I raised my hands anyway.

"Look. Tell me what's going on and I'll try to fix it. Pointing a gun at me isn't helping the situation."

"Shut up, bitch! Ain't none of your Goddamned business!"

"Wait, Trigger. She's a fighter. She can make us some money to pay back her stupid-ass brother's debt."

The other guy cocked his head, never taking his eyes off me. "What you mean, Bridges?"

"Think about it. Pres wants us in the big fights. If she's already in training, she'll make a good entry. She'll look the part and know what to do and how to act. She'll even look like she can win."

"Hmm." This Trigger seemed to mull it all over. "She don't gotta win. Right? Just has to be there."

"Like a little bitch like her'll be a threat. Even the chicks who're stupid enough to try to fight are twice her size."

"Fine," Trigger said. "Give her the address." Bridges scribbled an address down on the back of a business card. What the fuck? These guys had business cards? "You be there tomorrow night. All's you gotta do is show up to fight. That card will get you in. You can bring a manager with you if you want, but don't get no ideas 'bout goin' freelance. This works out, you fight for us. Southern Discomfort."

"Wait. What exactly is this?" I didn't take the card right away. I had no idea what I'd be agreeing to, and I didn't want them to mistake me accepting a card with me cooperating with them.

"Underground fights," Bridges said. "They happen every week. Only these fights are high end. On private property. Rich assholes host them, and the betting is insane. You gonna fight for us. We take half your cut if you win. All the winnings if you don't."

"I am *not* illegal fighting. That would make my chances of getting into anything UFC exactly zero. I'd be an outlaw."

Trigger swung his gun in an arch. Jonas was sitting beside where Trigger stood, and he brought the gun around to smash into my brother's temple. Jonas whimpered and crumpled to his side on the chair.

"You'll do what I say, or I'll do the little fucker right here! You get me, bitch?"

"OK, OK! Take it easy! What the fuck?"

"He owes Southern Discomfort about ten large for the coke he lost. The better you make your fight, the more money will change hands. You work it right, you can make back that money in one night. You don't, and you'll be doin' it again. And again. Until you pay it off." Bridges was more levelheaded than Trigger. The other guy didn't say much. I got the feeling he was the real muscle. I was certain they didn't want a gun going off in a residential area, but I couldn't take the chance with Jonas the primary focus.

"Fine. But I can't do it tomorrow. I have to know who I'm fighting and how they fight. It takes time to train."

"It ain't one specific fight," Bridges explained. "This is a tournament. You fight 'til you lose. Last one standing wins."

"No way I win something like that."

"No. But the bets the club makes will be what gets our money back. You last as long as you can. We'll do the rest."

"And when we tell you to lose, you fuckin' take the beatin' and lose. Or the little shit over here dies," Trigger said, his voice belligerent where Bridges was calm and even.

Bridges handed me the card again and I took it. And just like that I knew my dreams had gone up in smoke. But this was my little brother. I'd do what I had to. Then I'd figure out what really went down and, if anyone in that fucking club had double-crossed Jonas, they'd better hope I got beat senseless. Because if I didn't, I'd be coming after them.

Chapter Two
Fury

"You guys sure you got this? I feel like we're so fuckin' outnumbered it's laughable." I knew we more than had this, but something just didn't sit right with me tonight.

"You got Shadow and the ringside participants," Samson said calmly. "Hardcase and me got the crowd. We'll focus on the big bettors. You and Shadow just concentrate on the shit happening at the ring and getting each other out alive. Get me?"

"Fine," Fury muttered. "But for the record, something feels off."

"Noted," Samson replied. I hated not being in control. And this was a situation I definitely could not control. Illegal fights were a fucking nightmare to stay on top of. Unless you were the man running the fights, you had no idea what to expect. "Just concentrate on you and Shadow. Something goes sideways? Iron's holding back. He can assist wherever we need him."

"Not sure I want the men who fuck for a livin' watchin' my six," I growled. "They get distracted by pussy, me 'n' Shadow are the ones fucked."

"You're just jealous," Hardcase said with a chuckle.

"Yeah, but he's kinda pretty," Iron piped up. "When he ain't bein' all intimidatin'. If we can get the girls to not run screamin' when he enters the room with 'em, he could fuck for a livin' too."

"If I gotta do this myself, boys, I'm killin' every motherfuckin' one a' ya," Samson said evenly. It wasn't a threat, but a clear promise. "Shotgun says he's sure at least three competitors here are dummies from the fight ring. They may look the part, but they don't know jack about fightin', and they damned sure don't want to be here. We thought the bottom-ranked four looked promising, but it's hard to say. Rumor is one of them's a woman. We should give her a good look first."

Normally the banter would help me relax, but today wasn't the day for it. There was an itch between my shoulder blades. Like I had a target painted on my back. Something was epically off, but I had no idea what. When Samson mentioned one of the fighters being a woman, it nearly made my skin crawl. This particular fight ring stacked the odds in their favor by putting in what looked like rank competitors but who were really just people they'd kidnapped off the streets, or forced into fighting through blackmail or threat of bodily harm to a loved one. They were there to take a dive when told. Or to win by any means necessary. Anything to run up the betting.

"For the record, Fury," Samson said, "Jax asked to go. Said he wanted to have your back."

That surprised me. Jax, or Jackson, was my son. I'd been in his life, but we weren't close. His mom and I split before he was born. She'd surprised me with his birth picture and a note that he was mine. I'd never questioned it, just showed up to hold my son for the first time. She'd died from breast cancer two years ago, and Jax had come to live with me. Our relationship was blooming, but we still had a way to go. The boy was just too much like me.

"You know some women enter these things on their own, right? They like the challenge, and some of 'em are pretty fuckin' good," Hardcase said, bringing the subject back to women. Of course.

"Yeah. And more than one of 'em have died or worse," Samson replied. "Most of those were caught up in this ring, and El Diablo wants it stopped. Not in this city." Everyone in Black Reign knew El Diablo absolutely would not tolerate a woman being abused. They also knew better than to defy his orders. As gentle as he could be with women, he was equally brutal to anyone who seriously crossed him. Man or woman.

The fights were getting ready to start. The ones going first obviously had the clear advantage. The fighters going later might not get to see how their opponent fought, but if they made it to the second round, they knew what to watch out for. The fighters going first would have some of that advantage, but they might also get fucked-up enough they needed the hour or so between their matches to recoup. This particular competition had ten competitors, all ranked by their past performances. Shadow was our fighter for this tournament. Of the participants, he kept himself high on the list but not so over the top that he had every fighter gunning for him. He was ranked number two. The number one and two fighters got a bye in their first round. Which meant they got to watch four matches before Shadow had to fight. Four fights to get the feel of the surroundings at ringside.

As I glanced up at the board, I saw they had lined up the fights. All the names were on the board and their rankings beside them. One name stood out and that feeling of unease grew even worse.

Brawler.

Now, it could be a coincidence. Because, likely there were no female competitors, other than the one Samson mentioned. Though, this one was ranked tenth among the ten fighters. No. Couldn't be. Then again, if anyone could manage to get into this kind of trouble, it would be that fucking little bitch, Noelle.

No. I wouldn't think about that. She wanted to make it to UFC, and she knew I could get her there. There was no way she'd risk me kicking her to the curb. At least, she better not. If she did, I'd turn her over my knee and beat that sexy little ass until it was glow-in-the-dark red.

"What is it?" Shadow was prepping for his match, his dark eyes taking in everything around them. "Somethin' got you spooked?"

"Don't know," I said. "I just got this feelin'..." I trailed off as the announcement for the first match started. Brawler was in the first match. They didn't say anything about gender, but then they rarely did unless it was some kind of women's erotic wrestling. Besides, these types of fights rarely had women in them. They never lasted long, and they always had to fight men. Especially in the one-night tournaments. I'd seen more than one woman die or be so badly beaten they were unable to defend themselves against being brutally raped before my brothers and I stopped it. This time, it would blow our cover, and I couldn't afford it.

"Fuck," I muttered. "Can you see that Brawler they just announced?"

"Yep." Shadow shook his head. "Brawler's a chick. Guess you were right, Samson. First fight has a woman. Though she looks like she can hold her own."

"I swear to fuckin' God, if that's her..."

"You know the club sponsorin' her? Southern Discomfort. Not very original, but cute."

"No clue." I pushed forward. "Come one. There's four matches before you fight. Let's check this out."

"On your six."

We reached the cage just as the match started. At first I wasn't sure. The big guy she fought was between me and the fighter. He was so big, all I could see of the girl he fought was her legs as she moved. That shuffle was nauseatingly familiar.

The big guy swung a roundhouse, which the girl ducked. When she did, I honest-to-God thought I was gonna puke. No way that bright orange hair belonged to anyone other than Noelle.

"Mother fuck," I bit out. "I'll kill that fuckin' bitch when this is over!"

Shadow stood beside me, crossing his arms over his massive chest. "If you mean Brawler there, you may not get the chance. Looks like she's way overmatched. The guy's obviously insulted he had to fight a girl, so yeah. He's pissed."

The crowd was loud and obnoxious. I had to rein in my temper to keep from punching more than one motherfucker out. If this operation hadn't been so important…

"You drop that shoulder, girl, he's got you," I muttered under my breath.

"Who is that girl, anyway?"

"She's my protege. She's got potential to make it big in UFC, but not if she gets injured."

"Or killed?"

I just glared at Shadow. The big man just shrugged. "Can't say I like it my own self, boss, but she's obviously capable of making her own decisions." The crowd groaned as she scored a huge hit to the guy's knee, and he went down. Not all the way, but most fighters would have dived right in and pounded the guy. Not Brawler. She immediately backed off and kept dancing around a little, keeping herself aware of her surroundings. Apparently, she was fighting more than just the one opponent in the ring. As the guy struggled to his feet, favoring his right knee, I let my gaze track the ring area.

"Look," Shadow said, indicating a group of guys in leather cuts with Southern Discomfort on the back. They kept gesturing to the girl.

"They're communicating with her," I said, squinting my eyes to better bring the guys into focus. "What'er they doin'?"

"Urging her on? Can't tell."

"She knows better," I muttered. "He's easily twice her size, and the match just started. She went after him now, he'd just toss her off him like a fuckin' rat."

"Smart girl."

"I fuckin' trained her, you asshole. She ain't makin' that kinda mistake."

Shadow grinned but just shrugged again. "You think she's one of the plants from the fight ring?"

"Don't know. Doubt it. She'd come to me if she was in trouble." But would she? I'd tried to keep everything strictly professional. Would she think I didn't give a damn?

Again and again, the guy lunged for her. Each time, Noelle -- Brawler -- sidestepped or ducked, using her footwork and speed to her advantage. If she could tire him enough or keep injuring that knee, she might have a chance.

She landed another blow to his knee, and he went down harder than before. Again the crowd roared but became belligerent when she didn't jump in to finish him.

"Not yet..." I silently coached her, willing her to hear me when I knew it was impossible.

She kept it up, making him chase her around the cage. Sweat dripped from her opponent as the pain and his own temper got to him.

"I'll fuckin' kill you, you fuckin whore!"

Noelle just kept it up, ducking another haymaker and landing her own punch to his kidneys and punting his leg behind the knee as she kept moving across the ring. The man roared in pain and anger, all pretense at form gone now. He was out for blood, and I could see Noelle knew it.

She managed to scurry away from him again, though he tagged her shoulder. She didn't react, but I knew it was a solid blow. Likely deadening her arm. Thankfully it was her right arm, and Noelle was a southpaw.

Again, she landed a blow, this time a kick to his head. He staggered back, shaking his head. "Not yet…" And, again, she seemed to know exactly what to do, backing off slightly until he started forward again. This time, she took the fight to him, lunging in to tag his ribs and land an uppercut to his chin. His head snapped back, and she did it again before retreating. She shook out her shoulder, drawing his focus to that side of her body. "Smart. Keep it up."

When the guy roared and launched himself at her this time, she pounced. Using his own momentum against him, she swung a roundhouse kick at his head so that the force of his forward movement drove her kick even harder. She caught him with her heel square in the nose.

"Now! Now, Brawler!" I yelled as loud as I could.

Either she heard me, or she knew it was time, because Noelle launched herself on top of him, punching with her good left hand over and over. When he tried to defend himself, she managed to land several solid hits with her right hand until he guarded that side as well. Somehow, he'd landed with his legs underneath him, and Noelle used her body weight to keep them pinned as she pounded the fuck outta him.

It wasn't long until she landed a hard left hand that finally knocked him out. Three more punches with no defense on her opponent's part, and the ref called it. Someone pulled Noelle bodily off the guy as she was still screaming and hitting with all her might, not stopping until she was forced. Immediately, she went limp, tucking her legs until the guy let her down. She backed into a corner and stayed there until she was declared the winner. Instead of raising her hand in victory or celebrating, she walked off, grim-faced but in good shape. She walked toward the Southern Comfort guys, but didn't stop. Instead, she went back to her designated area and grabbed a towel.

"What now, boss?" Shadow asked. "You gonna make sure she's all right?"

"Can't. We gotta prep for this fight."

"I got this," he said. "That girl's in pain. You can see it on her face."

"Ain't my problem right now, Shadow. You are. You get hurt, and Cain'll have my hide."

The big man chuckled. "That's true. But Cain knows I can take care of myself in this kind of situation. I was built for fighting."

My gaze snapped to him. "This ain't no game, Shadow. Those men would as soon kill you before you got in the ring as not."

"Fully aware," he said, not fazed in the least.

"Come on," I said. "Ain't got time to fuck with her. She came into this on her own, she can go out on her own. Either way, after tonight, I'm done with her."

"Uh-huh." Shadow chuckled as he walked back to our pit. "Let me know how that goes."

I stayed for a while, watching as Noelle took off her gloves. She left her wraps on and used a towel to wipe her face off. Then she calmly reapplied the Vaseline to her face and readied for the next fight. Thankfully, I didn't see any cuts to her face or obvious bruising except to her right shoulder. With any luck, that could work to her advantage.

Then I realized what I was thinking. The longer she kept this up, the more likely she was to get hurt. My gut clenched, and I wasn't sure why. I'd already decided I was cutting her loose after tonight. As I continued to watch her, she glanced up, then did a double take. Yeah, she noticed me.

I refused to drop my gaze first, needing her to know how angry I was at her. Her lips parted, then her face flushed. She closed her eyes and winced hard before opening them again and meeting my gaze. She nodded once, knowing she was gone from my gym in that moment. Then she went back to work, readying herself for her next match. Which, I realized, was Shadow.

"Mother fuck," I muttered. "Just Goddamned mother fuck!"

I stomped over to her, leaning in close to inspect her face. As her trainer, it was an automatic reaction. "You hurt?"

She shook her head, her gaze darting around. "What are you doing here? You can't be here!"

"I could say the exact fuckin' thing to you, *Brawler*." I let my anger show. She might as well know how much fucking trouble she was in.

"Look, you need to go away. Leave me alone."

"Why? I'm your trainer. Right?"

"Not tonight."

"Not *after* tonight either."

She winced and looked away but nodded. "I hear you."

"Why, Noelle? Why would you throw away your future for a quick buck?"

Her head snapped back in my direction. "Because none of your fuckin' business, that's why."

I nodded. "Fine." Then I pointed to Shadow where he was readying for their match. "You see that big motherfucker over there? He's the number two guy in this tournament. That means you face him next. Guess who's gonna win that match?"

She shrugged, but I could tell she was more than a bit nervous. "I took down one big fucker. I can take this one down, too."

"No," I said calmly. "You can't."

"Anything's possib --"

"No, Noelle! It's not possible this time. Not with that guy. He's not like anyone else here. He's number two for a reason."

"'Cause he can't beat the number one guy?"

"No. Because he *wanted* to be in the number two spot. You can beat the guy in the number one spot, but you can't beat Shadow."

"You know him?"

I stood up straight, crossing my arms over my chest. "I'm his trainer as well."

Her mouth formed an "O" of surprise, then she ducked her head. "Yeah. I guess I can't beat him."

"Bow out. Take a dive. Don't care, but you get yourself outta that ring and get your ass the fuck home," I said, pointing my finger at her chest. "This ain't no place for you."

"No fuckin' shit," she muttered. "I'm doing what I have to do, Fury," she said. "If that means your guy pounds me, then he'll pound me. But I have to fight."

"Fine. Just don't say I didn't warn ya." I stomped off. Back to Shadow. This was all fucked up. *All the way* fucked up."

"She don't seem too happy with the situation," Shadow murmured as he finished wrapping his knuckles and putting his gloves on.

"She ain't."

"What's the game?"

I shook my head. "Proceed as planned. She don't bow out, beat the fuck outta her."

Shadow gave me a scowl. "I'll fight the little thing, but I'm not gonna hurt her, Fury. And I seriously doubt you mean that."

"Fuck you."

He slammed his fists together as he jogged in place, keeping himself warm. He threw a few punches, shadowboxing and kicking. He looked like he always did before a fight. Focused and determined. I knew there was no way he'd hurt Noelle, but there was no way he'd let her win either.

The next two matches went by quickly, the expected fighter winning both times. Then it was time for Shadow and Noelle to fight. Shadow. An experienced combat warrior, proficient in many different forms of martial arts as well as pure street fighting with me in his corner. I wasn't allowed in the UFC or MMA associations any longer, but I knew my shit. Then there was Noelle. A scrappy wannabe MMA fighter with no one in her corner, weighing a hundred pounds to Shadow's three hundred. She seemed to be with those punks from that MC, Southern Discomfort, but they also seemed to be taunting her more than helping. For the most part she ignored them, focusing instead on her opponent. Just as I'd taught her to ignore a heckling crowd. This was so one-sided as to not even be believed.

"Fuck." That was a word I'd forever equate with

Noelle. Mainly because, deep down, she'd become more to me than simply a girl I was helping. I genuinely cared about her. I'd never let her see it, and I wasn't even sure myself what I meant by "care" as a description of my feelings, but I did. I didn't want Shadow to hurt her. In fact, just the thought made me rabid to kill the big motherfucker.

"Don't look at me that way, Fury. You're the boss on this one, and we've known each other for a lot of years. But don't make the mistake of thinkin' I'm tame or anything. I can still beat you the fuck up if you try anything with me."

"Get your mind off me and on your opponent, Shadow. She's young and inexperienced, but she's still got the best instincts of any fighter I've trained. Including you. She can't beat you if you're on your game, but she will definitely take advantage if you fuck up."

"I'm not worried about her, Fury. I'm worried about you when she takes a hit. Are you sure your head's in the right place?"

"What? Of course, she's gonna take a fuckin' hit! She's in a fuckin' cage! Hell, I've hit her more than once my own damned self."

"Yeah. But only to teach her or to teach her a hard lesson. This shit's real. Can you handle it?"

"I did through her other match."

"That's because she didn't really get hit. If I'm gonna win this thing, I gotta either knock her out or make her submit. Either way means hurtin' her."

"Just get on with it," I bit out. "We've got one shot at this. We can't be made."

Shadow grunted and stalked toward the ring, his fight persona taking over.

Chapter Three
Noelle

I'd never in my whole Goddamned life seen such a big motherfucker as the man I was getting ready to fight. Not only was I getting ready to get my ass beat, it was probably going to happen in the first ten seconds. One glancing blow from this guy would probably break something. Those bastards threatening Jonas had basically told me I had to last at least a full minute against him. They told me if I did, it would pay Jonas's debt in full.

I glanced over at Fury. His face was implacable, no emotion whatsoever as he gave final instructions to his fighter. All the while, he looked at me with that steady, cold gaze I'd come to know so well. I wouldn't lie to myself. It fucking hurt to know he was going to let me get my ass handed to me. How could the only advice from him be to quit? Fucking quit! My whole entire life had been about going the extra mile, doing anything I had to do for my family. In this case, my brother, who wasn't helpless, but couldn't help himself in this situation. He'd been mulling for that fucking club without knowing exactly what he was doing. All he knew was they paid him, and that let him contribute to the bills. He felt like he was helping. I should have been paying more attention, but I'd been caught up in my own stuff. Family should have come first, and this was something that would forever haunt me.

I stepped into the cage as they introduced me, not taking my eyes off the big fucker Fury had called Shadow. He was all business. No give in his expression as he jogged lightly in place, shaking out his arms, keeping loose. In my mind, I heard Fury's voice when he wouldn't give me the words himself.

Sixty seconds, Brawler.

Breathe.

Stay ahead of him. Don't get trapped. Don't get hit. Use your speed. Don't grapple.

Sixty seconds. Then tap out.

The whistle blew, beginning the match. Like a speeding locomotive, Shadow charged toward me. He gave a battle cry meant to stun me as he lunged for me. I know it was meant to stun me because it almost did. Only blind instinct had me scrambling under him, sliding between his legs and landing a solid punch to his inner thigh. It felt like I'd punched a tree trunk. Shadow didn't seem fazed by the blow so much as he'd lost sight of me. Never a good thing in a fight.

I scrambled to my feet and moved around the ring, always making him move to keep me in sight. The other men I'd fought in the past, like my other fight here, had been enraged when I landed a solid hit. Like it was a blow to their pride or manhood or some shit. This guy just brushed it off. Both any pain it caused and the fact that he'd been hit by a girl. No way was I wearing this guy down in the usual manner. I'd have to outlast him. And keep him from hitting me.

Again, he lunged. This time he brushed my hip but was unable to get a solid hold. I sprinted out of the way, turning to jog backward once I was out of his reach so I could keep an eye on him. Fucker was slippery.

"You can't run forever, girl," he rumbled in a low voice where only the two of us and the ref could hear.

"Well, I ain't lettin' you hit me. You'd break me in half."

"True," he said, continuing to dance around the cage lightly. "Bow out."

"Can't."

He shrugged. "Don't say I didn't warn you."

I was ready for his speed this time. When I saw him move, I broke right, kicking out with my left foot to land a solid blow to his left thigh. Again, I might have just hit a brick wall for all the good it did, and now my foot was numb. I kept moving, doing my best not to show I wasn't at a hundred percent.

Shadow gave me an annoyed look and stalked toward me this time. In a way, that menacing move was more intimidating than his casual use of speed. No one that big should be able to move that fast, but he did. He was also scary as fuck. It was like watching the monster from a horror movie coming for you only to find out you were knee-deep in cement.

I backed away, trying to keep him spinning in the ring, but he anticipated my move. This time, I had to duck under him again. I didn't make the mistake of trying to hit him again, but kept moving. Good thing too, because he'd been ready for that same move. Had I stopped to punch, he'd have had me. I felt him tug at my hair, but he didn't have a good grip on it, thank God.

I didn't stop moving. I sprinted around the ring, looking for an opening. One quick glance at the clock told me I still had thirty seconds to go. No way I lasted that long.

The moment my eyes were off Shadow, he pounced again, just like I knew he would. This time, I sprinted hard, running up the side of the cage two steps before launching myself over his head. Somehow, I managed to twist in the air and wrap my legs around his neck. The momentum made him stagger backward but didn't bring him down. Not for the first time, I cursed my lack of height and weight. I was strong, but no amount of bulk was going to make me strong enough to defeat someone his size outright, and it would just slow me down. In this case, though, I wished for just a few extra pounds. Twenty might have done it.

When I realized he was going to regain his balance, I let go, shoving off his shoulders with my feet and leaping back to catch the cage wall. I had no intention of staying there, just wanted to break my fall. Which I did. By the time I was solidly on the ground, Shadow was moving toward me again.

Catching the cage was a mistake that cost me a precious second. Before I could get out of the way, Shadow had me, wrapping those beefy arms around me, constricting my breathing. I was seconds away from the full minute, but with my body working so hard, breathing was essential. I doubted I would last those few seconds.

Again, instinct ruled me. I snapped my head forward, catching Shadow in the nose with my forehead. The shock made his body seize and his hold on me loosen slightly, but not enough for me to get away. So I did it again, this time kicking out with my dangling feet. That proved to be just as devastating a blow as my head because I caught him in the groin. Twice. While it didn't put the big fucker to his knees or anything, it did cause him to relax his hold just enough for me to wiggle free.

I scampered away, once again, that instinct driving me. The big fucker just jumped up like nothing had happened. Holy shit! What was the man made of? I know I whimpered, but I only had seconds left. Just seconds.

He was on me again. I ducked a swing, then threw an all-out roundhouse kick, knocking the heel of my foot into his face. Somehow, I managed to hit him at exactly the right angle, my heel catching his temple solidly and with all the force I could have mustered.

Shadow went down. Hard. He didn't move. I didn't wait to see what happened next. I jumped on Shadow and started pounding him, just like I'd been trained. Until the ref split us, I was supposed to beat on him.

Only the ref didn't step in to push me off. In fact, the crowd was eerily silent. I glanced around to see shocked faces all around. Then I heard Fury's voice, soft but distinct.

"Mother fuck."

Then the crowd exploded. Some yelled in fury, others in joy. I imagine someone had won a shit ton of money, but I had other problems to deal with.

Someone finally pulled me off Shadow. Only it wasn't the ref. It was those fuckers who'd threatened Jonas. They dragged me off Shadow by my hair. I tried to get my feet under me but couldn't. The next thing I knew, there were five men from Southern Discomfort beating the shit outta me. My ribs exploded in pain. I tried to protect myself as best I could by tucking into a ball, but whatever part I exposed trying to protect something else, they beat on. I kicked out, landing a solid hit to someone, but the others kept beating on me. This was personal. Them trying to kill me. If I didn't get up, I knew I was dead.

* * *

Fury

If I live to be a hundred, I still won't know what the fuck had just happened, even though I watched it happen in real time with my own fucking eyes. One second Shadow was going after Noelle again. The next, he was flat on the floor out fucking cold.

The chaos that followed was a fucking nightmare.

"Get the fuck out," Samson snapped over the earpiece. "Hardcase and Iron are on their way to you."

"They're gonna kill her right here, Samson," I snarled. I wasn't about to leave Shadow to the tender mercies of the fucking mob, but I couldn't watch Noelle die either.

"Then wake that big fucker up and fuckin' help her!" I wasn't sure I'd ever heard Samson angry. In general, the man seemed to have no emotions. He sounded pissed.

I smacked Shadow a couple times, but he was just fucking out. Then I looked around and found a bucket of water they used to scrub down the floor when it got excessively bloody. I grabbed it and tossed it over Shadow. He came to with a gasp and sat straight up.

"The fuck happened?"

"Got your ass kicked by a girl," Samson said through our earpieces. I was surprised Shadow still had his in, but he scowled and grunted. "Fuck me."

"No," I said. "But those fuckers are tryin' to kill Noelle."

Shadow got to his feet, and we both threw ourselves into the battle. Shadow grabbed two of the fuckers and bashed their heads together so hard, I was sure it caved their skulls. Whatever the damage, they crumpled to the ground. I had another one by his ear, tugging the thick gauge so hard I thought it might rip through his ear lobe. It held. Then I yanked. Hard. The fragile skin didn't stand up to that. The man howled in pain as blood poured from his shredded earlobe. The other men realized there was a new threat.

Considering they were half our size, they backed off. Even four to two wasn't fair odds for them. Wisely, they backed off.

I helped Noelle to her feet. "Can you make it out of here?"

"Made it here, didn't I?" she spat.

"Noelle," I said in my most threatening voice.

"I'm fine. Just get out of here before they swarm you."

"Where's your ride?"

She pointed back through the crowd where she'd been readying herself for the fight. No way she made it without getting jumped. I imagine lots of people had lost lots of money on this fight. I was surprised they hadn't tried to get to Shadow. Probably because he was now back on his feet, and no one wanted to be the first to attack. Noelle was a better target.

"Keep her in the middle," Samson barked. "Iron and Hardcase are approaching from your seven o'clock."

Seconds later, I spotted my other two brothers shoving people out of the way to get to us. Shadow shoved open the cage, and we all jumped down. There were a few who tried to fight us or to reach for Noelle, but most were just scrambling to get to the bookies, wanting their money. Seeing us together, helping Noelle out, some yelled at Shadow, accusing him of taking a dive, but few actually got close enough to strike, and the one or two who did tasted Shadow's fists.

It took several minutes to make it out of the mob and back to our rides. I grabbed Noelle by the waist and tossed her into the back of the pickup Mechanic had brought with various equipment including radios and, of course, guns and ammo.

"I have to get my car!" Noelle protested, trying to climb down. I shoved her back.

"Later. You go back now, you're dead."

She didn't argue, but I could tell she was upset. Several bruises had started to form on her face and arms. She was going to have a one hell of a black eye before morning.

"Let's go," Samson said, starting up his hog. The others followed suit.

"Keep your head down," I said to Noelle. "Do not peek over the fuckin' edge. I'll come get you when it's safe. Just hunker down and fuckin' stay put." Thankfully, she nodded and curled on her side in the bed of the truck. My gut clenched at the sight she made. In that moment, she wasn't my protégé or even a fighter. She was a small, hurt woman in need of protection.

Everything inside of me screamed that she needed me to be that protection, and there was no way I could let myself. If I did, she'd just burrow farther under my skin. I had to face the fact that, somewhere along the line, I'd started thinking of Noelle as mine. It wasn't sexual. At least, it hadn't started out that way. But more than once in the last few months I'd gotten my rocks off imagining that lithe little body of hers under mine as I fucked her hard and long and fast. Knowing she was strong and could take anything I wanted to give her was a huge turn-on, but it was more than that. Everything about her had appealed to me from the second I met her. She was hard-working, determined, and strong. She didn't let anyone push her around or tell her what she could or couldn't do. And, Goddamnit, the woman was fucking beautiful.

Her skin was pale as eggshells, and she had flame-red hair that formed little corkscrews when she didn't pull it back tightly. Her eyebrows made an orange slash above startlingly pale blue eyes. But she was barely into her twenties. I was easily fifteen years her senior. I had a son who was closer to her age than me!

As our convoy sped off, I wondered what I'd do with Noelle when we got back to the Black Reign compound. She clearly had some things going on in her life I didn't know about. She wouldn't like it, but...

"Samson, I want Shotgun to see what's going on with Noelle. Law trouble. Financial trouble. Something underground. Anything. It has her attached to it, I want to know about it."

There was a small silence, and I might have winced a little. Samson was VP. He only took orders from El Diablo, and I'd given him what sounded suspiciously like an order.

"Agreed. I'll get him on it." Then he continued, "Watch your fuckin' tone next time."

I started not to reply, but he was right. There was a chain of command. I needed to follow it like everyone else. At least, some of the time.

"Will do, VP."

The night was sultry, the wind soothing to my frayed nerves. More than once, I saw Noelle's head pop up from the back of the truck. It was obvious she wasn't happy, but I wasn't about to ask Samson to call a halt to find out the trouble. Then I saw her beating on the back window of the truck and narrowed my eyes. The window slid open, and she stuck her head in. It was an older-model, single-cab truck. With Mechanic driving and Iron in the front seat with him, there was no room for her up front, but the next thing I knew, she was being hauled through the back, and the window shut.

"What the fuck's goin' on?" I snapped the question.

"Your girl's wantin' to go back. Says she needs to get her brother." That was Iron's voice.

I paused. Brother? How did I not know she had a brother? "Where is he?" I asked.

"Her house. She says he's being held by that fuckin' gang until the fights are over.

"This why she's fightin' in the first place?"

"Seems so, brother."

I was about to bark an order when Samson beat me to it. "We'll get her brother after we get her to the compound. She's hurt, and we're not prepared to protect one civvy, let alone two."

Someone keyed the mic in the truck, because I heard Noelle in the background. "I can take care of myself! Jonas can't!"

Fuck! I glanced at Samson, his face an impassive mask with no give to it. He didn't say anything, and they all kept riding. The windows of the truck were tinted so I couldn't see what was happening, but the truck swerved more than once before Iron's voice came back over the mic.

"Need some instructions, Samson. She's insisting we go back."

"Negative," Samson said instantly. "We take her to the compound, get a couple more brothers, then we'll go back. But not without preparing."

Immediately, the truck gave a lurch, and our tight formation backed off, giving the truck room so we didn't all get taken out. Samson was the only one who stayed close. He rode up to Iron's side, trying to see in. The other man rolled down the window to give the VP a view of what was happening.

"Pull over," Samson snapped. He backed off just

in time because, as the truck slowed, Iron's door opened, and the big man tumbled out. I pulled up to Iron who jumped up and waved me off and toward the truck. Samson was already on the driver's side, but the second the door shot open, Mechanic was half out of the vehicle, hanging on by the door. Seconds later a small leg kicked out, the foot connecting with Mechanic's jaw. The force was enough to stun him into letting go of the window, and he tumbled from the truck. How he managed to not get run over by the truck or Samson, I had no idea. Once I had Noelle, however, she'd pay for that one.

Then the truck sped off. She caught the door and shut it, whipping the vehicle around to head back to Palm Beach, crossing the median and speeding off.

"Goddamn it!" I swore as I stopped my bike next to Mechanic.

"Iron," Samson's voice was calm as ever. "You good?"

"Yeah. I got reinforcements coming to meet you. Just need an address."

"Mechanic?"

"I'm good. Just dazed. Girl packs quite a wallop."

"Fury, see to Mechanic and Iron. Get Shotgun her address. I'll follow her there."

"Swing by and pick me up, Shadow," Iron said. "I'm not hurt at all, and you need backup."

"Fury?" Samson said, asking if I agreed. As the club doctor I had authority over a patched member's medical ability to go on a run.

"Ain't had time to examine him, but if he says he's not hurt, I'd feel better about you having immediate backup."

"Examine me when we get back," Iron said.

"You'll see I'm telling the truth."

"Let him go," I said. I had to admit, I was glad Iron volunteered. I'd never send a brother out less than a hundred percent, but I wanted as many people on Noelle and her brother as possible.

Samson didn't question further. Instead he gave the order for Shadow to pick him up. Iron climbed on the back, and they took off. That left me with Mechanic. "Can you ride?" I asked him.

"Yep. In fact, follow Samson. We can see what the fuck is going on, and I can spank that little punk's ass for kickin' me outta the truck."

"I'll do the spankin'," I snapped, then quickly amended, "She's my fighter. I'm her trainer."

Mechanic snorted. "Uh-huh."

"Don't even think about it, Fury," Samson snapped, obviously knowing what we were intending on doing. "Back to the clubhouse with Mechanic. You want to head back this way when you drop him off, bring your truck. But Mechanic goes back to Reign."

"I'm good, Samson," Mechanic insisted.

"Not takin' chances with both of you. Iron took the least traumatic fall. After we settle this, both of you will be gettin' a thorough exam."

"Fucker," Iron swore as he climbed on behind me.

"He's right, even if I don't agree with him," I said. "Let's go. Only ten minutes to the compound."

We took off.

"Sent word ahead," Iron said. "The brothers are on their way, and a prospect has your truck ready and running."

I grunted my thanks and sped down the road.

Chapter Four
Noelle

The second I pulled up to my house, I knew there was trouble. I also knew I was in no shape to handle it like this. Three cars were pulled up outside the house. Which meant at least six members of the gang Jonas had gotten involved with.

As I sat outside, I pondered the best way to deal with the situation. Calling the cops was my first inclination. But call them for what? I had no idea what was going on. I also had the feeling Jonas would be going to jail as well as everyone else. Maybe even the only one going to jail because no one else was going to willingly admit to selling drugs. Jonas would out of fear of the gang. Then they'd be obligated to arrest him.

With a sigh, I got out of the truck and marched up the sidewalk steps to the house and toward the opened door. I could hear Jonas scream before I made it to the door. All my instincts screamed at me to hurry, but my training told me differently. I needed to approach this methodically or we'd both be killed.

I opened the door quietly, and the scent of blood hit me. Then the sound of a fist hitting flesh followed by male laughter.

"Look at the fuckin' dummy cryin'," one cackled. "Fuckin' retard."

"Shoulda known better'n to give a dummy a job like this," another one said. "Was bound to fuck up and spend it all. What'd you do, dummy? Buy fuckin' pussy?" Another round of laughter.

"Probably the only way the stupid little retard fucker like you could get pussy."

"I'm n-not a d-dum-my," Jonas cried. Someone

hit him again, and he yelped.

"Shut up you fuckin' *dummy*!" Everyone laughed again.

"This is all your fuckin' sister's fault," someone else said. "All the fuckin' bitch had to do was last sixty seconds. Sixty seconds! Then she beat that motherfucker in fifty-eight seconds! Not only did we lose the match bet, but we lost the side bet because the match didn't make it the full minute!" Another several thuds as they hit my brother, and whimpers from Jonas.

I wound through the house until I came up on the first thug. He was skinny. Young-looking. I was on him before he knew I was there. He was tall, but coming up behind him, it was easy to wrap my arms around his head and snap his neck. Of course, when he fell, I was unable to muffle the noise, and three guys were immediately on me. None of them had the bulk or strength of the men I was used to sparring with, so I got in several blows. One guy took a blow to the head as hard as I'd hit Shadow with, and he went down, hitting his head on the corner of the brick fireplace. Probably another lethal blow.

"Get the bitch!" one of them snapped. Two more guys headed in my direction. I knocked one silly with the heel of my hand hard under his chin, snapping his head back. He staggered and tripped over the guy next to the fireplace and went down hard. That was the best I could do, though. One of the big guys managed to snag me in a bear hug from the front. Before I could snap my head forward and catch his nose, another one had my hands in zip ties at my back. They used more than one, obviously taking no chances I could snap them and get free. Then it was just a matter of time before one of them knocked me down and they tied my feet the same way. The one I'd always thought of as the leader before, Bridges, tied a gag around my head. It was some kind of dirty rag I cringed to think about. He was casual about it, not rushing, but he was rough with snappish movements.

"You killed two of my men," he said, his voice husky with what was probably barely controlled fury. "For that you'll pay."

I tried to scream. I did kick out, but it was no use. I was well and truly fucked.

"Now," he said. "For killing Crab, Jonas is gettin' a beating. Crab wasn't really worth takin' a life over, but he had his uses. So you, you little whore, get to watch and know it was your fault he had to suffer."

Jonas whimpered, meeting my gaze through eyes that were starting to swell shut from the beating he'd already received. I wanted to tell him I was sorry. Wanted to tell the bastards to take out their anger on me, but I couldn't. I desperately tried to get rid of the gag, but it was no use. Bridges had tied it tightly, and he was good at tying knots.

I kept fighting, keeping my gaze on my brother's. He begged them. Begged *me*. But there was nothing I could do.

Those fuckers kicked and beat Jonas until blood leaked from his nose, his mouth. Even his ear had a trickle of blood running from it. Jonas, being the gentle soul he was, never once tried to fight back. It would never have occurred to him. He tried to protect himself, but it did no good against the four remaining men.

Bridges took out a knife then. A big, serrated blade that promised pain. And death.

"Now. The fuckin' retard is gonna pay for the second man you killed. Then I'm gonna fuck you up.

The boys'll have a go after I'm through." He sneered at me. "If there's anything left after that, the big bastard can have you. Hope he paid you well for that little stunt you guys pulled. Every son of a bitch at that fight's lookin' for the two a' ya. They catch either of you, you'll be wishin' for my tender mercies."

Then he raised the knife above Jonas. My brother was barely conscious. I shook my head, knowing there was no way to stop the inevitable.

Motorcycle engines sounded outside. Multiple bikes. Loud and obnoxious. For some reason, the sound made Bridges hesitate.

"See who those motherfuckers are and ask them to leave or make them have an accident," Bridges spat out.

"Uh, Bridges," Trigger said, parting the curtain with the barrel of his pistol. "It's those fuckers from that Black Reign club."

"Black Reign? What the fuck 'er they doin' here?" Bridges scowled, but he didn't do anything more to Jonas.

"Maybe they lost money too?" Trigger guessed, looking back over his shoulder. "They're comin'. Whaddaya wanna do?"

"How many of 'em?"

Trigger shook his head. "Too many. At least ten. Looks like more bikes headed this way." Then he leaned forward. "What the hell? Bridges!" He motioned for the other man, pointing with his gun. "Look!"

Bridges dropped Jonas, standing and stomping to the window. Jonas groaned, blood and spit bubbling from his lips. One eye was completely swollen shut, the other was unfocused and rolled from side to side.

"You've got to be kidding me. What's that big

fucker doin' here?"

"Looks like they were in cahoots. You were right, boss."

"Your fuckin' black bastard's here, whore. Ain't got time to fuck you and leave him a little present. But I'll be back to finish the job with more of my brothers soon enough." He moved through the house to the back door. "Come on, guys. Get the fuck outta here." Trigger stopped and reared back his big, booted foot, landing a vicious kick to Jonas's head. I tried to scream, but the gag blocked most of the sound. Jonas didn't move.

Then, the bastards were gone, and another group of men was entering my home. Unlike the other bunch, these guys were big and knew how to fight. I could tell that by the way they entered the house. The first one I saw was bald with a thick beard. His eyes were flat and cold as he swept the house, pausing only briefly on me and Jonas before moving on. Behind him was Shadow. Only this man wasn't the same one I'd fought in the cage. Had I entered a locked, enclosed area with this guy, I'd have begged for mercy. This man was a straight-up killer.

He knelt, his eyes still taking in the room, and undid my gag. "Any still here?"

"I think they all left," I managed to get out. "Help Jonas. He's hurt bad."

Two more men went to Jonas while the first guy came back and checked on the two men I'd killed. "Those two are dead," the first guy said. "What about that one?" He was referring to Jonas.

One guy shook his head while the other one reached for my legs to cut the zip ties around my ankles. Shadow undid my wrists, and I immediately crawled to Jonas, sobbing his name as I went. There was no doubt he was dead.

"Should I call a cleaner?" asked the one still kneeling beside Jonas.

The bald guy knelt in next to me. "You don't know me, but my name's Samson. I'm a friend of Fury's. We have two choices. You can call the cops and report this for what it was. A break-in you interrupted. No idea how that will go, but it's an option. Or we can make it all disappear. We'll be respectful with your brother's body, and you can have a service later if you wish. But there will be no body. No proof of death. Everyone here will just disappear as if they'd never been here. You can report your brother missing in a few days, and life will go on." When I looked away from him, he caught my chin and made me look at him. "It's your choice, but we have to make a decision now."

"How do I explain this to the police? Will you tie me back up or something? How would I even call them?"

"Can't answer that, Noelle. All I can do is give you the option to get it all over with now."

I knew it was all shady as fuck, but Samson was right. The way he'd offered was the better option. If they could pull it off.

"What if you leave evidence? Then I'm in even bigger trouble."

"Honey, we don't leave evidence. When the cleaning crew comes through here, there will be nothing left. Of anything. No one will ever find the bodies or any evidence anyone was ever here other than you and your brother." I looked away again. "I'm sorry it has to be this way, but we don't have much time. The longer we're all here, the more attention we draw, and there's more people looking for you and

Shadow than these punks."

I nodded. "Yeah. Figured." I looked up at Shadow. "I'm so sorry I dragged you into this."

"Honey, it ain't your fault. You beat me fair and square. Unfortunately, even if we swore on a stack of Bibles, ain't no one gonna believe that."

I looked back at Samson. "Do it," I said. "I just... I can't be here when you do."

"I swear, we'll be respectful with him."

"Where do I go?"

"With me. Back to the Black Reign compound." Fury strode toward me, bending to scoop me up in his arms. I sucked in a breath. Other than to punch me or take me down to the mat for a sound beating, the man had never touched me before tonight. I'd always known he was freakishly strong, but he lifted me like I weighed no more than a puppy. I suddenly had no idea what to do with my fucking arms. One went automatically around his neck, but I stopped short of linking my hands. I started to move my arm, but he growled. "Don't. Hang on to me while I get you to the truck."

Given permission, I wrapped my arms around Fury and buried my face in his shoulder. And the sobs came.

* * *

Fury

She was fucking breaking my heart. In all the time I'd known Noelle, all the times she'd been hurt or had the wind knocked out of her, or lost a match she should have won, I'd never seen her cry. Grimace in pain? Yes. Be pissed as hell? Certainly. But she'd never cried. Now, she'd let go like her whole world had disappeared right in front of her. Maybe it had. I'd never taken the time to get to know her outside of the ring, therefore I had no idea how much her brother meant to her. I didn't know their story, and I desperately needed it for no other reason than to be able to comfort her. Which was a totally foreign concept for me. I didn't *do* feelings.

I brought her to my truck and gently set her inside the cab. When she looked up at me, tears streaming from her eyes down swollen cheeks, she looked nearly panicked.

"Fury?"

"I'm driving, babe. Just gotta get you secured here. Can you put on your seat belt?"

She just nodded but didn't make an effort to do it. With a sigh, I fastened it myself and shut the door. Immediately, she curled her legs up on the seat and lay over on the armrest, her face in the bend of her arm.

"Get back to the compound and lock yourselves in," Samson ordered. "Probably best if she stays put for a few days. The less time she's outside those walls, the better. There's plenty for her to do within those walls."

"She ain't gonna like it," I said, knowing that once she was over the shock and violence of the night, she'd want to come back to her house and at least get her things. Maybe go through her brother's things.

"Don't matter if she does or not. She needs to be safe until we eliminate the threat to her and, make no mistake, these guys are a big fuckin' threat."

"I hear you," I said. "I can manage her. Just keep me in the loop. I want a piece of these fuckers."

"I'll run it by El Diablo. He's going to want to talk to her, you know. We need to find out exactly what happened so we can get a better handle on exactly what's hanging over her."

"Figured. I'll do a quick assessment of her

injuries tonight, but tomorrow, I'm going to want some X-rays. See if El Diablo can wait until tomorrow night. She needs sleep to heal. The more the better."

"She's gonna need more than sleep, brother. She's gonna need someone strong to watch over her. That gonna be you?"

"She's my fighter. My responsibility."

Samson gave me an impatient look. "She don't need a fuckin' trainer, you dumb shit. She needs someone to protect her from the bad shit in her head. Nightmares. Thoughts that this is somehow her fault, because it *will* happen. You're a fuckin' doctor. You know this!"

I shook my head. "She's strong. Once she gets this crying jag over with, she'll be good."

"Fuckin' asshole," Samson muttered. "Fine. Shadow will be by to see you guys tomorrow. You *will* let him in. He already feels bad about losing to her and not because he lost to a girl. He knows they cost a lot of people a lot of money, and they'll be more likely to come after her than him. He's willing to take on the emotional role since you ain't."

I scowled. No one was getting close to Noelle if I could help it. Especially not with her in this kind of vulnerable state. I knew I was talking bullshit, but I wasn't ready for this emotional garbage yet. I'd ease my way into it. She'd be fine. "What the fuck ever. But he doesn't interfere with her treatment. I'm the club doc. I have full authority over making sure her injuries are treated and healing."

"Just get the fuck outta here and get her settled." Then he muttered, "Motherfucker."

I had no idea what that was about, but he could piss off, VP or not. I'd take care of Noelle in my own way. I knew what was best for her.

The ride across town to the compound was made in silence, broken only by the occasional whimper from Noelle. It was starting to freak me out. Not because I didn't think she had the right to be so upset, but because Noelle just didn't get upset. I felt like I needed to pat her back or pull her close or some shit, but just like she didn't get upset, I didn't comfort. That was a nurse's job. I was the doctor. I just fixed shit.

Tentatively, I touched her head, stroking a caress over the braids in her hair. "You good, Brawler?" Fuck. Of course, she wasn't good! What the fuck was I doing?

She shuddered slightly, then raised her head, seeming dazed to find herself in the moving vehicle. "Where're we goin'?"

I was relieved she hadn't answered my question. If that made me a pussy, that was fine by me. At least she was talking, and I didn't have to do anything mushy.

"The Black Reign compound. You'll be safe there."

"Black Reign." She sounded dazed. It occurred to me I'd never really mentioned anything about the club. I hadn't tried to hide it, but I never talked about it with outsiders.

"Yeah. It's my MC. All kinds of shit there, but we don't let no one in who don't belong."

"I don't belong," she said softly.

"You do now. I'll get you in and settled, then I need to take a look at you. See where you're hurt."

"I'm fine."

"If I had a dollar for every woman who's used that word to describe herself when she's anything but…"

Instead of getting a rise out of her like I'd hoped,

Noelle just uncurled herself to sit straighter in the seat, then turned her head away from me to look out the window. We rode the rest of the way in silence.

When we finally pulled into the compound, I bypassed the main building and took us straight to the back where my clinic and suite was. It would be closer to the clinic if she just stayed with me. It wasn't like I didn't have the room. Besides, I could keep an eye on her this way in case she was more injured than I thought she was.

And I was *really* good at rationalizing.

As I climbed out of the truck and hurried around to Noelle's side. She started a little when I opened her door, like she hadn't been aware of what was going on. As I helped her out of the truck, Celeste and Lyric approached. Celeste had a speculative look on her face while Lyric just scowled.

"Is this the poor girl from the fight?" Lyric asked. Normally, she was sweet and easygoing. She looked angry.

"Yeah," I said. Noelle didn't resist when I took her hand to help her out of the truck.

"We've made up a room for her at the main house next to Shadow." She glanced at Celeste. "I thought he was looking out for her."

My gaze snapped to Lyric's. "Who told you that?"

She crossed her arms over her chest, giving me an almost belligerent look. "Shadow did. What the hell's going on?"

I shoved the truck door shut and walked toward my clinic entrance, never letting go of Noelle's hand. "Well, he told you wrong. She needs to be close to the clinic in case she needs medical attention. Since it's my clinic and I'm the club doctor, I get final say here."

"Shadow seemed pretty adamant," Celeste said. "He insisted on us helping so she'd feel comfortable being in a strange place with so many men."

"There's women here," I said with a shrug.

"You can't count club girls," Lyric said. "They'd eat her alive."

"No," I said, turning to the women after I keyed in my code. The door swung open smoothly. "She can take care of herself, especially with club girls. She's just had a trauma. Been a long fuckin' night."

Celeste smiled at Noelle gently. "What happened? Think it's anything a big ole slobbery puppy dog could cure?" Celeste addressed Noelle directly, ignoring me completely. To my surprise, Noelle gave her a half-hearted grin.

"Thank you, but I'm not sure I'm fit to be around anyone right now."

"I know we're strangers, Noelle, but Lyric and I have been through our own bad stuff. Lyric probably more than me. She was beaten and had her child threatened. But Black Reign took us in. They're all good people here."

"Except for some of the club girls," Lyric said with a roll of her eyes. "But if you're the badass Shadow said you were, they've met their match." Again, that got a small smile from Noelle. "Our daughters would love to meet you. When you're ready."

"Not sure Wrath will think she's appropriate for Holly," Celeste said. I was about to tell her to go to hell, Wrath's wrath be damned, when she got a wicked grin on her face. "Holly would absolutely *adore* you. She'll insist you teach her to fight, though. So she can take Wrath down when he tries to be all bossy. Also because she knows it would annoy Wrath. What she doesn't know is, Wrath would secretly love it."

"You seem to have an unusual relationship. The three of you." Noelle spoke quietly, but I could tell there was interest in her eyes. Which was good. I could leave her with these women and not have to saddle myself with actually taking care of her full time. Just not right now. She needed a doctor, and that was my job.

Rationalizing.

"Oh, we do," Celeste said. "Wrath is the big bad biker, and Holly is exactly like him. My daughter has leukemia, but she's nearing the end of her treatments. In fact, her doctor says one more treatment and, if things keep progressing like they have, she should be good. All her blood work seems to have leveled out, and she's holding her own."

"That's wonderful," Noelle said, sounding genuinely happy for Celeste. "I'm sure Wrath is her fierce protector. He might not want her learning to fight."

"Are you kidding? He'd love it. He won't *act* like he loves it. He'll make a big deal about how Holly doesn't need to fight. She has him. But as long as the docs say it's OK, he'll be all for it."

"I'd like to meet her. Sometime. I just… right now…" Tears filled her eyes, and she tried to blink them back. Then Celeste and Lyric both stepped close and pulled her into their arms. To my utter horror, Noelle burst into tears again. Fuck my life.

"Do you want to talk?" Lyric asked softly. "You don't have to, but just know we're always here. All you have to do is tell your man here you need us. Or, if he's being an ass, tell El Diablo."

"Who's that?" Noelle sniffled.

"He's the president of this MC," Lyric said.

"Don't worry about being able to find him," Celeste said. "He has a way of just turning up when you need him most."

"That's kind of creepy." Noelle tried to laugh, but it just came out as another sob.

Lyric tilted her head, brushing stray curls from Noelle's face. "Now that you mention it, it kind of is." Celeste giggled, but looked immediately contrite. Then they both giggled. "But it's not creepy. You'll know when you meet him. He's very protective."

"You know, he actually offered to make me his woman if Wrath didn't want me," Celeste said, shaking her head. "I'm pretty sure it was because he considered me 'MC Royalty' because of my dad or something, so there were ulterior motives, but he still did it. And he has the girls calling him Uncle El. How sweet is that?"

"El Diablo is many things," I said, needing to interrupt before Noelle decided to take off with the well-meaning females, "but he's not sweet. Now excuse us. I need to make sure Brawler here isn't hurt worse than she's letting on."

"Brawler?" Celeste said, pulling back a little. "He calls you Brawler?"

Noelle shrugged. "'Cause he says sometimes I have no fighting style. I'm just a fucking brawler." Surprisingly, she winced a little. Had that hurt her feelings? God! This was going to fucking drive me to the looney bin!

Lyric looked up at me and scowled. "Yeah. You'll be getting a visit from El Diablo. Sooner rather than later." She reached out a hand for Noelle. "You can come with us. We'll protect you better than that sorry asshole."

"Sorry, ladies," I said, tugging Noelle closer to

me and stepping in front of her a little. "She's coming with me. Doctor's orders."

"What happened out there?" Celeste asked, looking up at me with more than curiosity. She genuinely wanted to know. Not to be nosey. Because she wanted to help Noelle.

"Long story. Club business." I shrugged, but Celeste's face grew hard.

"I don't care if you are the club doc or not, Fury. This woman needs tender care. There's not a tender bone in your body."

"She'll be fine with me."

"And don't you dare throw that club business line in my face about this!" I might have misjudged Celeste. I'd never seen this side of her before. Lyric was nice enough, but there was an edge to her. She could fight if she had to, and there wasn't a club girl in the place who could best her if she had to fight them. But Celeste had always been pure sweetness. How she'd managed to mother a little hellion like Holly, also known as Maddog, I'd never know. At least, I hadn't been able to reconcile the two. Now? Yeah. Maybe Holly came by it honestly.

"Look. I'm Noelle's trainer. She's an MMA fighter. What happened tonight wasn't so much a physical trauma for her as a mental one. She lost someone close to her."

"Oh, no," Celeste gasped, reaching to take Noelle's hand in both of hers. "I'm so sorry, Noelle," she whispered.

"We'll help you," Lyric said, eyeing me closely. "She'll need as much support as she can get."

"I got this," I said, entering the clinic and stopping in the doorway to prevent them from entering behind me. "I've got to examine her to make sure she's not hurt worse than I think. Patient confidentiality and all." I tried to take the sting out of my abrupt kicking them out by smiling, but I was pretty sure it just came out smug. I controlled the door and who got in the clinic. Lyric and Celeste weren't getting in.

Both women were decidedly not happy about the situation, and I knew I only had a short time to pull Noelle out of her funk. Otherwise, Samson might persuade El Diablo to let Shadow have a hand in her care. I had no idea why the man took an interest in Noelle. If it was more than simple guilt, he could just think again.

As I headed through the clinic to the back where my suite was located, I tried to focus completely on Noelle as a clinician. She walked gingerly, favoring her left side. She also had several bruises coming up on her pale skin. The bruising around her eye wasn't as bad as I'd first thought it might be. Minor swelling under it, but I'd still need to rule out an orbital fracture. If her ribs were broken, there wasn't much I could do other than make sure she didn't have lung problems afterward, which meant she needed to rest until they had a chance to heal.

"I'm fine. Really," she said, not looking at me. "I'd just like a shower and some rest."

I nodded. "Not a problem. Can I take an X-ray of your chest first? If you've got broken ribs, I need to know. Hurt to breathe?"

She shrugged. "A little. I've had worse."

"So, the rib pain isn't bad?"

"It hurts. I'm not going to lie. But after the Brown fight, it hurt way worse."

"Yeah. Same side." I thought for a moment. "You might have reinjured yourself. You just cracked two ribs then. If the bone was weak, it could have broken again."

"If it did, it's not as bad. And I'm not short of breath at all. Just a little tender when I walk."

"OK. One X-ray. If it's good, you can take a bath and sleep. Otherwise, I'll have to take you to the hospital for more tests."

She met my gaze steadily. Not aggressively, but in a way that said she'd do exactly what she wanted, and I wasn't getting a say in it. "One X-ray."

I sighed. "I'm only trying to do what's best for you, Noelle. You're hurt. I'm a doctor."

"And I didn't even know that," she muttered. "I didn't know anything about your life other than you got kicked out of UFC and banned from all MMA competitions. I just figured you had anger issues."

"I do. But there's a reason for it. I've learned to control it. Mostly. Thanks to the people in Black Reign. And yes. I'm a doctor. I have no desire to go into private practice other than here, so I only have the clinic for people in the club or associated with it. If El Diablo approves."

"Sounds like El Diablo runs all your lives."

I shrugged. "His club. His rules."

"OK. I'll buy that."

"So. X-ray." I looked at her. She had on a sports bra and boxing shorts with tighter Spandex shorts underneath. "Anything metal in your clothing?"

"Not that I know of."

"Good. I won't make you undress." I nodded to a dimly lit room and ushered her inside.

The images took all of five minutes to complete. A quick look at the area she was hurting in didn't show any breaks, but I'd send these to a radiologist friend of mine for confirmation. I didn't want to miss anything.

"No broken ribs. No pneumothorax. We'll let it go for now." I handed her a couple of pills and a bottle of water. "For the pain. Nothing too strong, but it will help you sleep." She took them without complaint.

I took her to my room. It was spacious with a California king bed in one corner and a living area between the bed and the bath. There was a kitchen on the other side with a countertop bar separating the two areas. The open layout only had walls to close off the bathroom. I needed it that way.

The bathroom had a huge shower and a sunken tub inside a space big enough to fit three bathrooms. I had cabinets and shelves along the walls to store everything from my clothing to cleaning supplies. A washer and dryer sat in the very back corner.

"Use the shower or tub. Or both. If you need an ice bath, I can fill the tub in a few minutes." I pointed to a chute just over the tub's rim. "Designed specifically for the purpose of ice baths when I needed one."

"Wow," she said. I got the feeling that, had she not been so exhausted both mentally and physically, she'd be more impressed with her surroundings. "This place is amazing."

I shrugged. "It's home." She nodded, then stood there, fidgeting. "You need help?"

She glanced up at me. "No. I'm good."

"OK. I'll leave it to you, then. Do not lock that door. If you need help, I'd like to be able to get to you without breaking down my door."

I didn't move. She glanced up at me, then turned her back and stripped off her T-shirt before tugging at the pins holding her hair up in those impossibly tight braids. I sighed, knowing it was a horrible idea, but also knowing I was doing it anyway.

"Here," I said. "I'll help. Just... stand there."

She took a deep breath and let it out slowly, her shoulders slumping and hunching in on herself. "I can do it myself."

"Yeah. But it hurts you."

"Lots of things hurt," she said absently. Her body shivered, but it wasn't from the cold. She was barely holding herself together.

I pulled the pins gently from her hair, and the ties at the end. Then picked out the braids with my fingers. Once I was done, I let my hands fall to her hips. She didn't move away. Instead, she leaned back against me slightly. For some reason, my stupid hands slid around her waist to cross under her breasts, and I rested my chin on her head.

"You OK?"

She shrugged, but nodded. Taking another deep breath, she turned in my arms. "Will you help me with my sports bra? I'm not sure I can do it with my ribs this sore."

I swallowed, looking down at her. Those impossibly blue eyes looked up at me with such a combination of hunger, need, and pleading, I didn't know what to do. "I'm not sure that's a good idea."

"Please, Fury," she said, one tear sliding down her cheek. "Just this once. I'll never ask you for anything again."

"You're not in the right state of mind, Noelle. I'm not taking advantage of you. Let's just get you a hot shower and to bed. If this is still what you want, we can talk about it in the morning."

She turned around, nodding forlornly. God, she was breaking my heart. Gingerly, she tried to pull her bra over her head. Her side was red and turning purple where the bruise was. I knew it had to hurt.

With a sigh, I helped her get it the rest of the way off. When she went to drop her shorts, I stayed her hands.

"Leave them," I said gruffly and gently urged her into the shower.

When she would have turned, I stepped in behind her and grabbed her shoulders. Last thing I needed was to see her tits. Not now. Hell, not at *all*! I'd tried my best over the past year to not view her as a desirable woman and only see the fighter. But I'd had my fantasies. Noelle was at least fifteen years my junior, but she called to me in ways I didn't want to think about. 'Cause I could easily imagine having the nastiest, raunchiest sex I'd ever had with anyone with Noelle. She was strong, her body honed in battle. Just like mine. Noelle was a woman who could take anything I needed to give her and come back for more.

In the shower, she just stood there, the water cascading over us in a gentle fall. My boxer briefs were soaked and did nothing to hide my raging hard-on. Noelle didn't say anything. I just stood there with my hands on her shoulders.

"Come one, Brawler. Wash yourself. I'm here in case you get dizzy. Don't want you to fall."

Finally, she reached for the shower gel, then squirted a generous amount on her hand. Slowly, she washed herself, being careful when she touched a particularly sore spot.

She leaned her head forward and let the thick fall of water wet her hair before she brushed it back with her arm and reached for the shampoo. She lathered, then conditioned it before giving her hair a final rinse. Just the simple act of taking a shower had her whimpering when she used a bruised muscle. I wanted to help her, but knew if I had to touch her that much, I'd not stop there. Not with us like this.

I reached around her and turned off the water, snagging a towel I'd hung over the glass enclosure so it was within easy reach. Wrapping it around her body, I guided her out of the shower and snagged another towel.

"Wrap your hair up, and I'll brush it out and dry it for you."

She looked up at me. "Do you even know how to do that?"

"It's a fuckin' brush. How fuckin' hard could it be?" I was being mean, I knew. Noelle didn't seem to mind. In fact, she smiled.

"I like the grouchy side of you better." Then a tear tracked down one cheek before she dashed it away. "Not sure I can take much more of the kind and caring side."

"I can be nice."

"Yeah. But it's not your default setting." She ducked her head. "Not something I've seen a lot of."

She was right, I knew. And it had been on purpose. I didn't want to get to know her. Didn't want her to get to know me. I would have pawned her off on someone else if she hadn't had all the talent she did. But she was just too good for me to pass up. Noelle had a real shot at making it to the big fights.

If word got out about this fight, I doubted any manager in the big leagues would touch her. "You never needed it before," I admitted.

"And you think I do now?" She turned her head to look at me, a bitter look on her face. "I'm the strong one. I can take a hit and get back up."

"Fully aware of that. This ain't a normal hit. Now, get dressed for bed and come sit down. I'll do the work with your hair, then we can go to bed."

"We?" She glanced over at my big bed and

something like satisfaction bloomed in my chest. "You think I'm sleeping in that bed with you?"

"Nope. I know you are. It's plenty big enough for us both without either of us being even close to touching. You might need me in the night, and I'm not taking a chance of you being on your own if there's some injury I've missed."

"Fine," she muttered. "Just fucking fine."

She grumbled as I brushed her hair, but her eyes grew heavier with every stroke of the brush. She had so much hair, there was no way to not dry it. And, naturally, there was no way to completely dry it. She complained that, with all the curl she had, completely drying it would make a mess in the morning anyway. Instead, she braided it into one long, thick, orange-red braid and drew it over her shoulder. I helped her into bed, then walked to the other side.

"You need the bathroom light on in case you need to get up?"

"Might not be a bad idea," she admitted. "I don't usually have to get up, though."

I left it on and crawled beneath the covers myself. I'd put on boxer briefs and a T-shirt. More than I usually wore, but what else was I going to do? I wasn't sleeping naked with her anywhere close. Especially not in the same bed.

She had on one of my T-shirts and, I hoped, panties. Not nearly enough, but I couldn't say anything without admitting how much I wanted to fuck the shit outta her. I was enough of a bastard as it was without her worrying about that. Even if she had basically offered herself to me.

"Good night," she said softly before turning on her side away from me.

"'Night."

As I lay there, I knew I'd lied to her earlier. There was no way in hell we were revisiting the thought of us having sex in the morning. Or any morning after that.

Chapter Five
Noelle

My whole entire body hurt. It was pitch-black except for a small light across the room from a slightly opened door and a clock on the nightstand. I struggled to remember where I was and what was going on. Warmth surrounded me, which tried to combat the soreness and pain, but couldn't quite do it. There was a warm, pleasant scent of pine and ocean air that was at once familiar but strange in this setting.

I groaned, trying to roll over... only to be stopped by a heavy weight around my waist.

"Where you think you're goin'?"

Fury.

"Bathroom," I squeaked.

"Take it slow. You'll hurt worse today than you did last night."

Like I hadn't been in this situation on more than one occasion. My side hurt like a mother bitch, and my face pounded. I'd hurt worse, but this was personal. I got up and padded slowly to the bathroom. Every step reminded me of all the pain of the night before.

"You feel dizzy, you call out. You hear me?" Yeah. The situation might be all fucked up, but the tone was nothing new.

After doing my business, I took a look in the mirror. My face was swollen on one side, but, thankfully, my eye wasn't swollen shut or anything. The rest of my body was a mass of bruises. Thanks to my fair skin, everyone and their mother could see I'd had a rough go of it.

Sighing, I washed my hands and turned off the light as I stepped out of the bathroom. The room was dark except for the blue LED from the clock screen beside the bed. I shuffled to the big thing where I knew Fury was waiting.

"I thought we were sleeping on opposite sides of the bed," I asked, trying to remember the conversation from the night before.

"We were. Until you ended up practically on top of me. I just waited for you to settle, then let you sleep."

"But you had your arm around me. And I was facing away from you."

"Yeah. You turned over and took my arm with you. Every time I moved it, you'd get restless. You seemed to need the security, so I let you have it."

I shook my head. "I'd say you were lying, but since I don't remember much I'll have to take your word for it."

"That's right. Now, did you take any painkillers while you were up?"

"No. Didn't know that was an option." I sat gingerly on the edge of the bed only to feel him get up.

"I'll be back. You want pills or a shot?"

"I hate shots." God, I sounded whiny. But then, I got that way sometimes after I'd lost a match and was licking my wounds.

"Shot'll work faster."

"Just give me some pills. Tylenol and Motrin are fine."

He grunted and left the room. A couple minutes later he came back with a bottle of water and two pills and shoved them at me. "These got a bit more kick than over the counters. Swallow."

"If I had a dollar for every time I've heard that," I snickered half-heartedly.

Fury turned his back and scrubbed his hair with his hands. "Keep it up, and you'll hear it again," he muttered.

I paused in the act of taking my medicine before finally tossing back the pills and swallowing a healthy gulp of the ice-cold water. I remembered begging him to take me last night. I'd wanted the rough sex I knew would follow. Fury had a certain reputation, but more than that, I always craved rough, dirty sex after a match. No matter how badly beaten I was, I needed it to settle myself down. It wasn't always pleasurable or satisfying, but it wore me out. I'd never had a man turn it down. No matter if he was attracted to me or not. Until Fury. It hurt more than I could say.

"No man I've ever encountered would have turned me down last night." I spoke softly, but I knew he heard me.

"I don't fuck injured women, Noelle," he said, not facing me. "You didn't want to admit it, but you were injured both physically and mentally. No way was I touching you."

"And now?"

"You're still hurt. Probably more than you were last night because the soreness has had time to set in." Finally, he turned, his dark eyes meeting mine with a kind of fierce lust that took my breath. "Besides, I'm your trainer. I don't mix business with pleasure."

I shook my head. "You're not my trainer. Not anymore. You said so yourself. And I'm thinking I've retired anyway, so unless you just don't want me…"

His lust was soon replaced by anger, a fierce expression that nearly made me back up a step. Somehow, I found my backbone and lifted my chin.

"Don't test me, Noelle. You might find more than you bargained for."

"I'm not testing you. You're not my trainer anymore. You fired me last night. The only reason I wanted to fight in the first place was because of my brother. To give him a better life and the medical help he needed. Now..." I had to stop, my voice breaking. I couldn't show weakness. Not now. I cleared my throat, taking another swig of water. "Now, there's really no point."

"How about for yourself?" he snapped. "You could make it big if you follow my instructions."

"Again, Fury. *You fired me.* Even if you hadn't, you were banned from competitive stuff. You can't come with me, and I refuse to train under anyone else, or have anyone but you at ringside with me." I shrugged. "The end. Even if I wanted to go on, I doubt I could. They always find out about illegal fights. After last night, everyone in the whole UFC will know who I am. And no one will touch me."

"You're delusional if you believe that. You beat a man with size, strength, and skill better than just about anyone in MMA today. I wasn't lying when I said you couldn't beat him. You *shouldn't* have beaten him. You might never beat him again, but believe me when I tell you, UFC will want you even more."

"And I'm not going with anyone else as my trainer. So we're back where we started."

"Fuck," he swore as he turned and paced across the room a couple times. "Goddammit, Noelle!"

"What? Tell me I'm wrong. Or have you been lying this whole time?"

"You know I haven't," he snarled. "You saw the headlines. The articles about how I nearly beat a man to death."

"Not just a man," I said. "The fighter, his trainer, and the ref. So I know you're not lying. I'm not continuing without you. You've been my trainer for three years. You weren't my first, but you're the only one who gets me. The only one I trust completely. I'm not continuing on with anyone else, even if they let me in." I spread my arms out. "What's your excuse now? If you're not attracted to women like me, just fucking say so. You're not the first man to think I look like a freak."

"You don't look like a freak, Noelle. Dammit, can you just... go to bed? We'll talk about it in the morning." He looked tired, but, more, he looked... *trapped*. I'd seen that look in the eyes of women I'd fought. Men, too. Normally, this was the point where I'd take my opponent down, pound them into submission or unconsciousness. But with Fury, I wasn't sure if that was the right thing to do. Not in this instance. But I really didn't know what else to do. I wanted sex with Fury. Not a relationship. A relationship was pointless with a man like him. Even if he tried to do one, there would be a woman who came along he couldn't resist. Because I was telling the truth. I was a freak. I was in top fighting form. There was no way to be anything other than a freak.

"No. We won't. You'll be gone before I wake up, and I won't see you again in a situation where we can talk about it. I know how you work. Hell, you might even pawn me off on your buddy, Shadow, just so you don't have to address this."

Unexpectedly, Fury took two steps toward me before stopping. His fists were clenched, the veins in his arms and neck standing out in his rage. "You won't fuckin' go near him without me! Do you understand?"

"No! I don't fucking understand!" I yelled at him, whipping my shirt over my head. It was his shirt, and it swallowed me whole. Under it, I was completely naked. I'd had no chance to grab clothing from the house before we'd left so he was seeing all of me.

"Either fuck me or let me go. But understand me when I tell you, I'm getting laid at the first possible opportunity. I may not be a feminine flower, but I'm sure if I walk around here naked long enough, someone will offer to do the job."

Fury growled and whipped off his own shirt. In the moonlight drifting in from a nearby window, I saw his muscles ripple all over his body, even in the dim, silvery light. Tattoos decorated his chest, images I'd seen nearly every single day for the last three years. They might be obscured in the darkness, but I knew every one of them. Fury was... magnificent. To me, he always had been. He'd just been unattainable. My flawed hero. Now, he stalked toward me, looking every bit his namesake.

"There's not a fuckin' man in the fuckin' place who'll touch you, Noelle," he growled. "I'll kill 'em if they even look at your naked body."

Before I could say anything else, Fury pulled me into his arms. His mouth came down on mine with furious intensity, though he held me gently, careful of my injured ribs. Tongue sweeping between my lips, he took what he wanted, kissing me like he was staking a claim. Maybe he was. All I knew was that I was naked, in his arms with my breasts mashed against his equally naked chest. This was someplace I never thought I'd be. It was like my ultimate daydream coming to life. Sure, I'd often wondered what this would be like, to actually get the chance to fuck Fury, but he was my trainer. It was never going to happen, and he'd never indicated in any way he was attracted to me. Maybe he wasn't now. Not many men would refuse a woman throwing themselves at them.

He pulled back, his hand fisting my braid and holding my head where he wanted it. I looked up into his eyes, trying my best to read him. I was an expert at reading people in the ring. In a sexual situation, not so much. Sure, there was lust, but was it because he had a willing woman, or did he truly want me?

"I'm not doing this with you, Noelle," he said softly. "I can't and still respect myself in the morning."

"*You're* not doing this," I said, gripping his sides and digging in my fingers to hold on to him. "*I'm* doing it. I'm not asking for anything after this. I just need sex. I want it with you."

"But any man will do?"

I opened my lips to say yes, but he put his hand over my mouth. "Don't lie to me, Noelle. I can always tell when you're lying." Instead of answering, I closed my mouth and lifted my chin defiantly. Fury merely nodded. "Fine. I'll do this. But under two conditions."

"Name them."

"First, we do this my way. I'm not going to hurt you more than you already are."

"And secondly?"

He was silent for a long moment. So long I wasn't sure he'd answer. "You don't go looking to fuck any other man in this compound. You need to fuck, you come see me."

"So we're... what? Fuck buddies now?"

"There doesn't have to be a name for it," he snapped. "I just don't want you fuckin' my brothers, OK?"

I nodded. "I guess I could see how that would be awkward."

"We're clear, then?"

"Crystal."

Fury lifted me into his arms and planted a knee on the bed to lay me in the center. The rest of the room was shadowed in darkness, but the moonlight seemed to fall across the bed, right where he'd put me. I looked up into his eyes. They glittered when he turned his face just right. I thought I saw hunger in their dark depths, but I wasn't sure. He settled his weight on top of me, and I felt his cock mash against my mound and belly. He was long and thick, his arousal evident as it pulsed between us.

He stroked my cheek gently, not saying a word before his lips found mine again. This time, he kissed me slowly. Gently. There was still an edge to his touch, but he was gentle with me. I wasn't sure how I felt about that, but I soon forgot about anything other than the sensations building inside me.

I moaned and arched against him, wrapping my legs around him. I dug my heels into his ass, but he only slid his cock over my mound instead of getting it out of his briefs and tucking it into my pussy's entrance.

"Stay still," he murmured between kisses. "I'll fuck you in my own time. My own fuckin' way." The words were gruff, but the tone was gentle. Those kisses of his were drugging. His short beard tickled my face slightly, but it only added to the erotic sensations. The longer he kissed me, the more I craved him.

Fury's arm tightened around me while one hand cupped my breasts. He was careful with my bruises, but still managed to pull and tug my nipples with enough roughness to fill that need inside me for hard, nasty sex. When he slid down my body to take the other nipple in his mouth, sucking and nipping it, I gasped and whimpered. How could he manage to give me what I needed without hurting my battered body?

Then he swapped. He bit the other nipple sharply, stretching it out before letting go only to take it in his mouth to lick and suck before nipping it again.

Over and over, he did this until I thought I'd go out of my fucking mind. And he was just playing with my tits! I was beginning to think I was in over my head with this man. Fury had always been my fantasy, even if I never acknowledged it, not even to myself. But this was proving to be more than I'd ever dreamed. And the man was far more potent in person than in my dreams.

"Tell me if I go too far," he said, his voice a soft whip of command.

"Feels good," I whimpered. "Exactly what I need."

"Good." His praise was like a rough purr. He continued teasing and tormenting my nipples for a long while. Twice I nearly came, but he backed off before I could. "Patience," he said around my nipple. "We've got the rest of the night and half the fuckin' morning. You'll come when I let you."

"Fury," I gasped, my fingers sliding through his hair. "God!"

He just grunted but moved his way down my body. The contrast in how rough he was with my nipples and how gentle he was as he moved down my torso was stark. Instead of nipping or petting me, he skimmed his lips over my skin, sometimes pausing to place a gentle kiss. I was so caught up in the pleasure, I almost missed what he was doing. Because he was kissing each bruise down the length of my torso.

"Fury?" I tugged at his hair until he looked up at me just as he reached my pelvis. He kissed both hip bones, then took a long, slow swipe over my pussy lips and clit. "Fury!" I screamed his name, my head falling back but my fingers tightening in his hair.

"Like that, baby?"

"Yes!"

He gave my clit a sharp nip before sucking it gently. I yelped, but the slight pain quickly morphed into something wonderful. Then he tugged my pussy lips one at a time, pulling each of them just to the edge of pain before he flicked my clit once again with his tongue. I was just about to beg him to do more when he covered my pussy with his mouth and plunged his tongue inside me.

Pleasure exploded through me, but not enough to get me off. Just enough to make me crazy. I screamed, bucking my hips, trying to get the friction I needed on my clit. Fury growled at me, swatting my pussy with the flat of his hand.

"Still."

"But --"

"Only 'but' is the one I'm gonna heat up as I fuck it if you don't do as I tell you."

I gasped as the image he'd just put into my head fully sank in. Fury. Taking my ass. "Ahh! Fury!"

"Don't you dare fuckin' come!" He pulled his mouth from my clit but slammed three fingers inside my cunt, holding them deep but not moving.

"Fury, I can't --"

"You can because I fuckin' said so! Hold it!"

Strangely, he was right. It was just like when I trained with him. I did what he said because he said so. There simply was no other alternative. My pussy pulsed and ached, but I couldn't fall over the edge. My body broke out in a sweat, my breathing coming in little pants. But I didn't come.

"That's my girl," he praised, dropping his face back to my cunt to lick my clit again, flicking it with wicked lashes of his tongue. Then he pulled his fingers out of my cunt and pushed off the bed with his hands, crawling up my body to blanket me once again.

I felt his cock on my belly and wanted it inside me. Fury kissed me again. This time, I didn't lie back and let him do what he wanted. I lunged for him, meeting his tongue with mine. He reached for the nightstand, opening the drawer and pulling out a condom. His body lying on top of mine, he opened it. Reaching between us, he rolled the condom on his cock before tucking it beneath me and into the entrance of my pussy.

"You ready, Brawler?"

I gripped his sides tightly, my fingers sinking into the hard muscle. "I've been ready for this for a long fucking time, Fury."

"Remember. After this, you need to fuck, you come to me. You go to another man and..."

"Yeah. I get it. It's over."

"No," he snapped, letting the head of his cock penetrate me but went no farther. "You go to another man, you're signing his death warrant. 'Cause I'll kill any son of a bitch who touches you like this."

Before I could question him, he slid completely inside me in one hard thrust. I gasped and sucked in a breath to scream, but nothing came out. I just kept looking into his dark brown eyes, the breath seizing in my lungs. He didn't move. Didn't do anything but stare at me. I'd seen that look too many times. He was assessing my condition. Both mental and physical. Finally, after I'd had time to get used to the size of him, he nodded, then rolled us over so that I was sprawled on top of him.

"Fury?"

"You control this, baby. I'll fuck the shit outta you, but you're going to have all the control. I absolutely will not hurt you doing this."

I nodded, then lifted myself, bracing my hands

on his chest as I started to move my hips. At first, I went slow, getting used to the feel of him. I had to admit, this was much better than just having a guy use my body to get himself off. I wasn't too righteous to admit that was what I'd been doing either. I wasn't about to look too closely into the reasons for that, though. Not now.

Moving my hips faster and faster, I finally leaned back to brace myself on his thighs. I threw my head back and sighed, enjoying the feeling of fullness between my legs.

"Such a fuckin' beautiful sight," Fury growled. "Never seen a woman move that way and it be so erotic."

I moaned as I rose up to face him. "Don't lead me on, Fury. I don't need it nor want it. I just want you fucking me into oblivion."

His hands bit into my thighs, nowhere near any of my bruises. "I don't say somethin' I don't mean, sugar. Your body is a finely tuned machine. As much as muscles are a turn-on for women, they can be for men too. You're sleek and defined, your body built to take a hard pounding. When your bruises heal, I'll show you exactly what I mean." The wicked gleam in his eyes made my breath catch. He definitely meant every word. Which didn't make sense at all.

"But --"

"Sugar," he said, pulling me down to kiss me. "We'll talk about it later. Right now, I need to give you this as much as I want it."

I couldn't wrap my mind around it. I'd expected him to enjoy himself. But I hadn't expected him to say all those words. It did funny things to my insides. Like, made me want to hope for more than he was offering. Hadn't he said we'd be fuck buddies? OK, so I'd said that, but he hadn't disagreed.

"Get your head with me, Noelle," he snapped, reaching up to find my clit with his thumb. "I want you totally in the here and now. Focus on how my cock feels inside you. How my hands feel on your body. Listen to my voice. Talk to me."

"I -- Fury," I sighed. "It feels so good. *You* feel good."

"What do you need?"

Good fucking question. I honestly didn't know. Well, that wasn't exactly true, was it?

"I need..." I took a breath and swallowed. "I need you to fuck me hard."

"That's pretty generic, Noelle." He surged upward into my pussy with a hard jerk. It was technically what I'd asked for, but not what I meant. "This what you meant?" It was jarring, but what I went looking for when I needed sex. Before I could stop myself, I shook my head. "Then tell me what you mean."

"You won't do it," I said softly.

"Why won't I?"

"Because you already said you wouldn't hurt me."

He raised an eyebrow and gripped my hips to steady me. "Why do you need to be hurt, Noelle?"

"I don't know," I said. Embarrassingly, it came out nearly a sob. "Because I deserve it?"

"Why do you deserve it?" He didn't deny me, merely asked a question.

I shrugged. "Lots of reasons."

"We'll talk about that later. Right now, what do you need? You were pretty close to coming before."

"You were in control," I whispered.

"I see."

Carefully, he rolled us over. Instead of continuing to fuck me with him on top, he got off the bed and tugged me with him.

"Where're we going?" I almost dreaded what he'd tell me. I wasn't sure if I could take it if he decided to fuck me in front of his brothers. I'd had men do that before, and I'd let it happen. It wasn't the pain I needed, but it worked in some respects. Instead of heading out of his bedroom, however, he pulled me to the bathroom vanity.

"Hold on to the counter and lean forward," he commanded. When I did, he slid his cock inside me. Instead of moving, however, he just stood there, my pussy throbbing around his dick. "Now. Talk to me. Do you get off on the pain?"

"Sometimes," I admitted.

"But not always." When I shook my head, he continued. "Is it to punish yourself for something?"

I froze, catching his gaze in the mirror with mine. He gave me a level look, one of patience. He wasn't going to rush me, but he wasn't letting me get by without answering him either.

With a shrug, I looked away. "Maybe."

He nodded. "OK, then. This only goes as far as you need it to. But, understand me, Noelle, you will come. I won't settle for less. I'm not going to beat you for my own pleasure, and I'm not going to just fuck you to get my rocks off. This is for you. What you need. Later, after we've talked about this and set more boundaries, we'll see what happens next."

That surprised me and my eyes found his in the mirror again. "You mean, you'll still do this with me?"

"I will. I happen to know you can come your brains out if the right person is in control."

"You've done this with a woman before?"

"Once. A very long time ago."

"Why did you stop? Don't most people stay in that lifestyle once they enter into it?"

"You mean BDSM or some shit?"

"Well, yeah."

"No. Not at all. Some do. Others find it's a phase in their life and move on. Just because you start doing something doesn't mean you have to continue. Same with us. We'll start out with an S and M relationship, but whether or not it continues like that depends on you."

"Just..." I shook my head slightly. "Just don't humiliate me. Some of the men I was with liked to take me in public and make fun of me. I got some relief with it, but it was more painful emotionally than any beating I ever got. Not saying I didn't deserve it, but I just found that I can't do it again."

"That's not something I'd ever be able to do to you, Noelle. Ain't saying we wouldn't enjoy ourselves at a club party with all the other couples fucking, but it would be more to show you off than anything else. Now. Tell me your safe word."

"I -- uh --"

"You do have a safe word. Right?" I was too ashamed to admit I'd never used one. When I said nothing, he just looked at me a long time. I wanted to look away but couldn't. I'd seen that look before. He was furious at me. When he finally nodded in acknowledgment, still not breaking his stare, he said, "Fine. Your safe word will be 'red.' If I hurt you or take you too far, you say it, and we back off."

"But you won't stop?"

"No. Not unless it's what you want or need."

I didn't quite understand that answer, but I agreed anyway. "OK."

"Now. keep your hands on the vanity unless I say otherwise."

When I nodded, he shook his head. "Words, Noelle. You have to say the words."

"OK. Yes."

Fury started moving in me again. Slowly, building me back up to that fever pitch he'd had going before. One hand went to my nipple, the other to my clit. He stroked my clit while rolling and tugging at my nipple. I couldn't take my gaze from his in the mirror. Fury was still watching me intently. He started to move then, rocking his hips back and forth slowly while he continued to stroke my clit and alternated between my tits to pull and tug at my nipples. The pain wasn't much, but it was enough to make my pussy tighten around his cock.

"There we are," he murmured at my ear. "I feel you squeezing me."

"This isn't like anything I've ever done before. It usually just hurts. The pleasure is there but... different."

"Don't think about it. Just let me do what I want to you. I promise I'll take care of you." When I nodded, he delivered a sharp slap to my pussy, right over my clit.

I gasped, then moaned when he did it again. My clit was swollen and puffy from his ministrations earlier. When he delivered a third slap, he lingered, rubbing his fingers over my clit and around the place where we joined as he continued to fuck me.

"Your little pussy is wet and swollen with how horny you are," he said. "So fuckin' wet." He brought his fingers to his mouth, tasting my juice. I knew I was wet. I could feel it trickling down my inner thighs, even as he fucked me. I kept my pussy shaved for practical reasons, but it made me so much more sensitive. Now I appreciated it, because I'd never been more turned on in my life.

"I can feel it," I whispered. "So ready for you."

"Damn straight you're ready. Your little cunt is as hot as a furnace around my dick. You're getting close to coming, aren't you?"

"Not as close as I was before, but this is... oh, my God, this is so much different!" I was becoming a little desperate. I needed more of what Fury had given me so far, but I needed the pleasure not to end either.

He gave my pussy another smack, this one harder than the others. Again, it was right over my swollen clit. "I think I can keep you there. Until it's time for you to come. I think you like having your pussy spanked while it's getting fucked."

"Fury!"

"Don't come! Not until I say!"

He gripped my hips in both hands, continuing to fuck me but with even greater speed and force. The sound of flesh hitting flesh echoed all around us. His face in the mirror grew harder with each passing minute. The veins in his neck and arms stood out in stark relief against his skin as he pounded into me, his fingers biting into my hips as he did.

Without the added sensation of his slaps or him playing with my tits, the pleasure started to fade a bit. My pussy was still wet and swollen. Needy. But I wasn't anywhere close to coming like I'd been only a few moments before.

Then he swatted my ass. Hard. I gasped. Just like that, the pleasure was back in full force.

"Oh, my God! Do that again!" I all but screamed out the demand. Thankfully, Fury complied, swatting my ass with his palm over and over until it stung with every hit of his hand.

"That what you need, baby? You need that ass reddened like a naughty child?"

"Fury! Yes! Oh, God, yes!"

He continued to spank me as he fucked me. It wasn't long before I was panting, my skin once again slickening with sweat in the effort to hold off my orgasm.

"Now, baby," he snarled. "Come on my fuckin' cock! Take me with you!"

His permission was all I needed. With a shrill shriek, I let myself go. Never before had I come so hard or so long. It was like the muscles in my lower body seized up, pushing the pleasure on and on, never letting it die down.

"Mother fuck! You're squeezing my fuckin' dick!" One of his hands left my hips to circle my throat. He pulled me back until I was standing straight with my back against his chest. His hand squeezed on my neck almost to the point of discomfort, but he seemed to know exactly where that line was. Funny thing about it, the sensation made me come all the harder. The edges of my vision blurred, and I wasn't sure if it was from the hold he had on my neck or the fact that I hadn't been able to suck in a breath because of the intensity of my orgasm. He let go of my neck and wrapped both arms around me tightly, holding me to him. I still had spots in my eyes, my ears roared, and I still couldn't breathe. I felt Fury's cock pulsing inside me where he'd emptied his cum into the condom. I had the fleeting thought that I'd wished he'd come inside me. But that was stupidity.

Finally, *finally*, I sucked in a breath. Immediately, all sensation came rushing back to me. Which triggered another orgasm, though this one was not as intense.

My legs collapsed, and had Fury not been holding me up, I would have fallen. But never before had I ever felt so depleted. So sated. Had I been lying down, I probably would have passed out.

"Easy, baby," Fury murmured. "I've got you. Just relax for me."

I did, going limp in his arms. He lifted me and carried me to the bed. When he laid me down, he instructed, "Don't move. I'll be right back. True to his word, he was back moments later with a warm, wet cloth to clean between my legs. Then he slid in beside me, pulling me close as he moved us to the middle of the bed.

"Talk to me, baby. You good?"

"Better'n good," I said, my words slurring. "Never felt anything like that in my life."

"Good. Now sleep. Tomorrow, we'll talk."

I dreaded that talk, but it didn't seem to matter. I took a deep breath, taking Fury into me, then sighed, and I was out.

Chapter Six
Fury

The phone woke me from a dead sleep. It had been way too long since I'd slept that deeply for that long. A quick glance at the time as I answered the call told me it was past eleven in the morning.

"Yeah," I said, my voice gruff from sleep.

"Better get your ass to the main house. We got company." Samson was cheerful as always.

"Mother fuck," I groused. "Anything to do with last night?"

"Yep."

"How many?"

"Less than they think they need."

"Give me five."

"You've got three."

I ended the call and tossed the phone back on the dresser. Noelle was still sound asleep, draped over my chest. A feeling of immense satisfaction filled me, and I wanted to puff my chest out. Yeah, we had some things to talk about, but this felt... good. Really good. Better than I'd ever thought possible, especially with Noelle. She wasn't supposed to be here. She was supposed to make it in the big time where I couldn't. She was my chance at redemption. Now, she was in my bed. After I'd fucked her into an oblivion she'd needed.

Which brought up a problem. Noelle had issues. Severe ones I needed to help her work out. I had the feeling she didn't want to acknowledge them, but she was going to. If she still needed pain to get to orgasm, I'd find a way, but not before I figured out why. If she even knew why.

I peeled her naked body from mine and carefully

laid her on the mattress. She mumbled in her sleep, and I brushed hair away from her face. God, she was beautiful! How had I managed to keep myself blind to that fact all these years?

I leaned in to kiss her temple. When she mumbled again, I whispered, "I'll be back soon, baby. Sleep as much as you can."

Tugging on my jeans and T-shirt, I watched Noelle, hoping she'd settle. If she didn't, I'd take her with me, because no way was I letting her out of my sight if I didn't know she was sound asleep in my bed. Not after last night. She'd need my reassurances as much as I needed to give them to her. Thankfully, she hugged my pillow to her and slept on. It was time to bust some motherfuckers.

It took the full five minutes I'd told Samson I needed for me to get to the main house. He glared at me, but I just flipped him off and leaned against the wall. In the middle of the great room where we held club parties and where visitors were allowed, eight members of that fucking Southern Discomfort stood getting belligerent with Samson.

"I know you motherfuckers know what happened to our brothers," the one who appeared to be the leader accused. He had gotten close to Samson, jabbing his finger into the bigger man's chest. "You and that bitch were in cahoots."

"You might want to consider you're in another club's house."

"Yeah? You might want to consider there's eight of us and more on the perimeter. Not to mention that we don't much care who we have to go through. Rumor has it you've got women and children in here. Maybe we'll just take a couple of them back with us. Show them how a real club does things." The man looked back at his brothers and smiled. They all snickered. Samson didn't.

"I hearin' you right? You threatenin' our families?"

The guy stepped closer to Samson. Was the guy fucking nuts? "Ain't threatenin' nobody. I'm tellin' you now, you turn over the bitch and that black bastard she fucked us with, or we'll take you all down."

"Now, that's not very nice, is it, Samson?" El Diablo stood at the top of the stairs overlooking the room from the railing.

"Not at all, boss," Samson said, never taking his eyes from the man in front of him.

"Who is he?"

"President of a club called Southern Discomfort," Samson said. "Calls himself Chow."

"Ah. I see. You're the ones taking orders from the Brotherhood alongside Kiss of Death."

The man froze. "How do you know about the Brotherhood?"

El Diablo tsked. "Now, you really should know your enemy before you waltz into his home and threaten his family. You might run up against someone bigger and meaner than those you work for."

"Ain't nobody meaner than the Brotherhood."

"Are you sure about that? Really sure? What exactly were your instructions?"

"No one gave me fuckin' instructions! We came here to avenge our brothers! Now, turn over the bitch!"

"Interesting." El Diablo crossed to the stairs and descended them one slow step at a time. Somehow, he made the move menacing. El Diablo was the boss, and I respected the fuck outta the man, but this was a side I never wanted to see. "You came in here, all on your own. Into the lair of the Brotherhood's mortal enemy.

And you not only dare to make demands, you threaten our women and children. Am I hearing you correctly?"

"Ain't nothin' wrong with your ears," Chow said, giving El Diablo a smug look. The other men in his club chuckled. When Chow pulled his gun out, they followed suit. Chow taunted El Diablo, looking at him like he was saying, *"Whatcha gonna do about it, big guy?"* All the Southern Discomfort men did.

"That's what I thought." Then El Diablo proceeded to show the motherfuckers what he was gonna do about it.

Before the men had a chance to do more than smirk, El Diablo drew his gun and shot Chow twice. Once in the heart, once between the eyes as he fell. The brothers designated as soldiers each took out a target in the same manner as El Diablo. Then Samson went from man to man and shot them each once more in the head. It was over almost before it really began.

One thing I respected about El Diablo was that, once he made a decision, he followed through. He was one deadly son of a bitch, but he always protected women and children, especially those he'd claimed as his own. For whatever reason, he'd done that with everyone at Black Reign, including the club girls. He might or might not fuck them, but he always protected them from the outside. If they brought down the wrath of someone inside Black Reign, he dealt with it inside the family. Which usually meant letting the parties fight it out as they saw fit.

Outside, in the night, there were the sounds of gunshots and men screaming. I wasn't certain what El Diablo's purpose was with this gang -- other than eradicating them -- but he'd given orders regarding them. Specifically, there were certain members he wanted brought to him alive. I wasn't an officer in

Black Reign, but, like everyone else, I served my purpose to the club. Currently, it was helping El Diablo ferret out the fight trafficking ring bringing in a steady stream of two or three fighters a week to the underground fights to fix matches without having to pay someone to throw a fight. I didn't know for sure, but I suspected Noelle was supposed to be part of that ring. Their sacrifice. She was supposed to make it far enough to give Shadow a run for his money, but she wasn't supposed to win. If she'd made it sixty seconds, they would have collected big. I should have been comforting her instead of fucking her.

El Diablo watched Samson closely, waiting for something. It was eerily quiet in the clubhouse common room while the commotion outside played out until it finally died down.

After a while Samson gave a short nod, then turned to El Diablo. "Prisoner acquired. They'll be here in five."

"Very well." El Diablo crossed to his favorite chair next to the fireplace and sat. He rested his gun on his leg and settled in to wait.

Shadow moved up beside me. "What's goin' on?"

"You mean other than the message he's sending?" Shadow gave me a "duh" look. "No fuckin' idea. El Diablo doesn't do anything without a reason, though."

"This have to do with the trafficking ring or your woman?"

"Never said she was my woman." I'd known Shadow a lot of years, and the younger man always saw through me.

"Brother, you didn't have to say anything. And for the record, we've all known since you started training her she was off-limits."

"Fucker," I muttered.

As we stood there, Hardcase and El Segador -- The Reaper -- entered the room with their prisoner. Bridges. That kind of surprised me. Why keep Bridges alive when El Segador had killed the president of Southern Discomfort?

"Ah, Mr. Bridges," El Diablo said pleasantly. "So good of you to join us." As always, El Diablo was polite and well-spoken.

Bridges leveled a steady look on El Diablo but said nothing. He had the look of a man who knew he was going to die, could do nothing about it, and had accepted his fate like a man.

"Just get it over with, you bastard," Bridges growled.

"I'm hurt," El Diablo said, placing a hand over his heart. "Did you think I meant you harm? One little incident, and a man gets a bad reputation."

"I'm not stupid," Bridges said. "I know who you are and your skill set. You've never missed a mark you aimed for, and you don't make mistakes. You know my hands are dirty, or I wouldn't be here."

"A man who doesn't mince words. Straight and to the point. I respect that." He nodded at Bridges in acknowledgment. "You're right in that you don't get to live. How long it is before you die depends entirely on you."

"I have a feeling it's going to be a long night." Bridges sighed but met El Diablo's gaze steadily.

"Only if you choose. Cooperate, and you can be at peace."

Bridges and El Diablo stared at each other hard for several seconds. Finally Bridges glanced away and shook his head slightly as if feeling himself in an untenable position. "In the past, when I've been placed in similar situations, I endured. You were the one person they told me to avoid at all costs."

"If you're thinking of taking your own life, it would be a futile effort. Not only have my men made that impossible, but they won't kill you if you make a try for me."

"I'm aware of that. They even found the cyanide capsule I had as backup." As if for proof, El Segador lifted a small, oblong object in a sealed bag for El Diablo to see before tucking it back into his pocket. Then Bridges continued. "I was sent by the organization to infiltrate the area. I started with the MC Kiss of Death. When you eliminated most of those, I moved to this gang. It wasn't going to work, but I was gaining money the organization needed to solidify their hold on the local government."

"Continue," El Diablo commanded when the man stopped.

He shrugged. "The reason the boys were so upset when your man lost that fight was because they'd bet everything we had that, even as small as she was, the woman could last a full minute before she lost. Not only did she win, but the match lasted less than a minute. We lost everything. I was back to where I started."

"And the trafficking?"

"We either paid off men to lose fights, or brought in homeless people off the streets to fight. And, yes, we blackmailed our share, too."

"Did any of them live?'

Bridges raised his chin. "No. I couldn't let word get out the fights were rigged. Not if I wanted to continue to raise money. It wasn't the quickest or the most lucrative way to make money, but it was the most consistent, and as long as everyone died, the safest. Only a handful of fighters actually took a dive, and they were silenced the second they were in private after the fight. Everyone else usually died in the ring." He said all this matter-of-factly, like it was no big deal. I didn't know if it was because it really wasn't a big deal to him or if he was just relaying the information to El Diablo in a concise manner. I could tell by looking at the man he'd accepted his death. He was simply choosing the quickest method. Better a clean death than a slow, painful, messy one.

"Did you plan on killing me after that fight?"

I turned toward the sound of the voice behind me. Noelle walked into the room, moving straight toward Bridges. Me and Samson both blocked her path, though she tried to push past me. I simply wrapped my arms around her middle and pulled her against me. She was ten feet or so away from Bridges, but it was way too close for my peace of mind.

Surprisingly, Bridges answered her. "Yes. When we came to your house last night, it was to kill both you and your brother. Though not for the reasons the others thought."

"They thought it was because my brother had stolen drugs from you and, since I failed to win the match and repay those losses, you were killing him as an example, and me just because?"

"Unfortunately, that's correct." Bridges didn't look smug or even contrite. He was simply stating a fact. "But neither of you were going to survive even if you had won. You were going to be killed because you knew the fights were rigged."

"But I didn't know --"

"You knew *yours* was," Bridges interrupted.

"Mine wasn't rigged," Noelle quickly replied. "I

just had to last sixty seconds with Shadow. My struggle was just making it that long without getting killed."

"And then you were supposed to tap out."

Noelle tilted her head, hesitating as if that information had just dawned on her. "Yeah," she said slowly. "Guess I overlooked that part."

"You would have put it together eventually. I couldn't take the chance you'd let word leak to anyone else. Because, let me tell you, sweetheart, there is no way there's a person who was there wouldn't recognize you. They might not believe your version of events, that you were just supposed to last sixty seconds, then tap out. But they'd believe the fight was rigged. Hell, most of them do now. Especially with you being holed up here in the same compound as the man you beat."

"I'm not with Shadow."

"It doesn't matter. People believe what they want to believe."

When I tightened my hold on Noelle and turned to take her away before the killing started again, El Diablo stayed me. "Not just yet, Fury."

"She don't need to see this."

"I didn't say she would. But it's not time to go yet." El Diablo's tone was conversational, like he didn't have a care in the world. It was something I always admired and respected about the man. He could hold on to his temper even in the worst of circumstances. Mine burned hot, sometimes overriding good sense. It was why I did what he asked now. "How many men are held back by the 'organization,' as you called it?"

"After you found and took out Money, the rest of the club disappeared. I found a couple of them, but I have the feeling they were meant to be found."

When Bridges mentioned the man who'd targeted Shotgun's woman, Esther, El Diablo still didn't react. I'd been part of the party who'd taken down the rest of Kiss of Death. At least, all we could find. So far as I was aware, there was only one person left of that club. Pretty Boy. It bothered me, though, that we hadn't known about Bridges.

"They were. You didn't answer the question, though."

Bridges shook his head slightly and sighed. "As far as I know, Pretty Boy and Drago are the only two left. But they're the ones rounding up people to fight. Now that the fight avenue is shut down, they'll be selling the people they have. Or killing them. Unless they can manage to pull out one more match. There was one scheduled for tomorrow, but they had no intentions of going. My guess is they'll try to recoup their losses there."

That got a reaction from El Diablo. "Drago?" he snapped. "They've let that fuck live?"

"The organization says he's useful," Bridges offered by way of explanation. "Even if he is a sadistic motherfucker."

"Fucking Malcolm has some explaining to do." El Diablo said it under his breath, as if to himself.

"Malcolm has no say in that matter. He was overridden. And he's a wildcard."

El Diablo's head came up, his eyes boring into Bridges. "You better fucking explain."

"All I can tell you is what they told me. And, I gotta tell you, they probably knew it would come to this, so it's probably all bullshit they wanted me to feed you."

"That would be how they work. Tell me."

"They're backing off Palm Beach. You can have

the local government and any sources of income. You've made this a place too hot for them. They fear outing themselves after so many centuries in the shadows. Looking elsewhere for their game of world domination seemed to be their best option."

"That it?" El Diablo didn't look impressed. He looked hard. And I knew he was going to kill. He shot me a quick glance, and I turned my body, taking Noelle with me. The second I did, there was a sharp gunshot. Noelle jumped but didn't scream. I walked her from the room, keeping myself between her and the violence behind us. It was one thing to walk in on a room full of dead bodies, quite another to see a man you'd just been talking to dead, possibly with half his face blown off.

"Fury," she whispered my name.

"Not now, baby. Let's get back to our room. We'll talk about it later."

"Meet me in Church in an hour, Fury," El Diablo said mildly. "We're going to draw those two out and be done with this once and for all."

"One hour," I affirmed. "I'll be there."

Chapter Seven
Noelle

I wish I could say I was horrified by what had just happened. The fact that the head of this club -- or president... whatever -- had just killed a man right in front of everyone, and that either he or even Fury had killed all the men lying in the middle of the common room really should have bothered me. It didn't. Which I was compelled to point out to Fury since he was hell bent to get me away from the whole affair.

"You know, I could give two fucks those guys are dead. I wanted to kill that prick Bridges myself."

"I know that, Brawler," he said softly. "I didn't want you to have to."

"You do know I'm a fighter, right? Violence is an ordinary thing to me."

"Know that, too." He continued on until we got to our suite. And when did his room become *our* room in my mind?

When we got there, he opened the door and practically dragged me inside. "We got shit to plan and do, but right now, I need to fuck you more than I need to breathe." Almost before he'd stopped speaking, his mouth was on mine, his hands tugging at my clothes.

My head spun with the effect of his drugging kisses, my need skyrocketing in seconds. I tugged at his clothes, trying to shrug out of mine even as I tried to help get to his bare skin. Moments later we were both naked, grabbing at each other in a desperate frenzy.

Before we could make it to the bed, Fury brought his fingers to my dripping pussy. "So fuckin' wet!"

"Ready for you," I whimpered. "Ready!" I flung my arms around his neck and hopped up into his arms. My legs went around his waist, and I rubbed over his cock with my wet pussy.

He walked us to the bed, but I wasn't waiting a second longer. Reaching between us, I tucked the head of his cock into my entrance and lowered myself on him.

"Mother fuck! What the fuck 'er you doin', Noelle?" He sounded mad, but he didn't separate us as he crawled into the bed. The second we were securely in the middle, he started riding me. Hard. "Sweet fuckin' pussy, Noelle. So Goddamned sweet!"

"That's it," I breathed. "Fuck me hard, Fury. Take what you need," I whispered, my voice jarring with the force of his thrusts.

"I ain't gloved, baby." His voice sounded broken, but he didn't slow down, just wrapped his arms around me tightly and rode me harder.

I tightened my arms and legs around him even tighter. "Don't fucking care," I cried out, nearing my peak. "Fuck... fuck... FUCK!" With a gut-wrenching bellow, I came. Harder than I'd ever come in my life. My pussy spasmed around Fury, trying to milk him. And yeah, I wanted his cum inside me. I had no idea why, and I'd probably think of all the reasons why this was a bad idea later, but in this moment, getting him to come inside me was the most important thing in my world.

"Milkin' me so fuckin' hard!" Fury bellowed as he raised himself up on his stiffened arms and let out a loud roar loud enough it should have brought his brothers in force. Thank God it didn't. My hands found his upper arms and I clung to him, still feeling the effects of my orgasm. He was as deep inside me as he could get, his cock pulsing in time to the pulse beating frantically in his neck. Finally, he collapsed on top of me, his full weight pressing me into the mattress. It felt good. Safe and secure.

Fury's fingers sifted through my hair as we both struggled to get our breathing under control. His lips were pressed against my neck nipping and sucking gently, likely marking me. I didn't mind. This was what I wanted. What I needed. I just hoped it lasted a little longer, because I had no idea what I was going to do or how I was going to cope on my own.

"You good, Brawler?"

"Yeah, but I think my brawling days are over, Fury."

He stilled then, kissed the side of my face, gently cupping my chin and turning my face so I had to look at him. "You can still fight if you want to, Noelle. We can do whatever circuit you want. I'll always be at your side."

"I think I might like to teach kids self-defense or something," I said, finding the tattoos on his shoulder very fascinating. Anything to avoid looking into his eyes and seeing disappointment there.

"Wasn't expecting that," he muttered. "But yeah. I like the sound of that."

I looked up in surprise. "You're not mad? You don't think it's a stupid idea?"

"Hell no! We've already got kids in the compound. And it's considerably less dangerous."

That surprised me. "The danger never bothered you before."

"I never said that. Hell, the reason I took you on in the first place wasn't just that you had potential to go to the top. That bastard you were using before was gonna get you hurt big time. He knew your potential and knew there'd be a big payday in it for him, so he was pushing you to get there before you were ready."

"That's what I thought, too." I said softly. "Then you came in, told me your background and told me to check it out. You had no expectation you'd get a payday out of me but promised that you'd get me ready to fight in the UFC. You said you'd get me ready and hook me up with a trainer who could pick up where you left off seamlessly. I always wondered why you did that. Seemed like it was a waste of your time."

"Not if it kept you from getting hurt because of flaws in your training. Fighting is a dangerous sport, but you can lessen the risk of getting injured with good training and fighting practices. You're still gonna get hurt, but not because you didn't know how to prevent it or weren't in good-enough shape." He sighed, then rolled over, taking me with him. "I think I loved you from that first week I watched you training. I wanted to protect you, but I also wanted to take you out of the fight altogether. You want to spar, you do it with me. I nearly lost my mind when I had to let Shadow in that ring with you."

That shocked me. "I didn't even think you liked me."

"Oh, I liked you all right," he murmured, kissing the top of my head. "Too much. Still do. Hell, I love you, Noelle. Have for a long time. I was just too scared to tell you."

I looked up at him and grinned. "Afraid I'd kick your ass if you asked me out?"

He barked a short laugh. "Yeah. Maybe. But I wouldn't have asked you out. I'd have just taken you on the fuckin' mat when everyone left the gym. Ran through that scenario many times as we sparred."

"Why didn't you?" I knew I sounded a little forlorn, but I couldn't help it. "You were so far out of my reach there was no way I was brave enough to offer myself to you. Not until last night when I was so lost and broken. You'd said you wouldn't be my trainer anymore, and I just felt like I had nothing left to lose."

"Because I thought you really wanted a shot at the UFC. I knew I could get you there, but I'd have to trust you with someone else to take you that last step. I wasn't sure I could do that even keeping an emotional distance between us. But with you as my woman? No. I couldn't let anyone else have you, even if it was just professionally."

"I know what you said about finding me a trainer to take me the last step, but I never really thought I'd get there. If I had, there was no way I would have let you pass me off to someone else. I trusted *you*. Still do. Even if we don't continue this... relationship, I could never trust anyone else like this. I'd always be looking for you."

He pulled me on top of him so that I straddled him once more, his hands framing my face. "Believe me when I tell you we will definitely be continuing this 'relationship.' In fact, I want to make it a more official and permanent one."

"Permanent? We've only been doing this a day. How'd you go from hating my guts to a permanent relationship in less than twenty-four hours?" Fury wasn't intimidated by my scowl at all. In fact, he smiled and chuckled at me.

"Honey, you've been mine for the better part of three years. You just didn't know it. Hell, *I* didn't know it. I think it took Shadow and Samson to make me realize just how much I needed you in my life. They knew it way before I admitted it to myself."

We were silent for a long while. Then I asked the question I really didn't want to ask. "So, what happens now? You have a meeting soon. Right?"

He sighed. "Yeah. We still gotta find the rest of the people that fucker, Bridges, and his MC set up to rig the fights. If we don't, they'll likely sell them to some other fight ring. Or kill them."

"You know you can't go to the fights again, Fury. Or Shadow. They'll kill you."

"I know, baby. Don't worry. El Diablo takes the safety of everyone here personally. He's not going to send any one out unless the risk is acceptable."

"Then why would he call you for a meeting?"

"Honey, we all put our heads together for shit like this. Doesn't mean we're goin' in. Both me and Shadow will probably be their backup, but whatever El Diablo and Samson have planned will be well-thought-out with lots of backup."

"You trust him?"

"With my life, baby. And yours. That should tell you something right there."

I sighed and snuggled against him, my eyes drooping. "Fine. I'm still feeling a little battered. I think I'd like to take a nap while you go do your little meeting." I tried to sound like it didn't matter what he did, but it did. I was pretty sure he knew that too.

He kissed my temple. "I swear I'll fill you in on exactly what we're doing. I won't ever leave you in the dark. You're strong. You can stand with me."

"I can, and I will, Fury. No matter what. So if you're going, I'm going. You make sure your people know that."

He chuckled. "I hear you, baby. I'll make sure they understand." He looked like he needed to say more, but stopped himself.

"What?" I asked, not willing to let things stay here.

He sighed. "Yeah. There's something I need to

tell you. Not related to any of this, but it's something you need to know."

When he didn't immediately start, I prompted him. "And?" It wasn't like him to hesitate like this. He was usually pretty self-confident and just said what he needed to say.

"I have... a son. Jackson. Goes by Jax. His mom and I split before he was born, but I've tried my best to be in his life. Gwen died two years ago from breast cancer, and Jax came here to live with me. It's taken us a while, but we're getting closer. Good thing too, because now that he's old enough to prospect for Black Reign, and Samson and El Diablo are gonna bring him in."

"How old is he?"

"Just turned eighteen. And reckless. But he seems to be growing into a good man. Picks on Wrath's adopted daughter, Holly, mercilessly. But he also protects her."

"Is he a fighter too?"

"I've seen him working the heavy bag a few times. He has good form, but it looks more like he's just got good instincts. I've offered to train him, but he's refused so far. Not sure if it's just the thoughts of his old man being in charge or if he's just not interested."

"Maybe I can help him."

He gave me a wry grin. "Just don't let him take you away from me. He's only eighteen, but he's a charmer, if the club girls are any indication. I've had to warn more than one of them to stay away. Not sure how successful I was."

"You've got nothing to worry about, Fury. You're the one for me. Not your son or anyone else in this place. You."

I leaned down to place a gentle kiss on his lips. Which turned into a hot and heavy kiss. Which led to more sex. Yeah. I loved Fury. And I'd do anything to make him happy.

* * *

Fury

"Everyone, this is Rebel," Samson said by way of introduction. "He's from a club in the Panhandle called Devil's Boneyard and a friend of mine. He's gonna be our fighter."

Immediately there were objections.

"Another club?"

"There are plenty of us here who can fight."

"Yeah! What the fuck, Samson?"

"This ain't no Goddamned committee," Samson said in his even tone. Even, but everyone knew not to fuck with him on that. "I'm gonna need every single one of you motherfuckers doin' somethin' else. Now shut the fuck up." When everyone settled, he continued. "Archangel and Hardcase are going to be in the pits with Rebel. They will be responsible for keeping Rebel safe. The rest of us will be hunting. I want to know where the men and women used to either rig or throw fights are being kept. It's possible a fighter is paid to throw a match, but we're almost positive it's disposable people brought in separately. That way, once the fight is over, they can kill the only person who can tie a rigged fight to them."

"Who's them? Didn't we take out all Kiss of Death and all but two Southern Discomfort?"

"Yes. But it's only been a day. They'll be trying to make up the money they lost in Noelle and Shadow's fight."

"Quick question," Iron, who stood in the back,

raised his hand.

"Go ahead."

"Is Noelle up for grabs? 'Cause any woman who can take down Shadow, even if it was an accident, turns me the fuck on."

The place erupted in laughter. Samson's lips even twitched. When they quieted down, I responded. "She's mine. I'll be gettin' her property patch the second this is done. Woulda already but been too busy fuckin' the shit outta her to take care of it." Again the men laughed, and I suspected I had a shit-eating grin on my face. Noelle would hear about this and might even object, but I could get her to forgive me.

"Right," Samson said, shaking his head. He still looked like he was fighting a grin. "Anyway. The rest of you have your assignments. Shadow, Fury, and Noelle will be the only three not actively engaged in this, but they will be our backup as well as medical. Some of the fighters might be in bad condition."

"Your boy, Rebel, might be in bad condition," someone yelled from across the room. I couldn't see, but I thought it might be Jax. Fuck. He wasn't supposed to be here. "I can help up front."

Surprisingly, it was El Diablo who answered. "You'd be a great asset, Jax, but I need you here at the front gate of the compound. If there are any issues, you'll be in charge of coordinating reinforcements to meet us on the road, and to make sure the gates are open for us. You'll also be responsible for fortifying the perimeter in case we're followed or our enemies get here before we do."

I found Jax's gaze across the room. He was disappointed, but determined to do the jobs El Diablo laid out for him. "You can count on me," he said.

"Which is why he put you in that position,"

Samson said gruffly. "No parties while we're gone."

Jax and everyone else chuckled at that. Good Jackson knew he really was being given an important job. It was one more reason why El Diablo had my loyalty. He saw the needs of his people, and Jax needed to be included in the club.

"Not even a small one?" Jax grinned, but there would be no parties.

"Wait until this is all done, and you can party all you want, young man," El Diablo said with a chuckle.

Samson explained the areas each team was to patrol once at the fight. Once they found where the prisoners were being kept, or they found either Pretty Boy or Drago, they would give their position, and those holding back would intercept them, bringing out the innocents and taking captive the enemy. "Any questions?" When there were none, Samson nodded. "Let's ride."

This fight was in an underground parking garage. Escape routes were limited, which was probably the whole idea. If anyone pulled the same stunt they thought Samson and Noelle pulled, they'd be beaten to a bloody pulp with little chance of escape. If all went well, though, Black Reign would be out and gone without anyone the wiser. They'd managed to get Rebel in at the last minute by holding the number ten contender in the field, tied, gagged, and drugged. They dumped him in the bed of Fury's truck and had two men on him. Just in case the big fucker woke up.

Rebel was everything Fury hated in a fighter. Mouthy. Cocky. He just invited opponents to beat the shit out of him. Except the fucker was good. He thrived on his opponents losing their cool, but was able to pound them into submission if they didn't.

"Yo, Adrian!" The fucker yelled as he raised his

hands over his head in a very Rocky-like fashion. "We did it, Adrian!" That got him both cheers and jeers, but the big man just jogged around the cage, enjoying his win.

"Pull him back, Archangel," Samson snapped. "He may have one more fight before we can leave."

"You found them, then?" Hardcase murmured his question while Archangel got Rebel out of the ring. He followed closely behind the other two men.

"Yes. Drago and Pretty Boy. I'll have the location of the other prisoners soon. One of them is in the next fight. Iron, I'll need you to escort the guy to our setup."

"On it, vice."

"I was number ten. Which means I get to fight the number two fighter next, right?" Rebel grinned from ear to ear, jogging in place and throwing punches to keep loose.

"Hopefully, it won't come to that," Archangel said. Rebel didn't have a mic, but Archangel and Hardcase did.

"Hopefully? I was just gettin' into this."

"Yeah? See how into it you are if any of these fuckers decide you're a plant because you replaced the number ten fighter. You win, and it's liable to be a repeat of Noelle and Samson's match."

"Nah, they won't think that. I more look the part than Noelle. Plus, I'm a big guy. She's a little thing."

"A little thing who could kick your ass." Noelle had been watching him from a distance, but every time he did something stupid -- like taunting his opponent -- she swore viciously. "One of these days you're gonna run your mouth to the wrong fighter. I just hope I'm there to watch you get your ass kicked."

"Awww, your woman's a bit testy there, Fury." Rebel chuckled.

"She ain't the only one. Quit playing with them and beat the fuck outta 'em," I snarled.

"Hey. Don't talk to me. Samson's the one what told me to drag it out. Just doin' my job." And sounding a little too smug about it.

"We're clear," Samson said. "I want everyone the fuck outta here before this match is over and Rebel has to fight."

"Ah, man! You're breakin' my heart, Samson."

"Better your heart than your head, you crazy bastard. Get the fuck out."

"Fine," Rebel groused. "But I want to go on record as sayin' you Black Reign types are a bunch of pussies."

"Keep that up, and I'll let Archangel and Hardcase leave your ass."

"Might anyway," Hardcase muttered.

It wasn't long before they started coming to our base setup, about a quarter mile from the garage. The two men, who were really older boys, looked equal parts terrified and hopeful. They looked at me with suspicion, but allowed me to do a quick exam. Other than being a little dehydrated and a little banged up, they didn't seem too much the worse for wear.

"I think the kids are gonna be fine, Samson," I said, ushering them to the truck. "They could all use either some IV fluids or as much sports drink as they can handle. Not to mention a really good meal high in protein. Like the biggest Big Mac ever made." That got some chuckles from a couple of them. I grinned, then caught Noelle giving me a knowing look.

"What?" I asked, trying to act put out.

She just grinned. "You're not nearly the badass you want everyone to think you are."

"Yeah?" I lunged for her. She squealed, but let

me wrap my arms around her. I buried my face in her neck and inhaled. All those red curls of hers seemed to float around us in the slight breeze coming off the sea. "We'll see how badass I am when I get you home, wench."

She turned her head and nipped my earlobe. "I still think you're a badass. But you're my badass."

"Damned straight," I said, giving her a hard kiss. "Come on. Let's get ready. Once Archangel, Hardcase, and Rebel get here, we'll need to roll out."

"What's gonna happen to us?" one of the young men in the back of the truck said.

"You can go back to your families," I said, not really thinking through my response.

"But..." The kid looked at the other two in the back seat. "We ain't got families. Those guys took us from the docks. I was living under a pier and Ben and Gray were in a warehouse." He held out his arm, which was covered in sores. "My dad kicked me out after I got kicked out of my fourth rehab."

"Our old man was a bastard. We left after he beat our mom to death," one of the others -- I thought it was Gray -- offered. "We ain't got nowhere to go. Those guys who picked us up said we could live with them. We just had to win our fights."

Ben looked up at me, then away before speaking softly. "I think they were gonna kill us tonight after the fights. Whether we won or not. I heard 'em talkin'."

"We'll figure it out. We ain't gonna turn you out on your own with nowhere to go. But we don't put up with bullshit," I said, looking at the first young man. "Whether you're with us for a day or a month or until you die from old age, you're under our roof, you follow our rules."

"Somehow I get the feelin' you'll be harder than

my old man ever thought about being."

"What's your name?" I asked the kid.

"Mars," he said.

I raised an eyebrow. "That your given name or your street name?"

He gave me a defiant look. "It's the only name I have."

"Well, then, Mars. We don't give up on family. As long as you're with us, you're family."

"You think we can stay?" Gray looked hopefully at me, then back at his brother.

"Not up to me, son. I'm the club doctor, but whether or not we give you sanctuary is entirely up to the officers. So, if you're lookin' to suck up, I'd suggest you talk to Samson. He's the vice president."

"Shut up, Gray," Ben hissed. "What if they're like the last club? Maybe we'd be better off back at the warehouses. At least we knew the score. Who to avoid. Who was all right."

"Just give them a chance," Noelle said, sliding her body next to mine, her slender arms around my waist. "They're good people. And they really care about those they choose to let into their unique family."

As she finished speaking, Archangel hurried into the clearing where we'd set up our base. "We've got about ten minutes before we're all missed," he said. "We need to get out. Now."

"Everyone present and accounted for?" Samson said over the comm. "Iron? You guys got those two scumbags El Diablo wanted?"

"Got 'em both. Tied and ready to ride," he quipped.

"Then move out. We'll intercept on the road in ten."

Chapter Eight
Noelle

When we rolled through the gate of the Black Reign compound, Jax was, indeed, standing sentry. He had the whole place fortified with guards from what we could see. All along the perimeter, there were armed men moving, keeping watch over their area. At least, that was what Fury said. If he seemed just a touch proud, with his chest puffed out and everything, I didn't mention it. Man had a right to be proud of his son.

Once inside, El Diablo met us in the garage. Everyone congratulated everyone else on a job well done. The three boys had been given rooms and assigned a member of Black Reign to accompany them and to ask questions of when they arose. Archangel had taken Mars. The young man's eyes lit up at the sight of everything, and Archangel expressed quiet concern to Samson and Fury about the boy's recovery. While no one cared if someone did recreational drugs, abuse was an entirely different problem. The guy obviously had an addiction that had cut him off from his family. He was going to be an issue if he started the same game in the club.

The scary part started after the majority of the club left. Fury stuck around because he said it would concern him if Samson required his assistance in keeping the two men alive, but, otherwise, it was El Diablo, Samson, a guy named El Segador who was the scariest son of a bitch I'd ever seen, Fury, and me. I was sure I wasn't supposed to be there, but I wasn't leaving unless they made me. Samson did look at me, then back to El Diablo. He shook his head but said nothing.

Then they brought out the men they called Pretty

Boy and Drago. Pretty Boy gave me the creeps, and it wasn't his appearance. He looked like he'd had severe burns over his face and neck. His arms were covered by long sleeves, but his hands looked like they'd been burned as well. Drago looked more like a successful businessman. Much like El Diablo. Neither man looked like they'd break any time soon.

"Now," El Diablo said. "Before we begin this, I'm giving you one chance to give me what I want."

"Go fuck yourself," Pretty Boy said mildly.

El Diablo raised an eyebrow. "Not me," El Diablo said. "But you'll get your chance before you die." He looked at Drago. "How about you, Drago? We've known each other… how long now?"

"You know," Drago replied mildly. "Likely to the very second. That's just the thorough bastard you are."

El Diablo smiled. "True. So, you also know I mean what I say. This is your only chance to tell me what I want to know before I start taking you apart."

Drago actually grimaced while Pretty Boy just laughed maniacally. "Yes," Drago said. I understand. I'll give you what I can, but you know as well as I do, there are some things you just don't give."

"There was a time I believed as you do," El Diablo said. "With my closest allies and friends, I suppose I still feel that way. But the Brotherhood sold you out. They don't protect their own, and they don't have your back when the going gets tough. They send you out to do their dirty work, then target everyone you love, including wives and children, to keep you in line. Not for the good of the organization, mind you. All for those at the top." He stared at Drago. "The Brotherhood is dead. They're rotting from the inside out. I'm simply trying to minimize the damage they do to the rest of the world."

"Not sure that's possible. When they fall -- and, I agree, they will fall -- they'll take as many people as they can with them."

I didn't understand what they were talking about, but I didn't dare say a word. Or move. Or breathe, really.

There was a long pause. El Diablo and Drago seemed to be communicating silently. Though they appeared to be on opposite sides now, they understood each other. It was just a matter of wills now. And if one could convince the other to go in a different direction.

Finally, El Diablo spoke. "I want to know where Malcolm is," he said. Then his face grew as hard as I'd ever seen anyone look. As I watched, he turned from a man who welcomed everyone in Black Reign with a smile, to a man who would just as soon kill someone as look at them. I'd only ever seen him as the man who played with and took care of the children in the compound and made sure the women of his men were taken care of, even if that meant making sure their men were good to them. But in that moment, he was a stone-cold killer. "And I want to know where... *she* is."

Drago looked startled, then fearful. "You know I can't tell you where she is. I swore a blood oath. I can only die once, but my family... the others' families..."

Disgust showed on El Diablo's face. "The fucking Brotherhood," he spat. "So afraid of a little girl that they threaten the lives of innocents if she's found."

"She's one girl. One life compared to the lives of fifteen or twenty."

"She had no choice in the matter! Her only crime was being born to Malcolm, no matter how illegitimate!"

"Be that as it may, the council took the prophecy

seriously. They've locked her away. If she's found, they've vowed to unleash the devil on our families."

"Fortunately, I'm the devil," El Diablo said. "Even if they call me to carry out their plans, it doesn't mean I will."

"Not you. They have a new executioner. He's nothing like you, and he has fewer restrictions. He's a sociopath."

El Diablo nodded. "We'll see. Now. Tell me what I want to know."

Drago stood up taller, resignation on his face. "I will give you Malcolm's location. But not hers."

"I ain't givin' you shit," Pretty Boy said with a chuckle. "And I get off on pain."

"Very well," El Diablo. "Take them below. Start the process." He looked at El Segador. "Let Fury know before you need him. I want no mistakes."

"As you wish," the other man said in an almost formal manner. He turned to Fury. "I should be good for another sixteen hours. After that, come check in. I'll call you before if it's necessary."

"Understood," Fury acknowledged.

El Segador looked at me. There was death in his eyes. "This is the part we normally keep our women from. In your case, you needed to know what you were up against. It's up to you to ease Fury's mind. He's tough, but this is something he's not built for. He can kill. But not like this. Unfortunately, we must ask it of him from time to time." He shook his head. "Don't hate us. It's only to preserve the lives of people they'd kill willingly."

I wanted to cringe or at least back away, but I knew in my heart Fury needed me to stand strong. With him. As if I were looking in the face of an unbeatable opponent, I did my best to show no fear.

"Fury's mine. I'll protect him as much as he'd protect me."

"Good, little sister. You'll be a good woman for him. Help him be at peace."

When El Segador turned from me, Archangel gave me an appreciative nod. Apparently, the club was more than I'd first thought. On many, many counts. But they must truly care about their members. And Fury didn't take exception to what El Segador had said to me, which was a surprise. I looked up at him. His face was an expressionless mask. Much like when I went to battle and he was standing there, ready to see me fight.

"Let's go," I said. "I need you."

Fury nodded, then looked at Drago and Pretty Boy. Drago was stoic, but Pretty Boy looked completely insane. I had the feeling it was going to be a long few days.

* * *

Fury

What El Segador said shocked me. They actually knew what it did to me to have to keep their torture victims alive until they had the information they needed. I never knew they realized and regretted the pain they caused me. I'd always regarded it as my duty for the club. A club who'd given me just as much as I'd given them.

Now, as I entered my suite with Noelle firmly holding my hand, I reflected on how lucky I was. El Diablo had let me bring my son into the arms of Black Reign and had allowed him to prospect for the club once he'd turned eighteen. Not only that, but he recognized the young man's skills as a leader, and saw how well he organized himself and others. He and

Samson and the other club officers had nurtured that in Jax. They'd given him an important duty to perform tonight and watched to see how well he executed their orders. By all accounts, Jax had the place ready to fight off a siege army. He'd locked down everyone not a member or a prospect and thrown everything we had on the wall. I'd been so proud I wanted to give him a war bellow, but I knew it would just embarrass him. They'd also given Noelle a place of honor. They'd let her be there today when they didn't have to. Samson said he recognized her skills and that they could use every hand they could get, but I knew it was to help her feel like she'd have a place with us.

I closed and locked the door when we entered. Immediately, Noele began to take off her clothes. When she was naked, she helped me with mine.

"Come shower with me," she said. "Let's wash off the day."

I followed her, shedding my clothes as I went. She adjusted the water, then stepped inside, opening her arms to me as I followed.

"You know I love you. Right?" I took in the beauty of Noelle's body as she opened to me, stepping into my arms.

"I do. You know I love you, too?"

"I do. You're gonna be the death of me, though. The way you accept my club, me. No sane woman would do that, you know."

"Never said I was sane. I'm a fighter. Pretty sure that means there's a certain degree of insanity."

"Yeah." I chuckled. "I suppose it does."

Then I kissed her. Noelle melted in my arms, sliding her own around my neck. It didn't take us long to burn hot. Out of control.

The hot water beat down on us, making our

bodies slide together in an erotic glide. My fist bunched in all that curly red hair, holding her where I needed her as I took her mouth. Her hands roamed my chest and abs until she slid to my cock, circling its girth with her fist and pumping steadily.

She took a step forward and tucked the head of my cock against her entrance. She was so wet, it slipped inside her easily. The friction started the second I started to thrust. She was tight. Hot. Wet.

"Fury…" Noelle gasped my name, clinging sweetly. She tried to move faster, but I held her hips in a firm grip. There was no way I would last beyond a hot second if she moved on me.

"Still," I hissed. "Don't you fuckin' move."

"Then move faster!"

"I'm not comin' yet. So you're just gonna have to put up with slow and steady."

I pulled out of her, knowing she'd take control if I didn't keep the upper hand. Taking a bottle of shower gel, I squirted a generous amount over her tits. Her soapy skin was slippery under my palms as I rubbed the soap over her body. Her tits, over her flat belly, between her legs, then around to her ass. I held her close, enjoying the way our bodies moved over each other. It was erotic as hell, and not something I could sustain for long without fucking her.

My hands gripped her ass cheeks, squeezing and kneading. Occasionally, I'd slip my finger down the seam and ream her little asshole with one finger. She jumped and gasped out, but then pushed back against me, welcoming my touch.

"You want me to take you here?"

"You would, wouldn't you," she said. It wasn't a question.

"Baby, I'll take you anywhere, any way, any time

you'll let me. There's absolutely nothing I wouldn't do as long as it brought you pleasure."

I found her neck with my mouth and sucked, then trailed kisses over her jaw and cheek until I worked my way to her mouth. We kissed for long, long moments, our hands exploring each other while the water cascaded over us, washing away the soap. I stroked and probed her with my fingers, pinching her little clit occasionally. She was so fucking wet!

Kneeling in front of her, I shouldered my way between her legs. She parted eagerly. When I swiped my tongue through her folds, I groaned, and she screamed.

"So fuckin' sensitive," I rasped, scraping her clit with my beard before darting my tongue out to flick it.

"Mother fuck!" Noelle's fingers tightened in my hair, holding me to her. "That feels amazing! Don't fuckin' stop!"

I smacked her ass but kept licking and nipping at her pussy. I sucked each lip over and over before stabbing my tongue deep. Opening my mouth, I covered as much as I could with my mouth, taking long licks from her pussy. Several more times I slapped her ass, gripping the fleshy globes with my hands.

"Fuck me, Fury! Oh, God! Please!"

I stood, fisting my hand in her hair once again. Kissing her was a pleasure I would never deny myself. Whether it was soft and tender or hard and rough, her taste and responses never failed to turn me on. She loved it as much as I did, and it showed.

She tugged and stroked my cock, bringing it back between us once again. I thrust between her legs, letting my dick rub back and forth against her weeping cunt. When she got impatient with me, she put my cock in her pussy herself, gripping my ass for good measure so I couldn't leave the hot, tight haven of her little cunt.

Leaning back against the shower wall, Noelle wrapped one leg around my hip, opening herself up farther to me. I growled my approval and moved faster now, fucking her in earnest.

"So fuckin' good, baby. You feel so fuckin' perfect!"

She arched her neck back, thrusting her breasts upward. There was no way for me to ignore that. As I continued to fuck her, I dipped my head to suck one ripe nipple between my lips. I pressed and rolled it between my tongue and the roof of my mouth, making her moan. She quickly found the other nipple with her hand and squeezed it, pulling and tugging at the dark pink peaks.

"I've never seen a sexier woman," I said truthfully. "I love the way the muscles play under your skin. Reminds me I can take what I need from you without hurting you. You were built for me, baby. Only me."

"Then take me hard, Fury," she cried. "I fucking need it!"

I smacked her ass again, pulling her hard against me. I increased my speed, pulling her leg higher, until her knee hooked over my arm. The new position gave me better leverage to fuck her harder, faster.

"You love my cock fuckin' you, don't you?" I growled at her ear, nipping the lobe sharply. She squealed, but I felt the rush of wetness from her pussy.

"Fuckin' love it! Keep fucking me! Don't stop. Don't fuckin' stop!"

"Fuck!" I pulled out, spinning her around and shoving her against the shower wall. Hiking up her leg and placing it on a nearby shelf, I shoved myself back inside her pussy, gripping her hips and fucking her as hard as I could.

Flesh slapped against flesh, echoing in the shower and punctuated by our cries and grunts. I reached around Noelle to find her clit with my fingers, pressing hard and rubbing the little nub in circles while I fucked her.

"I want you to fuckin' come, Noelle. Milk me so I come in that little pussy."

"You want to come inside me again?"

"Always, baby. There'll never be anything between us ever again. Now, fuckin' *come*!"

With a scream, she did. Noelle milked my cock until I shot my load deep inside her. My cock pulsed angrily, needing to pump everything I had inside her sweet pussy.

When she trembled in my arms, her considerable strength giving out so she leaned back against me, limp and pliant in my arms, I pulled her close. My cock was still inside her. Though I'd just come my brains out, I was reluctant to separate from her. The only reason I could let my cock slide out of her was because I needed to clean her before we settled in for the night. It had been a long day and evening, and I wanted to hold her for a few hours before I had to go back to El Diablo. We were both breathing hard as I reached over to turn off the water.

I dried us both with a fluffy towel before carrying Noelle to bed and curling myself around her, covering us both so we were settled and comfortable.

She sighed, snuggling deeper against my chest. "What's gonna happen to those two men?"

"You know what's going to happen. Just forget about them. As far as you're concerned, they're gone."

"Do you think El Diablo will get what he wants

out of them?"

"I do. Anything El Diablo wants, he can get. The methods are never pretty, but they work. The worst part is that Drago knows what's coming. Pretty Boy... not so much."

"Who do you think will break first?"

"Not sure. If I had to guess, I'd say Pretty Boy. He thinks he's a badass, but he's not. Drago is too much of a hardliner to break. If he does, it will only be because he's delirious with pain and doesn't realize he's giving anything away. Which means that El Diablo has to break Pretty Boy."

"Can he do it?"

"Oh, yes. He can."

She was silent for a while, then said a firm, "Good. Bastard has it coming."

I had to chuckle a little at that. "Little bloodthirsty, are we?"

"Maybe. But he deserves it after what they did to my brother. Do you think I could have a little service for him? Maybe have some kind of memorial marker for him? I mean, just for me. Someplace quiet where I can go to talk to him and remember all the great times we had together. He was a great brother both before and after the accident."

"Absolutely, babe. We'll pick out a spot tomorrow."

"I appreciate all you and your friends did for me. If it hadn't been for you guys, I'd be dead right now."

"But you're not," I said fiercely. "You're here. Safe. With me. I'll always keep you safe, Noelle."

"I know." She stretched and yawned. "You're my hero, Fury."

"You're mine, too, Brawler. Now rest. I've got until tomorrow evening before I have to go check on the interrogation. I intend to spend as much of it as I can makin' love to you."

She giggled. "How can a girl say no to that?"

Marteeka Karland

Erotic romance author by night, emergency room tech/clerk by day, Marteeka Karland works really hard to drive everyone in her life completely and totally nuts. She has been creating stories from her warped imagination since she was in the third grade. Her love of writing blossomed throughout her teenage years until it developed into the totally unorthodox and irreverent style her English teachers tried so hard to rid her of.

Marteeka at Changeling: changelingpress.com/marteeka-karland-a-39

Changeling Press E-Books
More Sci-Fi, Fantasy, Paranormal, and BDSM adventures available in e-book format for immediate download at ChangelingPress.com -- Werewolves, Vampires, Dragons, Shapeshifters and more -- Erotic Tales from the edge of your imagination.

What are E-Books?
E-books, or electronic books, are books designed to be read in digital format -- on your desktop or laptop computer, notebook, tablet, Smart Phone, or any electronic e-book reader.

Where can I get Changeling Press E-Books?
Changeling Press e-books are available at ChangelingPress.com, Amazon, Apple Books, Barnes & Noble, and Kobo/Walmart.

ChangelingPress.com

Printed in Great Britain
by Amazon